WORTHY BROWN'S DAUGHTER

WORTHY BROWN'S
DAUGHTER

PHILLIP
MARGOLIN

HARPER

www.harpercollins.com

HarperCollins books may be purchased for educational, business, or sales promotional use. For information, please e-mail the Special Markets Department at SPsales@harpercollins.com.

FIRST EDITION

Designed by William Ruoto

Library of Congress Cataloging-in-Publication Data has been applied for.

ISBN: 978-0-06-219534-0

14 15 16 17 18   OV/RRD   10 9 8 7 6 5 4 3 2 1

For Doreen, who was with me when I started
Worthy Brown's Daughter, and is still in my heart

PART ONE

※

PHOENIX

CHAPTER 1

The river was insane. It boiled and surged between its banks, panicking the horses, terrifying the women and children, and forcing the men to hide their fear, which was considerable. The wagon master had ordered a halt for the night so the wagon beds could be caulked to make them watertight. As soon as the sun rose, several men tied ropes around their waists and swam the river to anchor a cable that would guide the wagons across to the far shore. The wagon master, who had taken many travelers along the Oregon Trail and knew a thing or two about fording rivers, guaranteed everyone in the party that the crossing would be perfectly safe. By the time Matthew Penny was ready, Rachel Penny was not so sure. She'd seen the river hurl huge logs about as if they were matchsticks, and none of the wagons had made it to the other side easily.

"I'm afraid," Rachel told her husband moments before Matthew drove their wagon into the swirling waters.

"Don't be. I'll make it, and I'll be waiting for you on the other side."

"It can't be safe to cross now," she whispered, not wanting their friends, Paul and Mary McCormick, to know how frightened she was.

Matthew grasped his wife's hand and held it firmly. "We're going to be okay. Be strong. Mary needs you."

Rachel was riding in the back of the McCormick wagon to comfort Mary, who was pregnant and ill. She wiped a tear from her cheek and threw her arms around Matthew's neck. Over his shoulder she could see dusty plains stretching out forever beneath a slate-gray sky filled with turbulent, merciless clouds. The landscape terrified her. The last thing she said was, "I love you."

Matthew held his wife a moment more before disengaging and taking his place on their wagon.

"See you on the other side," he told her with fake cheer. Then he snapped the reins, and the oxen walked reluctantly into the river.

Matthew was across in no time, without adventure, and he breathed a sigh of relief when his feet were planted on solid ground. He waved at Paul McCormick, a large man who was perfectly at home steering a team of oxen across a wide river. Behind Paul, Rachel smiled bravely through a gap in the canvas. Matthew threw her a kiss. The wagon rolled, and she ducked inside.

Emotions as strong as the current washed over Matthew when McCormick drove his team into the water. He loved Rachel and could not bear to be separated from her, especially knowing how terrified she was of making this crossing. But she would make it, and he would be here to comfort her and to chide her about how silly she'd been to worry. Then he changed his mind. He would hug Rachel, but he would not tease her. She'd sacrificed too much for him to be shown anything but love and respect.

Rachel had been perfectly happy in Ohio, where they were surrounded by loving families, but Matthew had contracted the wanderlust. It had come on him like a sickness, making him hot and restless and driving him west when all Rachel wanted was what they had already. Matthew had seduced his wife with promises of a better life in an Eden that would rival the original garden, and Rachel had given up everything to follow him to Oregon.

The McCormick wagon was halfway across when the cable snapped. Matthew saw Paul half standing and the wagon teetering for an eternity in the ferocious current. Then Paul was flung into the river, arms flailing, and the wagon was on its side, headed underwater. The oxen held fast for a moment, but the power of the river and the weight of the wagon dragged them off their feet. They snarled in the reins and fought the yoke, but the river had them. A sorrowful moan rent the air just before their muzzles disappeared beneath the foaming water.

For a split second the canvas flap blew out, and Matthew saw Rachel slam against the inside of the wagon. He screamed her name and was rushing toward the riverbank when two strong men wrestled him to the ground. He was still screaming her name when the wagon disappeared around a bend in the river, and he was screaming it again when the boy Harry Chambers had sent to fetch him shook his shoulder and wrenched him out of his nightmare.

"What!" Matthew exclaimed, bolting upright. The boy jumped back. Matthew stared at him without comprehension, his heart thumping.

"Mr. Chambers needs you at the inn," the startled boy stuttered. "He said they're fixing to lynch the salesman, and you got to come."

"What salesman?" Matthew asked.

"The one that stole the money."

Matthew had no idea what the boy was talking about, but a lynching was serious.

"Tell Harry I'll be right over," he said, and the boy took off.

The tent flap closed, and Matthew forced himself to stand. He was twenty-nine, tall, and well built, with clear blue eyes and dark hair that hung to his shoulders. His appearance would have been considered youthful had it not been for the lines that hardship and sorrow had etched into his face. When freshly bathed and groomed and dressed in a clean, unwrinkled suit, the attorney was quite presentable. Awakened from his deep, troubled sleep after riding for hours in the sweltering heat of summer, Matthew felt awful and looked worse.

In 1860, most of the Oregon counties where court was held had no hotels. Judges, lawyers, and litigants boarded in any quarters that were available, usually a one-room pioneer cabin where they learned quickly how to change clothing in bed to avoid embarrassing their reluctant hosts. The little town of Phoenix was unusual. When rumors spread that a railroad line might pass through it, the speculators had descended, bringing instant prosperity and a need for lodging. At one end of the town's only street was Harry Chambers's inn, a two-story clapboard lodging house and drinking saloon. At the other end was a large canvas tent sectioned off into tiny sleeping rooms on which its owner had bestowed the grandiose name the Hotel Parisian.

Matthew Penny was one of a small group of lawyers in Portland with a private practice. There were fortunes to be made in that bustling, waterfront town of roughly three thousand souls, but real estate, shipping, and commerce were strangers to Matthew's law office. His clients were not the wealthy merchants but small farmers and shopkeepers as likely to pay in produce or trade as in cash. This accounted for Matthew's sleeping on a dirt floor in a canvas tent.

Matthew's clothes and face were caked with dust, and his hair was matted across his forehead. He brushed away as much of the evidence of his travels as he was able, ran his fingers through his hair, trying for a semblance of order, and made a sorry attempt at smoothing down his clothes. Then he trudged off to the inn.

AS SOON AS MATTHEW ARRIVED at the end of Main Street, he heard the angry murmur of the crowd milling around the oak in the field in front of the inn. Matthew hurried over to Harry Chambers, who brought to mind one of the fat geese he plumped up for his guests. His immense belly—hidden behind a stained apron—rolled like the foothills, and rings of fat circled his neck. Chambers's sandy hair was thinning, and he sampled his wares more frequently than was advisable, so his bulbous nose was veined and red.

"I've been riding all day, Harry, and I'm exhausted. Why did you have that boy wake me?"

The innkeeper pointed toward a tall, gangly man who was gagged, trussed up, and held firmly by two angry farmers.

"That's Clyde Lukens. He stole two hundred dollars from a guest at the inn."

Chambers nodded toward a tall, rawboned man who held a length of rope, one end of which he'd fashioned into a noose.

"Abner Hardesty's decided to fix the problem without the inconvenience of a trial, and so far you're the only lawyer who's arrived for court."

"I'm a *lawyer*, Harry, not a *lawman*."

"Well, someone's got to do something, and no one would listen to me."

Matthew sighed. "Has Lukens confessed?"

"No, he's been screaming he's innocent since we caught him. That's why the gag. They couldn't shut him up any other way."

Hardesty threw the noose at the oak's sturdiest branch, and the crowd roared approval. When the prisoner saw the rope drape itself over the tree limb, his eyes grew wide and he began flailing in his captors' grasp.

The angry crowd frightened Matthew, but court would be held in the morning, and that was the place where civilized societies resolved their disputes. Matthew steeled himself and pushed through to the area shaded by the oak just as a horse was led into position beneath the noose.

"Mr. Hardesty, wait on Justice Tyler to hear these charges," he said, trying to keep his voice calm and commanding. "The judge will be here soon. If you hang this man without benefit of trial, you'll be committing murder."

Hardesty turned on Matthew. "Who the *hell* are you?"

Matthew's stomach churned, and he fought to keep from trembling. He wanted to step back. In truth, he wanted to run. But he held his ground.

"I'm Matthew Penny, sir, and I'm an attorney. Oregon has a constitution now. We're a member of the Union. Our courts are organized, and we have no need of lynch juries."

Hardesty spit at Matthew's feet. "That's what I think of the courts. We don't need 'em here."

A pistol shot brought everyone around, and Matthew found himself facing the Honorable Jedidiah Tyler.

From a distance, it would not have been unreasonable to mistake Justice Tyler for a fierce black bear. He was short and stocky, with massive shoulders. His large head was covered by dark, slicked-back hair and supported by a thick neck. Bushy eyebrows and a woolly beard covered most of his broad, flat face; and sharp, glinting eyes and a vicious hairline scar cemented an impression of animal ferocity that made his visage as terrifying as his courtroom demeanor. Tyler was a hard man with a wicked temper. More than one litigant had threatened his life, and he never held court without a pistol close at hand.

As soon as he had the crowd's attention, Tyler planted himself so that he looked as immovably rooted to the ground as the tree before which he stood.

"I'm Jed Tyler, a justice of your supreme court," he bellowed. Then he turned and faced Hardesty, who was five inches taller than the judge and lean and dangerous looking.

"What is your name, sir?" Tyler demanded.

"Abner Hardesty," snapped the leader of the lynch mob.

"Well, Mr. Hardesty, this is my judicial district, and there will be no lynching in it. This man will receive a fair trial. If he is convicted, I will decide his punishment."

"This ain't *your* district, mister. It's *our* town, and this son of a bitch is gonna hang."

The moment Hardesty tacked the period onto his belligerent pronouncement Tyler hammered the butt of his pistol against the hangman's skull. Hardesty's eyes bulged, and he sank to his knees before toppling over, unconscious. Tyler leveled his pistol at the crowd.

"Harry," the judge ordered calmly, "escort the prisoner to the inn and lock him in the storeroom."

"Stand back," Chambers hollered as he rushed to Tyler's side. "Let's do this legal, like the judge says. If this fella is guilty, he'll get what's coming to him in Jed Tyler's court."

Tyler's thunderous blow and loaded pistol had tipped the scales in favor of a fair trial, and the men holding Clyde Lukens made no move to challenge the judge's authority. When Chambers told them to bring the prisoner to the inn, they followed the innkeeper across the field with the salesman in tow.

Matthew felt weak-kneed as the adrenaline that had kept him upright dissipated. He said a silent prayer of thanks for the judge's intercession and started back to his place of lodging. Before he had taken two steps, Tyler stopped him.

"This man will need counsel, Mr. Penny, and you will serve in that capacity."

Matthew wanted to protest. He already had a client, and he needed time to prepare his case. But Tyler had a long memory, and Matthew would have to be crazy to defy the judge if he wanted to practice law in Oregon.

"Very well," Matthew said, but Tyler was no longer listening. Matthew followed the judge's gaze and saw that he was looking at a full-figured woman whose oval face was framed by ebony ringlets that were in sharp contrast with her milk-white complexion. The woman's lips were pursed in disapproval, and there was no doubt in Matthew's mind that her piercing green eyes were studying the judge. Then the frown turned into a smile of respect, and she nodded at Tyler before walking away.

DURING THE EVENING, THE NOISY bar/dining room that took up most of the ground floor of Harry Chambers's establishment was poorly lit by lanterns that cast shadows everywhere. Farmers, townspeople, litigants in Phoenix for a trial, and traveling salesmen packed the oak tables and bellied up to the long bar. Beer and hard liquor slopped onto the sawdust that covered the wood-plank flooring. The din made conversation almost impossible.

Chambers knew that this atmosphere was not fit for the better class of clientele to whom he occasionally catered, so there was a small room at the rear of the inn where his more refined guests could dine. A master carpenter had crafted the chairs and tables, a Persian rug that Harry had won in a poker game covered the floor, and a genuine crystal chandelier from Paris, France, hung from the ceiling. The chandelier was the pride of Phoenix and as out of place in the clapboard inn as a pig on silk sheets. More than one tough-as-nails mountain man had sneaked down the corridor from the bar to peek at it. The town's great mystery was how Harry had obtained it. Many had asked him, and his versions of the acquisition were varied, fanciful, and usually unbelievable.

Matthew followed Chambers down the hall to the storeroom, which was just past the private dining room. Harry fished a key from his pocket while Matthew lit the lantern that hung to the right of the storeroom door. The storeroom was pitch-black. After swinging the light around for a few seconds, Matthew found his client languishing in a corner, hogtied and gagged, his head resting on a sack of meal.

"Untie him, Harry," Matthew ordered.

"The judge said—"

"He didn't say anything about tying and gagging him, did he?"

"Well, no, but—"

"You were just supposed to make sure he didn't escape. How can he talk to me with a gag in his mouth?"

"I really don't—"

Before Harry could finish his sentence, Matthew pulled a bowie knife from under his frock coat and cut through the prisoner's bindings.

"Hey, I was gonna—"

"You were gonna stand there jawing. This man is presumed innocent. I want him treated innocent. Now, if you'll excuse us, a client's statements to his lawyer are confidential. You can't stay here."

When the storeroom door closed, Matthew turned to the prisoner, who was rubbing circulation back into his wrists. The man looked truly pathetic. He was bathed in sweat, and his sparse brown hair was in disarray. His gaunt face was scratched and bruised from the beating he'd received, his nose looked as if it had been broken, and his thin lips were split and caked with dried blood.

"I'm Matthew Penny of Portland. Justice Tyler has asked me to be your attorney."

"Thank God, thank God," the prisoner whimpered. "She's just doing this to get even."

"Who is? What are you talking about?"

"Her! The Jezebel, the Jezebel!"

CHAPTER 2

As soon as Matthew finished with Clyde Lukens, he got his horse from the livery stable and rode to the home of Glen Farber, his client in the case of *Farber v. Gillette*. Farber lived a few miles out of town in a log cabin with his wife, Millie, and their thirteen children, and he farmed from dawn to dusk just to get by. Farber's corded muscles were the product of a life of hard labor. Since there was no fat on his whip-thin body, his bones were visible as jutting elbows, conspicuous shoulder blades, high cheekbones, and a pointed chin. If Farber had been an implement, he would have been a knife, and his temper was as sharp and fierce as a fighting blade.

Farber had paid little attention to the rumors that the railroad was headed for Phoenix until Benjamin Gillette, a wealthy businessman, offered to buy some of his land. Farber jumped at the chance to make some easy money. If the deal had gone through, it would have been the first time in his life that anything had come his way without backbreaking labor. Then Gillette had second thoughts about the deal and Gillette's lawyer, Caleb Barbour, and pointed out a loophole through which he thought his client could slip. When Gillette decided not to honor his contract, Farber's first thought was to shoot Gillette and his lawyer, but Millie Farber beseeched her irate husband to seek legal counsel, and he eventually gave in.

It was late afternoon when Matthew arrived at the Farber cabin. After sharing a meal with the family, Matthew conferred with his client about the case. Mrs. Farber did her best to keep the children quiet, but the din in the cabin gave the lawyer a splitting headache that was still throbbing when he left his horse at the livery stable in Phoenix. Matthew decided that a glass or two of beer might ease his pain. He was walking toward the inn when a giant Negro materialized out of the shadows.

Matthew would not have been more surprised if he had encountered a creature from another planet. Black men were rare and unwelcome in Oregon. The new state constitution prohibited free Negroes from entering the state, making contracts, holding real estate, or maintaining lawsuits unless they were already residing in Oregon on the date that the constitution was adopted.

"Sir?" Matthew barked, startled by the sudden apparition.

"Are you Mr. Penny?" the Negro asked in a rich baritone that would have worked well in a church choir.

"I am."

"My name is Worthy Brown, and I work for Caleb Barbour."

"Yes, certainly," Matthew answered with relief, believing that the mystery of the massive black man had been solved. "Do you have a message for me?"

"No, suh, I wish to speak to you myself on a private matter."

Matthew took a harder look at Brown, whose purple-black skin was so dark it took sharp eyes to make out the man at night. The Negro was well over six feet tall and deep chested with broad shoulders that were stooped from years of fieldwork. Clearly, the man was nervous, but his hands were steady, and, though deferential, there was an air of dignity about him.

"I need to know about slavery, suh. Can a man be a slave in Oregon?"

"Our new constitution prohibits slavery, Mr. Brown."

"What if a man was a slave before he come to Oregon?"

"He would be a free man when he arrived here."

Matthew waited quietly while Worthy Brown mulled over Matthew's answer.

"Mr. Penny, I need a lawyer, but I don't have money to pay you. What I plan to do is tell you something, and I want you to promise me you'll be my lawyer if it's valuable."

"Certainly Caleb Barbour can help you with any legal problem you might have. He's an excellent lawyer."

"No, suh. Mr. Barbour can't help me on this."

"What's your problem?"

"I'd rather not say until you decide if my information will pay for your help."

"Mr. Brown, this is very confusing. How can I promise to be your lawyer if I don't know what you want me to do? What you ask may be illegal, or I may have a conflict that prevents me from representing you. Surely you see that I can't commit myself without more information."

"What I'm asking ain't illegal. I wouldn't ask no man to break the law. All I ask is that they keep their word," Brown concluded bitterly.

"Does this matter involve a conflict between yourself and Mr. Barbour?" Matthew asked. He was reluctant to involve himself in a dispute between a servant and a man with Barbour's connections.

"I don't want to say no more about it now. When you hear what else I got to say, you'll see why I can't go to Mr. Barbour."

"And that is?"

"He's gonna bribe some of the jurors in your case."

"What!"

"He's got a plan for getting someone on that jury who will fix the verdict for him."

"Who?"

"That I don't know, but they're meetin' behind the inn, tomorrow night. You see if I ain't telling the truth. Then you say if you'll help me."

"How did you come by this information, Mr. Brown?"

The Negro laughed, but there was no humor in it. "A slave ain't nothing but a piece of furniture, Mr. Penny. Mr. Barbour talks around me same as he would around a chair or a table, 'specially when he's drinking."

"Does Mr. Barbour keep you as a slave?" Matthew asked incredulously.

"I don't wish to discuss that now, suh."

"Very well. Tell me, did Mr. Barbour say whether Benjamin Gillette is a party to this bribery?"

"That I can't say, but I 'spect not. Mr. Barbour wants to win this case terrible bad. From the way he's been drinking lately, I think he and Mr. Gillette ain't getting on too well. Mr. Barbour is afraid he's gonna lose Mr. Gillette's business, and he can't afford that."

Brown looked around nervously. "I've been here too long, Mr. Penny. If someone sees us talking, it could go bad for me." He started to walk away.

"Wait. If I decide to help you how can I get in touch?"

"Don't worry 'bout that. If you gonna help me, I'll find you."

CHAPTER 3

Oregon's four supreme court justices spent part of their time as appellate judges and the rest riding circuit as trial judges in the counties of the state. A justice had to be not only wise but also rugged enough to endure long horseback rides, foul weather, poor food, and primitive accommodations. Jed Tyler was such a man. He was ruthless in business and brutal in court, a hard drinker and a fearless gambler who was well known to the whores who worked in Portland's brothels.

As he washed off the dust of travel and changed for dinner, Tyler thought about the woman on the edge of the crowd. She had vanished by the time order was restored in the field. Harry Chambers could have told the judge who she was, but Chambers was occupied with the prisoner. The mystery was solved soon after the judge entered Harry Chambers's back room. Seated between Benjamin Gillette and his attorney, Caleb Barbour, at a table for four beneath Harry's famous chandelier was the woman who had occupied the judge's thoughts.

Benjamin Gillette always looked as if he'd just gotten off the boat. This was an image he cultivated because it helped him succeed in business. Gillette was tall and heavyset. He sported a mane of white hair and a constant smile and he ate what pleased him.

Though he wore shirt collars and ties when appropriate, he never felt comfortable in them and tugged constantly to keep the stiff fabric away from his fleshy neck.

Oregon's wealthiest businessman had moved to Portland from California in the early 1850s, starting in the mercantile trade, branching into private banking and real estate, and using his California connections to gain control of most of the shipping on the Columbia and Willamette Rivers. It was railroading that captured his fancy now, and a lawsuit involving land in Phoenix had brought Benjamin to Harry Chambers's inn.

If Benjamin Gillette looked as if he had just gotten off the boat, Caleb Barbour looked as if he owned the vessel. He was six feet three inches tall and well proportioned. His wavy black hair and groomed mustache gave him the look of a music hall hero. Barbour had his stylish clothes hand-tailored, he gambled flamboyantly and whored discreetly, and he lived beyond his means. He had acquired this last vice in Georgia, a state from which he had fled just ahead of his creditors. Barbour had arrived in Oregon in 1856 and had quickly established his professional reputation. He had done well enough handling Benjamin Gillette's legal affairs for Gillette to ignore the rumors that his attorney's methods were often questionable.

"Jed," Gillette called out when the judge entered the room.

"Won't you join us, Judge?" Barbour asked.

There were only two tables in the room, and one was unoccupied. It would have been impossible for Tyler to turn down the invitation, even if he had wanted to.

"Thank you," the judge said.

"Have you met Miss Hill?" Gillette asked. "We've only just had the pleasure."

Tyler nodded to the lady. "I'm afraid I haven't had the honor of an introduction."

"I'm Sharon Hill, Justice Tyler, and I'm most pleased to make your acquaintance."

There was a throaty quality to Hill's voice, and the hand she extended was as smooth and delicate.

"Miss Hill has been regaling us with the story of your exploits with the lynch mob," Barbour said.

"Yes, tell us about the lynching," Gillette said.

"I hope that Miss Hill hasn't made too much of it," Tyler answered. "This fellow Lukens is accused of stealing. I simply made certain that his fate would be decided in a court of law."

"You're far too modest, sir." Sharon Hill said. "The man would be dead now were it not for you."

Tyler shrugged. Then he turned to Barbour. "That reminds me. I've asked Matthew Penny to defend Lukens, but I have no one to prosecute. What about you, Caleb?"

"If you think I can be of some help," Barbour answered.

"I've seen no one else," Tyler answered gruffly.

Barbour reddened briefly before regaining his composure.

"If I'm to prosecute, I'll need to know the names of the witnesses," he said stiffly.

"Talk to Harry Chambers," the judge answered. "I know nothing about the case."

"You might also talk to me," said Miss Hill, "since I am the victim of that despicable man."

CHAPTER 4

A session of court was great entertainment in Phoenix, where nothing much happened most of the year. There were no courthouses in any Oregon county in 1860, so court was held in the interior of Harry Chambers's inn in winter and in the field adjoining it in summer. On the morning of Clyde Lukens's trial, court convened under a bright sun and clear blue sky. A welcome breeze had chased away the sticky heat of the past few days, leaving the spectators, who were sprawled on their blankets in the grass, in a festive mood. Justice Tyler sat in the shade provided by the oak tree at a table that had been carried over from the inn. On Tyler's left was a chair for witnesses. The jurors had been picked from the spectators gathered in the field, and they sat perpendicular to the chair from which the witnesses testified in an improvised jury box composed of two rows of chairs.

Two more tables had been set up in front of the judge. At one of them sat Clyde Lukens and Matthew Penny. At the prosecution table sat the dapper Caleb Barbour, who was continuing his examination of Harry Chambers.

"When did you first learn that Miss Hill had been robbed?" Barbour asked the nervous witness.

"After she ate breakfast. She went up to her room. A few minutes later, she came down all upset and told me that someone had stolen her money."

"Did she suggest who the culprit might be?"

"Him," Chambers said. "Clyde Lukens."

An angry murmur passed through the crowd. Tyler was tempted to rap the butt of his pistol on the table to restore order, but he stayed his hand because of the tiny smile of satisfaction that played on the corners of Sharon Hill's lips. The state's star witness was sitting on a chair that the judge had ordered for her. Even in the plain dress she had chosen for her court appearance, she radiated sexuality, and the judge had to fight to keep from looking her way while Chambers was testifying.

"What did you do after speaking to Miss Hill?" Barbour asked.

"I brought her and a few men to Lukens's room and told him what Miss Hill had said."

"How did he react?"

"Well, his eyes got real big. Then he turned red and started yelling."

"What did he yell?"

Chambers looked embarrassed, and he turned to the judge. "Do I have to say the words, Judge? They're sort of rough."

"We're in court, and we must have the truth, no matter how rough it may be," Tyler told him.

Chambers took a breath and turned back to Barbour. "He was screaming at Miss Hill. He called her a Jezebel, and, well, he said she was a whore."

Angry conversations could be heard in the field. Tyler rapped his pistol and ordered the crowd to pipe down.

"Did you have to restrain Mr. Lukens?" Barbour asked.

"Yes, sir, or he would have done Miss Hill harm. He was wild."

"How did Miss Hill react to this assault?"

"She was as calm as can be."

"Like someone with a clear conscience?" Barbour asked.

"Objection," Matthew said.

"Sustained," Tyler ruled.

"What did you do after subduing Mr. Lukens?" Barbour continued.

"We searched his room."

"And what did you find?"

"The two hundred dollars Miss Hill said was missing. It was rolled up in his socks with seventy-five more dollars."

"What did Mr. Lukens say to that?"

"He said all the money was his."

"Really? Did he explain how Miss Hill would know that he had this money concealed in his room?"

Harry looked at Sharon Hill apologetically. She beamed a comforting smile at him.

"Well, Mr. Chambers?" Barbour said.

"He, uh, well, he said he told her about the money the evening before."

"Nothing further, Your Honor," Barbour said.

"Your witness, Mr. Penny," the judge said.

"Where did Mr. Lukens say he told Miss Hill about the money?" Matthew asked.

"In . . . In her room."

"Did Mr. Lukens give an explanation for his presence in the room of an unmarried woman?"

"Uh, yes, sir, he did."

"Enlighten us, please."

Chambers cast an anguished look at Sharon Hill. "He . . . he said, uh, that he'd spent part of the evening there."

There was angry whispering in the crowd, and Miss Hill's eyes blazed with indignation.

"Objection, Your Honor," Caleb Barbour shouted.

"Mr. Barbour opened the door to this line of questioning," Matthew replied.

"Tread softly, Mr. Penny," the judge warned in a low and threatening voice. "The objection is overruled, but if you sully the reputation of this young woman without cause, I will deal with you and the defendant."

"I assure the court that there is a valid reason for my inquiry," Matthew said.

"Mr. Chambers, why did Mr. Lukens claim he was in Miss Hill's room?" Matthew asked the witness.

"He said that she agreed to . . . to, er, be with him for money."

"To prostitute herself?"

Chambers nodded.

"No further questions," Matthew said as he reclaimed his seat.

Barbour jumped to his feet with a theatrical flourish. "We will clear up these scandalous allegations quickly. I call Miss Hill."

Sharon Hill walked to the stand with her head high and her back straight.

"Do you swear by Almighty God that you will tell the truth, the whole truth, and nothing but the truth?" Justice Tyler asked when she placed her hand on the Bible.

"I do," she answered forcefully.

"Please take the witness stand, Miss Hill. Mr. Barbour, you may proceed."

"What is your full name?" Barbour asked.

"Sharon May Hill."

"And where are you from?"

"San Francisco."

"Please tell the jury where you're headed."

"Portland."

"Were you traveling by coach when you arrived in Phoenix?"

"I was."

"You told Mr. Chambers that the defendant stole two hundred dollars from you. How did he come to learn that you were carrying this sum of money?"

Sharon Hill turned to the all-male jury. The eyes that had stared at Clyde Lukens with such malevolence were now soft, limpid pools that threatened to overflow with tears.

"I was seated opposite that . . . that man in the coach during the trip to Phoenix. At one point I searched my purse for a comb. We hit a rut. The coach bounced, and I lost my grip on my bag. The contents spilled on the floor, and he handed back my roll of bills."

"Did he say anything about the money?" Barbour asked.

"No, but he held it longer than necessary, and I thought that he eyed it with evil intent."

"Objection as to Mr. Lukens's intent and move to strike," Matthew said.

"Yes, Miss Hill, don't guess at what the defendant may have

been thinking," Tyler said, his tone gentle, as if he were repri-
manding a favorite niece for a silly, but minor, infraction.

"I'm sorry, Your Honor."

"Did anyone at the inn besides the defendant know that you
had this money in your possession when you arrived in Phoenix?"
Barbour asked.

"Not to my knowledge, and we were the only passengers."

"When was the last time you saw your money?"

"When I placed it in my chest of drawers on the evening we
arrived. I realized it was missing in the morning when I went to
my room after breakfast."

"Did you ever see the defendant in your room, Miss Hill?"

The witness seemed uncertain. "This may appear foolish, and
I wish to be fair."

"Just tell the unvarnished truth," Barbour prodded gently.

"Well, I believe I saw Mr. Lukens in my room, but . . . This is
confusing."

"Take your time," Justice Tyler said protectively.

"Thank you, Your Honor. I was exhausted by the long coach
ride, and I fell into a deep sleep after dinner. At one point I had
what I believed to be a dream. In that dream I saw Mr. Lukens
closing the door to my room. I now believe that I actually saw
him leaving my room, but was so tired that I fell back asleep and
thought I'd dreamed it."

Barbour pointed at Clyde Lukens with contempt. "This *gentleman* has claimed that he was in your room for—and I beg your
pardon for asking this—immoral purposes. Is that true?"

"Certainly not!"

"Except for his possible nighttime incursion, was Mr. Lukens ever in your room to your knowledge?"

"No, sir."

"Thank you, Miss Hill. I have no further questions, Your Honor."

Matthew walked to the witness stand and stood inches from Sharon Hill.

"You concede that Mr. Lukens's intrusion into your room may simply have been a dream?" he asked.

"Well, yes, Mr. Penny." Hill paused and furrowed her brow as if genuinely perplexed. "But how then did he come by my money?"

"Honestly, if it was his own," Matthew responded.

"Objection," Barbour called out. "Mr. Penny is testifying, and he's implying that Miss Hill is a liar."

"Sustained," Tyler snapped.

Matthew knew that Hill had gotten the best of him. Even worse, a quick scan of the jurors' faces showed quite clearly where their sympathies lay. Matthew decided to change his tactics.

"Miss Hill, why are you going to Portland?"

Hill seemed flustered for a moment, but she recovered quickly.

"I'm looking into business opportunities."

"What type of business?"

"Whatever presents itself. I'm keeping an open mind. A shop, perhaps."

"And you planned to finance the business with the two hundred dollars?"

"It's all I have in the world."

"Please tell the jury how you—a single woman—came by such a large sum of money."

Hill's composure broke, and Matthew was certain he had her. But when she spoke, he knew that Clyde Lukens was doomed.

"An inheritance from my father. He passed away, and I . . ." Her voice caught, and she fetched a handkerchief from her purse.

"I'm sorry," Hill said as she dabbed at her eyes.

"Would you like some water?" Tyler asked solicitously, reaching for a pitcher Harry Chambers had provided for the judge.

"No, I'm fine. It's just that I am only recently alone in the world."

"Mr. Penny, I suggest you pursue another line of questioning," the judge said. Matthew heard angry whispers in the crowd and sympathetic murmurs from the jury box. He knew he was defeated.

"Nothing further, Your Honor," Matthew said as he took his seat.

"The state rests," Caleb Barbour proclaimed before gallantly assisting Sharon Hill from the witness stand.

"Any witnesses, Mr. Penny?"

"Mr. Lukens, Your Honor," Matthew replied, even though he knew that Clyde Lukens could not be saved. His client must have sensed the inevitability of punishment. When he took the oath, his words were barely audible, and Justice Tyler ordered him to speak up.

"Did you steal from Miss Hill?" Matthew asked.

"As God is my judge, that money is mine. She's doing this to get even."

"Get even for what?"

"She's a temptress, a harlot."

There were angry rumblings in the crowd, and Matthew worried that there might be a second attempt to lynch his client.

"Explain to the jury what happened between you and Miss Hill," Matthew said.

"I will, I will," Lukens said, looking for understanding from the twelve stone-faced jurors and finding none. "We met on the stage to Portland. We were the only passengers. I'm a bachelor, sir. A salesman. I'm alone on the road most of the year. I . . . I couldn't help but notice that . . . Well, Miss Hill is a beautiful woman. Quite innocently, I assure you, I struck up a conversation. At first, that's all it was, a way to pass the time. Then she told me it was a shame that I had to travel the road alone when I could spend some time with her at the inn, if I had the price.

"I asked her what she meant. She was quite explicit. She wanted to know if I had any money. I told her about my two hundred and seventy-five dollars, which was partly profits from sales and partly expense money from my company. She quoted a price."

Lukens bowed his head. "I knew it was sinful, but she was so beautiful. I . . . I couldn't help myself."

"What happened at the inn?" Matthew asked.

"We agreed to check in separately. She ate in the back room, and I ate in the bar. I waited an appropriate amount of time after she went upstairs before following her. When I entered her room . . ."

Lukens paused to cast a quick glance at the crowd. He saw angry faces glaring at him. The jurors' aspects were no kinder.

"Go on, Mr. Lukens. What happened in Miss Hill's room?"

Matthew knew the story Lukens was going to tell, and, while he thoroughly disapproved of the man, he believed it was the truth. Unfortunately for Lukens, Matthew knew he was probably the only one in the field who would feel that way.

"She was in bed, naked. I joined her." He hung his head. "I couldn't help myself. It was as if the devil had taken hold of me."

"What happened next?" Matthew asked.

"The trouble. She demanded twenty-five dollars. I didn't have it."

"But you've told the jury that you had two hundred and seventy-five dollars?"

"I did, but it wasn't mine. Most of the money belonged to the company. I did have expense money, but how would I live? I told her I would get the money in Portland and pay her then. She was furious. I tried to explain, but she wouldn't listen. I begged her to understand. She said she did. She said she believed that I thought I could use her and get away without paying, but that I was wrong. Then she grew calm and smiled at me in a way that chilled my bones. It was the most malevolent smile I've ever seen. She told me to get out. I dressed and left."

"Whose money did Harry Chambers find in your socks?"

"My money, the company money."

"And you stole nothing from Miss Hill?"

"Nothing. I swear to God, it was mine."

"Your witness, Mr. Barbour."

Barbour looked at Lukens with contempt. "I will not waste the time of the court or this jury by questioning this . . . man."

Several jurors shook their heads to show their agreement with the prosecutor, and Lukens slunk back to his seat.

"Any more witnesses, Mr. Penny?" the judge asked.

"No, sir."

"Then you may make your closing argument, Mr. Barbour."

CHAPTER 5

The arguments were short and the jury deliberations shorter. Clyde Lukens had barely reached the inn when he was summoned back to hear his guilt pronounced.

"You are one of the lowest specimens I have ever encountered," Justice Tyler told the quivering defendant. "You crept into the bedroom of a defenseless woman and stole from her. Then you compounded your crime by trying to sully her reputation before this assemblage.

"Hanging would be a fit punishment for you. Unfortunately, it's not prescribed for the crime of theft. There is no jail in Phoenix where you can be incarcerated, and I will burden Mr. Chambers with your unsavory company no longer. Therefore, I sentence you to receive fifty lashes in public on your bare back."

Lukens blanched. "But that will kill me."

"You should have thought of that possibility before you broke the Eighth Commandment."

"It's my money. Send word to my company. Please. I can prove it."

"You've had your day in court, sir. Now you shall have judgment."

Tyler turned toward Abner Hardesty, who was standing on the edge of the crowd.

"You may have the honor, Mr. Hardesty. You will tie the prisoner to the oak and commence punishment. If he passes out, revive him. I want Mr. Lukens to savor the fruits of his wrongdoing. Court is adjourned until this afternoon, when we will select a jury for *Farber v. Gillette.*"

Lukens begged for mercy as he was dragged to the tree, but Tyler turned away. As he walked toward the inn, hands slapped the judge on the back. Matthew followed Tyler until he was clear of the crowd.

"Your Honor, if I may have a minute."

"Yes, Mr. Penny."

"Mr. Lukens has a frail constitution. Fifty lashes may kill him."

Tyler thought for a moment. Abner Hardesty was headed to the livery stable to secure a whip. Tyler called to him, and he turned back. The judge took him aside.

"I'm charging you with Lukens's punishment, but I'm also charging you with his safety. Theft, no matter how vile, doesn't carry a death sentence. If it appears that fifty lashes are too much for him, stop and come to me at the inn."

Hardesty nodded and went on his way.

"Does that satisfy you, Mr. Penny?" the judge asked.

"Yes, sir. Thank you."

Tyler felt a presence at his side and turned to find Benjamin Gillette and Sharon Hill.

"Will you join us for lunch?" Benjamin Gillette asked the judge.

"I'm afraid I must beg off. I have some work I must do before the afternoon session."

"Are you returning to Portland soon?" Sharon Hill asked.

"Not for a while. There are sessions of court in three more towns after I'm through here."

"Oh. Well, perhaps I'll see you when you're finished riding the circuit."

"It would be my pleasure," Tyler answered.

AS SOON AS HE FINISHED talking to Justice Tyler, Matthew went in search of Glen Farber. He spotted the Farber family among those who gathered around the oak in eager anticipation of the judicially mandated flogging.

"Do you think our jurors will hold it against us that you defended Lukens?" Farber asked anxiously when Matthew walked up.

"No, Glen, don't worry. I'll make sure they're not biased."

Farber could see that Matthew was upset. "He deserves what he gets," the farmer assured his attorney.

"He may have been innocent."

"If you believe what he admitted to, he's a fornicator and a cheat."

"You have a point," Matthew agreed. "And Mr. Lukens is going to pay, no matter what I think, but he'll need help when Mr. Hardesty has finished with him. Do you think your boys can help me carry Lukens to the river after the flogging so I can clean him up?"

"I don't know," Farber said, looking around nervously.

"Look, Glen, no one will think less of you if you help me. I'm your lawyer."

"It ain't you. I don't want nothing to do with that scum."

"No lawyer in Portland wanted anything to do with your lawsuit when they heard you wanted to sue Benjamin Gillette," Matthew reminded his client.

Farber looked embarrassed.

"The boys will help," Millie Farber said firmly. Millie was taller and heavier than her husband. Her wide hips and large breasts offered domestic comfort, but Matthew knew that her unwavering faith in God and the fortitude she required to raise her brood and deal with her husband had coalesced to form a will of iron.

"Thank you," Matthew said after waiting a beat to see if Glen would protest. "Do you think one of the boys could drive Lukens to a doctor in Portland in your wagon? I'd pay," he heard himself say, knowing that he could ill afford any extra expense given the precarious nature of his financial situation, which provided barely enough money for rent and food. But the Farbers were poorer than he and could not afford to let an able-bodied worker go for the time it would take to go from Phoenix to Portland and back. And there was the matter of the guilt Matthew felt for failing to save Clyde Lukens from the lash.

Glen cast a worried look at his wife, but she laid a hand on his forearm.

"Mr. Penny's gone out of his way to help us, Glen."

"I know, but I'm worried what everyone will think."

"They'll think we're good Christians. It's easy to help someone who obeys the Lord's word. But Jesus instructed us to show compassion to the sinner so he could be redeemed."

Farber didn't look convinced, but he knew better than to argue with his wife on matters of religion.

"I'll talk to John and Peter about taking Lukens to the doctor," Glen said.

"Thank you," Matthew answered, just as Abner Hardesty re-appeared, alerting the crowd to his presence by cracking his whip for practice. Lukens, who was already stripped and secured to the oak tree, looked over his shoulder and began to weep in anticipation of the pain.

"Excuse me," Matthew said, walking away from the Farbers to position himself where Lukens could see him. He felt it was his duty to bear witness, and he wanted Lukens to know that there was at least one sympathetic soul in the mob.

Matthew forced himself to watch every minute of the whipping, even though he wanted to close his eyes and cover his ears to block out Lukens's screams. He suffered with Lukens, and every crack of the whip and cry of pain brought home how badly he had failed his client.

Lukens did not stand up well. He fainted frequently and whimpered or begged while conscious. When it was clear that he'd had enough, he was cut down and left like a dog in the field. Matthew waited until most of the crowd had drifted away before nodding to Farber. Two of Glen's sons—one sixteen and one seventeen—carried Lukens to the river while the youngest ran to the inn to fetch the salesman's possessions and the eldest went for the wagon.

Matthew was no doctor. Millie Farber, who had patched up her husband and most of her children at some time, stepped in when Matthew's incompetence became obvious. While Millie worked on the salesman, Matthew penned a note to Dr. Raymond Sharp, explaining the situation and offering to pay for his client's care. When Millie had done all she could, the Farber boys lifted the moaning victim onto the straw in the back of the rig, placing him on his stomach and giving him a rolled blanket to use as a pillow. Lukens had been delirious or unconscious since the whipping, but he came to just as Farber's boys prepared to drive off.

"Wait," Matthew shouted.

Lukens turned toward the sound. He seemed dazed at first. Then he focused on Matthew, who gave him a drink from a canteen he'd placed near Lukens's hand.

"God, it hurts," Lukens moaned.

"Bear it as best you can," Matthew said. "I've paid these boys to take you to a doctor in Portland. He'll treat you."

A breeze brushed Lukens's back and brought a new spasm of pain. He gritted his teeth and squeezed his eyes shut.

"Damn you," he swore at Matthew. "This is your fault. You were seduced by that witch like the rest of them. If you'd fought for me—"

More pain brought Lukens up short, and he started to weep. His client's ingratitude stung Matthew, but he told himself it was the pain talking. He signaled to the boys, and Peter Farber snapped the reins. Lukens gasped as the wagon bounced along the hard ground. Matthew turned back toward the field and noticed a crowd regrouping. He'd spent his lunch hour caring for Lukens and would have to pick Farber's jury on an empty stomach. He remembered an old adage about no good deed going unpunished as he trudged back toward the makeshift courtroom.

CHAPTER 6

Harry Chambers's establishment stood near a narrow bend where the river slowed before rushing forward as a short stretch of white water. There were no windows in the rear wall of the inn and no moon to light the way, so Matthew used the muted sound of sluggish water churning around the debris that choked the passage to guide him to the riverbank. A log had washed ashore behind a stand of cottonwoods. Matthew sat on it and waited to see if Worthy Brown's information was correct. The gentle *shush*ing of the river made his eyes heavy, and the sultry night air worked like a sleeping potion. Matthew had almost dozed off when the sound of men approaching jerked him awake.

"Do you have the money?" came the nervous inquiry of a clearly inebriated individual known to Matthew as Otis Pike, a slender man in ill health who had been chosen earlier in the day to sit as a juror in *Farber v. Gillette*. Pike had seemed sympathetic to Farber's cause, and Matthew had been surprised when Barbour left him on the jury.

"Will I have my verdict, Pike?" asked a voice Matthew had no trouble identifying as Caleb Barbour's.

"I said I'd deliver, and I will."

"Have the others agreed?"

"Yes, yes. Now let me have my money. I don't want us seen together."

Matthew's initial impulse was to rise up and face the conspirators, but he was armed only with his knife, and he had heard that Barbour was a mean shot. After a moment of indecision, Matthew moved deeper into the shadows and crouched down. He listened to the clink of coins changing hands and a promise that more would be forthcoming when Gillette won his verdict.

Matthew's legs were beginning to cramp, and he worried about making noise if he moved, but Pike saved him by walking off. Barbour followed soon after, leaving by a separate path so as not to be seen with his coconspirator. Matthew considered following Pike to discover the identity of the other felonious jurors, but Pike had too much of a head start, and Matthew knew that there was a risk that he would be discovered eavesdropping. As he waited in the shadows for Barbour to get far enough away that he could risk standing, Matthew wondered if he should confront Benjamin Gillette. He had never heard a word that would suggest that Gillette was the type of man who would try to subvert justice, but Matthew could not be certain that Gillette was not in on Barbour's scheme.

When he could stand it no longer, Matthew rose up and stretched his cramped muscles. He had not slept well since leaving Portland, and he reckoned that there was only a slim chance that he would sleep tonight. As he headed back to his canvas room at the Hotel Parisian, he hoped that some miracle would bring him relief from his fatigue and a solution to his dilemma.

CHAPTER 7

Matthew Penny remained awake for most of his second night in the Hotel Parisian as he tried to devise a plan to deal with Caleb Barbour's treachery. If he went to Justice Tyler, Barbour and Pike would deny his accusation. His word alone would not win the day. Worthy Brown was a witness to Barbour's dishonesty, but no judge would take a Negro's word over a white man's, assuming that Justice Tyler would even listen to Brown. When the sun rose to signal the imminent opening of court, Matthew was still not certain what he would do, but an idea had begun to germinate in his sleep-deprived brain.

The trial in *Farber v. Gillette* took up the morning session, and the evidence in the land-sale case clearly favored Farber. When both sides rested, Matthew had no doubt that he would win the trial if the jury was untainted. As the plaintiff's lawyer, Matthew had the honor of giving his closing argument first. Then he was allowed to rebut Barbour when Gillette's lawyer finished arguing the defense case. In his first appearance before the jury, Matthew reviewed the evidence, establishing for jurors and spectators alike that Glen Farber's cause was just. He made certain to direct many of his remarks to Otis Pike, whom, he noted with pleasure, would not meet his eye. When he finished his opening argument, he took his seat and waited to see what Caleb Barbour would say.

Though the evidence supported few of his points, Barbour looked supremely confident as he argued Gillette's position, and there was a swagger in his step when he returned to his client's side. When Matthew rose for rebuttal, he planted himself directly in front of Otis Pike and addressed the jury.

"Gentlemen, Mr. Farber has relied solely on the evidence to maintain his rights in this case. He has not endeavored to influence your judgment by approaching you secretly."

Matthew watched with satisfaction as Pike and two other jurors lost color.

"The other side has not acted accordingly. They have not been content that you should weigh only the evidence. They have endeavored to corrupt your minds and pervert your judgments. Although you have sworn to Almighty God to render a verdict according to the evidence, they believe some of you to be so low and debased as to be willing to decide against the evidence for pay and let perjury rest on their souls."

Matthew paused. Behind him, he heard murmurs and movement in the crowd. The three jurors who had been caught out stirred uneasily. The other jurors looked confused or offended. Matthew pointed at Otis Pike.

"I know you have been approached, Mr. Pike. I know you agreed to accept a bribe on behalf of yourself and other jurors because I sat in the dark by the river behind the inn while you conspired with Caleb Barbour. You didn't guess that anyone else was privy to your cowardly conversation, but I overheard your foul bargain."

There was the click of a pistol cocking from the vicinity of the defense table and an answering click from Glen Farber's gun. Matthew had told Farber about Barbour's actions and what he planned to do. Farber had come prepared to do violence to protect his lawyer. Matthew turned and faced Barbour, who was on his feet.

"There is no terror for me in your pistol, sir," Matthew said, though in truth his insides were roiling from fear. "You won't win your argument by shooting me. You can win in only one way—by showing that you deserve to prevail under the laws of this state. You will never win this case by bribery or threats of violence."

Justice Tyler slammed the butt of his revolver onto the table several times and shouted for order. Then he pointed his pistol in the direction of both counsel tables.

"Put down your weapons, gentlemen. Remember, you're in a court of law."

Barbour hesitated for a moment before holstering his gun. Farber lowered his as soon as he was certain Matthew was safe.

"Mr. Penny has made a serious charge, and we need to settle this matter before I can instruct the jury," the judge said. "I'm going to adjourn court. All of the parties will meet with me in the back room of the inn in fifteen minutes."

Tyler told the jurors to stay in the field, but he forbade anyone to approach them, and he forbade the jurors to discuss the case until he had charged them. Then he walked toward the inn. A crowd surrounded Matthew and Caleb Barbour.

"I demand satisfaction, you bastard," Barbour said as soon as the judge was out of earshot.

Glen Farber took a step toward the attorney, but Matthew held out his arm and blocked his client.

"You tried to play dirty, and I caught you out," Matthew said. "Take your medicine like a man."

"I said I demand satisfaction."

"Demand away."

"So you're a coward as well as a slanderer."

Matthew was opposed to dueling, but he couldn't risk being branded a coward. In Ohio, if a man was rude, you could turn away from him, but Matthew had learned quickly that men in Oregon were likely to take liberties with someone who did not stand up for himself. The only way to get along was to hold every man responsible and resent every trespass on one's rights.

"Very well," Matthew answered softly. "And since it's your challenge, it's my choice of weapons."

"Choose, then."

Matthew drew his knife from under the folds of his coat and held it up for all to see.

"We'll fight with bowie knives in a sealed room."

The color drained from Barbour's face. Though deadly with a pistol, he had no skill with a knife. He was also a natural coward and a bully, and the idea of a knife fight terrified him.

"I won't fight with knives. They're not a gentleman's weapon," Barbour responded, managing to keep the fear from his voice.

"True, but you've accused me of being no gentleman."

"An accusation we know to be groundless, Mr. Penny," said Benjamin Gillette.

A large, dangerous-looking man stepped out of the crowd and

moved in behind Gillette as soon as the businessman inserted his considerable bulk into the argument. Matthew had never met Francis Gibney, but he recognized the bodyguard, who accompanied Gillette everywhere.

"Come, Caleb," Gillette said, "let this matter be decided by law. Nothing will be served by dueling."

"But . . ." Barbour started.

Gillette closed his hand on Barbour's forearm. "Enough," he said forcefully.

Barbour's fear of losing Gillette's retainer decided the question.

"Why don't you wait for me at the inn," Gillette said. Barbour didn't like the idea of leaving his client with Penny, but it was clear that Gillette wanted him gone, so he cast a disdainful look at Matthew and walked away.

"You know my reputation, do you not?" Gillette asked Matthew.

Matthew nodded, uncertain where this conversation was going.

"Then you know that I am very well connected in this state. If your argument to the jury is a trick to gain an advantage for your client, I will destroy you."

Matthew knew that his career depended on meeting Gillette's eye.

"Last night I saw Caleb Barbour pay a bribe to Otis Pike. The money was for Pike and some of the other jurors, with more to come if you prevailed."

"If you knew about this last night, why didn't you come to me?"

"I'll be blunt, Mr. Gillette. I didn't come to you because I didn't know whether Caleb was acting on his own or was following your orders."

Rather than get angry, Gillette looked suddenly tired. "If there was a bribe, I can assure you that it was not my doing. This case may be important to your client, but the amount involved is a pittance for me."

"Then why have you fought so hard against our claim?"

"If I give in to your client, every son of a bitch in the state will think he can back me down, and I'll spend my every waking hour in court defending frivolous lawsuits.

"But that brings me to something that's had me puzzled. Why would Caleb risk his career over such a minor matter? That's what's got me wondering about your accusation."

Matthew remembered what Worthy Brown had told him. "Caleb Barbour might risk everything to win this case if he felt that losing it could cost him your business. Farber's claim isn't frivolous, but Barbour convinced you it was. He gave you bad legal advice. That's why he bribed Pike. He doesn't want to look bad to you."

Gillette mulled over Matthew's answer, and Matthew was certain he'd scored a point.

"Would Mr. Farber be willing to settle his case?" Gillette asked.

"He might. I would certainly advise him to do so if the sum you offered was sufficient."

"Then I'll settle for the amount of your demand plus your attorney fees on the condition that Mr. Farber agrees to keep the settlement secret and you agree to let this bribery allegation die. Your accusations have tarnished my reputation as well as Caleb's, and I want the matter buried."

Gillette's offer was far more than Matthew had expected, but he did not show that he was surprised.

"I'll talk to my client," Matthew said.

GLEN FARBER WAS JUBILANT WHEN Matthew told him what his conference with Gillette had accomplished. Matthew was as elated as his client. The attorney fee would go far toward digging him out of the financial hole in which he found himself.

With Farber in tow, Matthew followed Benjamin Gillette to the inn. When they were almost there, he noticed Worthy Brown tending Barbour's horse and a mule he guessed was the servant's mount. Matthew was tempted to send a signal of gratitude to Brown but wise enough to do nothing that would put the Negro at risk.

Inside the private dining room, Benjamin Gillette told Justice Tyler that both parties wanted the matter of *Farber v. Gillette* settled. Matthew avoided looking at Caleb Barbour, who stood apart from the others, scowling angrily, his arms folded tightly across his chest.

"Do you plan to pursue your accusations against Juror Pike and Mr. Barbour?" Tyler asked Matthew.

"Mr. Farber and I see no reason to go any further with the matter now that the case is settled."

Matthew thought the judge looked relieved. The Oregon legal community was small and tight knit, and Matthew suspected that Tyler had not been looking forward to conducting an inquiry into the honesty of one of its members.

"Very well, Mr. Penny. Will you prepare the papers?"

"I'll get on it as soon as I'm back in Portland."

Tyler stood. "I'll tell the jury that the case has been settled. There's no need for you gentlemen to accompany me."

"Thank you, Judge," Gillette said. "I'm giving Miss Hill a ride back to Portland, and I know she's eager to continue her journey."

WITH COURT ADJOURNED FOR THE DAY, Harry Chambers's bar was packed. Glen Farber stood Matthew to drinks at the inn to celebrate their victory, and several others customers who had been thoroughly entertained by the afternoon's proceedings also treated the jubilant attorney. By the time Farber left for home, Matthew was tipsy and it was too late for him to start for Portland.

Matthew ordered dinner and settled in a corner of the barroom while Harry fetched his meal. His lack of sleep had caught up with him now that the adrenaline that had kept him going in court had worn off. He closed his eyes and rested his head on his arms, snapping to when Harry waddled over with a steaming bowl of stew.

"This meal is on the house," Harry said as he set the bowl on the table. "We were all rooting for Glen." Harry laughed. "You sure showed up Barbour. It's all anyone's talked about since you backed down that coward."

"I did, didn't I?" Matthew answered with a smile, which vanished as soon as Harry turned his back. Matthew had been elated after his rout of Caleb Barbour and the settlement he'd won for Glen Farber, but he suddenly remembered Clyde Lukens and the injustice the salesman had suffered. Matthew sighed. Law was like that. Victory and elation one minute, and a crushing defeat the next.

PART TWO

WORTHY BROWN'S DAUGHTER

CHAPTER 8

Matthew Penny paid eighty dollars a month to rent an office on the second floor of a three-story building on the fringes of Portland's commercial district. The rent was a little more than he wanted to pay, but the cost was offset by a high-ceilinged loft above the office, which was intended for storage but served as the lawyer's apartment. Matthew had furnished the empty space with a pine table and a rocking chair he'd taken in trade for legal services. He'd used credit to purchase a cot and a stool, which he used as a washstand. Each day, Matthew brought the water he needed from a nearby well, and, with a tin basin, a pail, a piece of soap, a toothbrush, a razor, a comb, blankets for the cot, and a few towels, his apartment was all rigged out.

Three weeks after his trip to Phoenix, Matthew was in his law office with his coat off and his sleeves rolled up, seated on a high stool, hunched over a slanted wooden desk, making copies of court papers that had to be filed by noon. Summer was hanging on, and the sound of steamer whistles, the conversations of passersby, and the clatter of wagon wheels invaded through his open window. When he looked up from his task, he could see sailing vessels bobbing at anchor at the end of a dusty street lined with two- and three-story whitewashed clapboard buildings.

Matthew's hand cramped constantly, and his eyes burned as he worked on the legal papers. He hated every minute of this scrivener's work, but he didn't have the money to hire a scrivener on a regular basis, so he did the small jobs himself. Matthew dipped his quill pen into the well, then shook off the excess ink carefully so none would spatter on his white shirt. The copies had to be duplicates of the original, and, worst of all, they had to be neat and legible. He sighed with relief when he had blotted the last copy of the last page dry.

A freckle-faced boy was waiting impatiently for the documents. Matthew told him what to do with them then flipped a coin to him when he repeated his instructions accurately. The boy pocketed his pay, opened the office door, and froze in midstep. Worthy Brown filled the doorway, a floppy, wide-brimmed hat held before him in his thick calloused hands.

The messenger squeezed past Worthy and bounded down the stairs, casting several curious glances over his shoulder on the way. Though the weather was warm, Worthy wore a red flannel shirt. His feet, which had been bare in Phoenix, were encased in badly worn, homemade shoes, which Matthew was willing to bet were brought out only on special occasions.

"I wondered when you'd come calling, Mr. Brown," Matthew said as he showed his visitor to a chair in front of his rolltop desk. The rolltop, the desk at which the scrivener's work was accomplished; two wooden chairs; and a potbellied stove that provided warmth in winter were all one could find in the way of furnishings in Matthew's office. Its sole decorations were Matthew's framed certificate to practice law and a landscape showing Mount Hood that Matthew had purchased from a street artist.

"I still don't have money for your fee, Mr. Penny," Brown said as his hands worried the brim of his hat in nervous anticipation of rejection.

"You needn't worry about legal fees. Your assistance in Phoenix was much appreciated. Now how may I help you?" asked Matthew, who had been wondering about Brown's legal problem since the Negro had tantalized him with his vague references to it during their clandestine meeting.

"Suh, Mr. Barbour has my child, and he won't give her up."

"I'm not certain I follow you."

"He aims to own Roxanne, but that ain't by our agreement."

"What agreement is that?"

"May I explain? I don't want to take up your time, but the story goes on some."

Worthy looked anxious, and Matthew saw that his hat brim was taking a beating.

"Mr. Brown, where children are concerned, I have an infinite amount of patience. Take all the time you want."

A look of gratitude suffused Worthy's features.

"Thank you, suh, thank you." Worthy took a deep breath and gathered himself. "My wife, Polly, she's dead," he said sadly. "But when she was alive, we was slaves to Major Whitman in Georgia. Then Major Whitman fell on hard times and sold us to Mr. Barbour for his debts.

"I was a field hand on Mr. Barbour's plantation, and Polly worked up to the house waiting on Mrs. Barbour. When Polly took sick and died of fever, Roxanne went up to the house to look after Mrs. Barbour. Roxanne be about ten then.

"Mr. Barbour was hard on Mrs. Barbour. She took to drink then she died. Soon after Mrs. Barbour passed, Mr. Barbour fell on hard times and sold off most of the slaves. One evening, Mr. Barbour fetched me and Roxanne and said we was going. Why he had to leave I don't know, but I know he was a dear friend of the cards, and I 'spect it was something like what happened to Major Whitman.

"We went off in the middle of the night so no one would see, me driving the wagon with Mr. Barbour's trunk and such in the back, Roxanne huddled in among his belongings and Mr. Barbour seated beside me, casting fearful looks every way until we was clear of Georgia. I didn't say nothing, of course. I just do like Mr. Barbour say. Soon, we was in Oregon, and I was working for Mr. Barbour like I done in Georgia."

Worthy looked embarrassed. "Mr. Penny, I can't read. Never could." Then he smiled proudly. "But Roxanne is very smart. While she was working up to the house in Georgia, she sneaked looks at Mrs. Barbour's books and she figgered out some reading by herself. I 'spect Mrs. Barbour helped, too, even though it was against the law for a slave to read. But Mrs. Barbour was a kind woman, and she took to Roxanne.

"After Roxanne got some reading in her, there was no stopping her. She was all the time trying to read and learn. Well, suh, one day Mr. Barbour left the newspaper in the house and Roxanne saw where there was a new constitution with no slavery. I pretended I learnt that in town, and I asked Mr. Barbour about it. All that did was make him mad. He said we was his slaves and that was that, but I kept at him and I wore him down.

Finally, he said if I worked for him for one more year he would free us. I helped clear his acreage and plant his crops. Roxanne done his washing and cooking. After he promised I never said no more about it. Finally, the week before court in Phoenix come the day to be free. Only Mr. Barbour said he never made no such promise."

Worthy's fist clenched, and his jaw stiffened with anger. "I didn't know what to do, but I thought on it all week. The day we returned from Phoenix I faced him again. I told him what you said 'bout the constitution saying no slaves. I said he'd given his word. Mr. Barbour been mad ever since you made him look foolish, and he was drinking more than usual. He fetched his rifle and ordered me off the property, only he wouldn't let me take Roxanne. He wasn't thinking right from the drink, and I was scared he would shoot me if I stayed, so I left, figgering to come back for Roxanne when he was sober and calmed down. I been back there twice since, and each time he told me he got investments in Roxanne and is gonna keep her till the debt is paid off."

"What kind of investment does he claim to have made in your daughter?"

"For clothes and feeding her and giving her a roof over her head."

"How old is Roxanne?"

"Almost fifteen." Worthy's voice cracked. "She is a very good child, Mr. Penny, very mindful. If you can see your way to helping me . . ."

Matthew saw how hard it was for Worthy Brown to ask for

help, and he raised his hand to stop the man's plea and allow him to keep his dignity.

"No need to go further, Mr. Brown. You and your daughter are clearly the victims of a terrible injustice, and I'll help you."

Worthy looked stunned. Matthew guessed that he had never truly believed that he would be able to convince one white man to take up his cause against another.

"Have you thought of taking Roxanne when Mr. Barbour is not at home?"

"Yes, suh, but we is colored, and there ain't no place we could hide. Then, too, I don't want to chance Roxanne getting hurt."

"So you've come to me."

Worthy sat up straight and laid the hat in his lap. He looked very serious.

"Mr. Penny, I believe things should be done legal and by agreement. I made my word with Mr. Barbour that I would work for my freedom, and I kept it. I want him to keep his word."

"Quite right, and we will make Caleb Barbour keep his word. I intend to file a petition for a writ of habeas corpus. That's Latin for 'bring the body,' and we will get the court to order Caleb to transport Roxanne to your arms. You have my word on it."

Worthy Brown sat ramrod straight for a moment. Then he clasped Matthew's hand, shaking it up and down like a thirsty man working the handle of a water pump.

MATTHEW SPENT ANOTHER HOUR ASKING detailed questions about Brown's history in Georgia and Oregon. When Worthy left, Matthew wrote a draft of his habeas petition, which he put away when the fading sun cast shadows across the room. There was an inexpensive café across the street that catered to sailors, working-men, and neighborhood businesses. After finishing off a glass of beer and a plate of sausage, potato, and cabbage, Matthew climbed the outside stairs to his office.

A chessboard lay on the floor of Matthew's apartment. It had taken Matthew a month and a half to make it. When he had finished the board, Matthew had begun carving the pieces. Two white knights and the white king's bishop stood on their appropriate squares. A half-finished queen's bishop lay on its side, unable to stand because Matthew had not yet whittled the base. It was almost dark when he sat down on the narrow landing that fronted the office and settled in his rocking chair to work on the bishop's miter. He whittled slowly on the half-finished chess piece until the night sky filled with stars.

Matthew put down his knife and walked to the railing. There was a constant din from the street below. Matthew welcomed the noise. It was a comfort to someone who lived alone and missed the company of the woman he had loved deeply. When Rachel was alive, he had never felt alone, even when he was by himself.

Time had softened the pain caused by his loss, but there were moments when a memory would blindside Matthew. At first, he had fought the grief that could make him howl like a dog. Then he came to believe that his grief was a tribute to the depth of his love for the woman he would never hold again, and he'd learned to let it flow through him like the river that had carried Rachel away.

Matthew pulled his thoughts away from Rachel and focused them on Worthy Brown. There had never been any question that he would take on Worthy's case. Some cases demanded to be taken: cases that nourished the spirit, uplifted the soul, and gave a lawyer the strength to pursue all of the tired, often petty, lawsuits that make up the bulk of a practice. For Matthew, the deciding factor had not been the loathing he felt for Caleb Barbour or the incredible inhumanity of the man's actions or the value of Worthy Brown's information to the case in Phoenix. What convinced Matthew that he had to represent the former slave was Worthy Brown's unwavering belief in the sanctity of contract and his willingness to resort to the legal system that permitted his people to be treated like cattle. Brown had demonstrated a belief in principle that transcended personal experience and an ability to understand the idea of law sorely lacking in many people of Matthew's acquaintance, including members of the bar.

What worried Matthew was the possibility that he would not succeed. They were in Jedidiah Tyler's district, and Tyler was still bitter about the defeat of the pro-slavery platform at the Constitutional Convention.

Matthew leaned on the railing and thought about the feelings of rage and impotence Worthy Brown had to harbor as a black man unable to save his own daughter without the help of a white man. Then he remembered his own feelings of impotence and rage, pinned to the ground, screaming helplessly, as the river took Rachel from him.

Matthew's chest seized up. Heat seared his cheeks, and his eyes began to water. He had not been able to save the most important person in his own life, but maybe he would be able to save the most important person in Worthy Brown's life; maybe he could spare Worthy Brown the pain of separation that Matthew himself felt so deeply. He stood up straight and took deep breaths. When he was calmer, he brought a lantern onto the porch, sat back in the rocker, and whittled away on the bishop's hat.

CHAPTER 9

While Matthew was working on the bishop's miter, Sharon Hill was sitting on the edge of her bed in the Evergreen Hotel, engaged in futile attempts to move the air in her bedroom with a folded newspaper. Her dress was rolled over her knees, and her bare legs were spread apart to catch any breeze that fortune sent through her open window.

Benjamin Gillette had been a perfect gentleman during the trip from Phoenix and had not questioned the lies she'd fed him about her past. For her part, Hill had plied the older man with subtle questions. Among other things, she'd learned that Gillette was a widower with a daughter who had just returned home from several years of schooling in the East.

When they arrived in town, Gillette had suggested that Hill stay at the Evergreen, Portland's most elegant hotel. Hill told him that the hotel was too expensive for her. As she had hoped, Gillette offered to assist her with the cost of her lodging until she established her business. Hill had protested, but not too strongly. By the time she had said good night to Benjamin Gillette, she was ensconced in a suite with a sitting room, a large bedroom, and a spacious bathroom with a deep, claw-foot tub.

Gillette had not tried to take advantage of her that first night, but he had since come calling for his quid pro quo. Hill had no illusions. She knew she would have to share her bed with Benjamin Gillette in exchange for the luxury of the Evergreen. And sleeping with Gillette was not much trouble. He treated her like a lady. More important, he was quick in bed and usually did not have the staying power for more than one ride.

Trading sex for money was something Hill had done for a long time to survive, but it was not something she had ever enjoyed. She smiled as she remembered the relief she'd felt when she'd closed the door to Warren Quimby's room on her way out of the seedy San Francisco boardinghouse that had been her home for so many years. There was a hundred dollars in her purse, which she'd taken from the metal lockbox Quimby hid in a secret compartment under the floorboards. Her pimp did not mind. He was dead, his leaden pallor testimony to the effectiveness of the poison Hill had used to dispatch him. She'd earned most of the hundred dollars by faking hours of pleasure under the sweaty bodies of the men who had used her. Quimby's only contribution to her labors had been the deft application of painful blows that left no marks and spurred her to greater exertion when the evening's take was too small.

A knock on Hill's door made her jump. "Who is it?" she called as she searched the room for her handbag, which contained the derringer she had carried for protection ever since the night a sadistic customer had beaten her unconscious.

"Francis Gibney, ma'am," boomed a deep voice. "I have a message from Benjamin Gillette."

Hill's heart jumped. "I'll be with you in a minute, Mr. Gibney."

Hill rushed to the mirror that hung above her dresser and hastily applied makeup. Then she did the best she could with her hair, which had been ruined by the soggy heat. When she had salvaged as much as possible, Hill straightened her dress, slipped on her shoes, and opened the door.

Benjamin Gillette's massive bodyguard was forty-five years old, well over six feet tall, and gave the impression that he was hewn from oak that had been seasoned in the woods he'd trapped in during his youth. His face was scarred, and part of his left ear had been chewed off in a fight. His easy grin could not disguise the fact that violence had always been a part of his life.

"Miss Hill," Gibney said, "Mr. Gillette requests the pleasure of your company this Friday evening at a reception at Gillette House to celebrate the arrival of the Oregon Pony."

"I believe I'll be able to attend," Hill answered.

As she spoke, Gibney's eyes roamed over her. There was nothing sexual in the appraisal, and Hill sensed a shrewd intelligence behind the brawler's exterior.

"I'll send a buggy at seven," Gibney said. Then he touched his fingertips to the bill of his navy blue cap before leaving.

He knows, damn him, Hill thought. *But would he tell?* That was the question. She thought that he would not. Gibney was from the world of the rough and tumble. That breed lived and let live. His insolent grin was the tip-off. He wanted her to know that he could spot a whore the same way a connoisseur can discern a fine wine.

Hill was excited by Gillette's invitation. This was the first time he had asked her to join him in society, a sign that her plan to get more from Gillette than temporary lodging was working. The old man was incredibly rich. Hill's scheme involving Benjamin Gillette ended with marriage, but snaring him would require a lot of work. She opened her closet and examined its contents. She had stolen two exquisite frocks from Quimby's wardrobe and all of the jewelry in the lockbox. She chose a low-cut silk gown of emerald green and a diamond necklace. They'd been snatched in a second-story job at some nob's mansion. Hill had worn them on a few occasions when she'd entertained upscale trade. She knew that she would look stunning, and she prayed that they would help to introduce her to a life of ease.

CHAPTER 10

Roxanne Brown served refreshments to the men seated in Caleb Barbour's parlor the way Mrs. Barbour had trained her to serve in Georgia, quietly and deferentially. Most of the men knew Roxanne from previous visits and ignored her, even though the topic of conversation was the Negro race. The Reverend Dr. Arthur Fuller, a visitor to Portland, cast an interested glance at Roxanne the first time she entered the room, but Roxanne was plain, so the reverend paid no more attention to her after his first inspection than he did to the table on which Roxanne set down his lemonade.

It was true that Roxanne's brown skin lacked luster; her close-cropped, kinky hair was indistinguishable from a boy's; her nose was broad and flat; and she hadn't much of a figure. But a person is more than the sum of her physical attributes. If the reverend had taken the time to study Roxanne more closely, he might have noticed that the serving girl was paying close attention to the men's conversation, and he might have discerned the keen intelligence hidden behind Roxanne's large brown eyes. There was, however, little chance that a man like Reverend Fuller would suspect the presence of intellect in a colored serving girl. Men like the reverend know everything and see only what they want to see.

"What do you think about the question?" Roxanne heard Caleb Barbour ask Fuller during one of her forays into the room. The Baptist clergyman was in town to lecture on the benefits of slavery at a rally in support of John C. Breckinridge, the presidential candidate of the pro-slavery Democrats. Many Oregonians had an interest in Breckinridge's candidacy because his running mate for vice president was Joe Lane, the former United States senator from Oregon.

Fuller smiled confidently at the men who had come to Barbour's home to meet him. A sturdy gentleman with sandy blond hair, blue eyes, and a ruddy complexion, he looked more like a healthy farmer than a man of the cloth.

"The answer is simple," Roxanne heard Fuller say. "Throughout history, slavery has been almost universal, and it is expressly and continuously justified by Holy Writ. If slavery is morally wrong, then the Bible can't be true, for the right of holding slaves is clearly established by the Holy Scriptures.

"In the Old Testament, the Israelites were directed to purchase their bondsmen from the heathen nations, except if they were Canaanites, who were to be destroyed. And it's declared that the persons purchased were to be their bondsmen forever and an inheritance for them and their children.

"The New Testament presents a view consistent with that of the Old. Both the Greek and Roman Empires were full of slaves. Many Greek and Roman masters and their slaves converted to Christianity while the Church was still under the ministry of the apostles. In matters purely spiritual, they appear to have enjoyed equal privileges, but their relationship as master and slave was not dissolved. The 'servants under the yoke' mentioned by Paul to Timothy as having 'believing masters' are not authorized by him to demand their emancipation or use violent means to obtain it. Instead, they're directed to 'account their masters worthy of all honor' and 'not to despise them, because they were brethren' in religion; 'but rather to do them service, because they were faithful and beloved partakers of the Christian benefit.' Similar directions are given by Paul and other apostles in other places." Fuller shrugged. "Had the holding of slaves been a moral evil, it cannot be supposed that the apostles would have tolerated it for a moment."

"But what about the Golden Rule, Reverend?" asked Jedidiah Tyler, who thought that Fuller was a pompous ass. Tyler had asked the question not because he disagreed with the minister's conclusion but because no one else in the room was willing to put forward a contrary view.

Fuller smiled tolerantly at the judge. "Good sir, the abolitionists have urged the Golden Rule as an unanswerable argument against holding slaves. But surely this rule is never to be urged against the order of things, which the divine government has established. A father may very naturally desire that his son should be obedient to his orders. Is he, therefore, to obey the orders of his son?"

"And what would a Negro do with freedom, if he received it?" asked Morris Goodfellow, a wealthy merchant who also fancied himself a scientist. "It's an established fact that Negroes lack the intellectual wherewithal to achieve any status above that of a simple laborer. Recently, I have read a scientific article that proves that

Negroes are clearly less than fully human. You must only regard the features of the typical Negro's face to see the truth of this conclusion."

Goodfellow pointed at Roxanne but addressed his host. "May I, Caleb?"

"Certainly. Roxanne, go to Mr. Goodfellow."

Roxanne cast down her eyes and walked over to the merchant, who began pointing at several of her facial features.

"Notice her zygomatic muscles are large and full. Now, this is important because—as Lavater points out—these muscles are always in action during laughter, and the extreme enlargement of them causes a low mind. Too, the Negress's jaw is large and projecting, her chin retreating, her forehead low, flat, and slanting; as a consequence, her eyeballs are very prominent and larger than those of a white man. All of these peculiarities contribute to the reduction of her facial angle almost to the level of a brute."

"I'm not certain I understand you," said W. B. Thornton, the Multnomah County district attorney, who was muddle-headed under normal circumstances and had decreased his level of comprehension further this evening by imbibing more liquor than he should have.

"Ah, but the implications are clear," Goodfellow replied. "Even the ancients were fully aware of this kind of mutual coincidence between the facial angle and the powers of the mind; consequently, in their statues of heroes and philosophers they usually extended the angle to ninety degrees, making that of the gods to be one hundred, beyond which it cannot be enlarged without deformity. Modern anatomists have fixed the average facial angle of the European at eighty, the Negro at seventy and orangutans at fifty-eight. All brutes are below seventy, with quadrupeds being about twenty."

"Are you done with Roxanne?" Barbour asked Goodfellow.

"Quite," Goodfellow answered with mild surprise, since he had forgotten that the girl was standing obediently in front of him.

"You may go," Barbour said. Roxanne left the room but stood quietly behind the closed door to the parlor so she could hear her master speak.

"I have to concur with Morris," Caleb Barbour said as soon as his servant was out of the room. The assemblage listened intently, as they usually deferred to his opinions on matters of the Negro because of his greater knowledge of them as a former slave owner. "I was in Atlanta when a traveling carnival came to town. One of the exhibits was an ape from Africa. The similarities between the ape and my Negroes were astonishing. Now, I am no scientist, so this is simply my uneducated opinion, but based on my observations, I would not disagree with a scientific paper that concluded that the Negro is somewhere between the ape and the white man and not quite a human being."

"AM I A HUMAN BEING?" Roxanne Brown asked herself later that night as she lay in her room in the rear of Caleb Barbour's house. Aside from her narrow bed, the only furnishings were a rickety wooden chair and a small chest of drawers. The tiny, windowless space had originally been a storeroom, and it was stiflingly hot because of the lack of ventilation. Roxanne would have gone out onto the porch if she could, but ever since Barbour and her father had quarreled, Mr. Barbour had taken to locking her in at night for fear that she would run away.

Mr. Barbour had given Roxanne a candle. Her room was pitch-black when she extinguished it. The darkness did not cool the room, but it was conducive to thought, and tonight she was thinking about what Mr. Barbour and his guests had said about her people and apes. Roxanne did not know what an ape was, but she suspected it was some kind of animal that resembled a Negro. Animals were less than human, and Mr. Goodfellow seemed to think that the way her face slanted indicated a closer relationship to the brute than the human. In her experience, most Negroes were treated more like animals than humans, but her father had assured her that the only difference between Negroes and whites was the color of their skin. He had seen the skeletons of dead white men and dead Negroes and the insides of injured white men and Negroes, and he had told her that there was no difference between the bones and guts of the races that he could see.

Was it the thoughts of white people and Negroes that made them different, then? Did white people have bigger thoughts? Whites had written all of the books she'd read in secret, and she knew of none that had been written by her own people. Was the capacity of blacks to think on things smaller? If so, how was she able to understand what she heard and read? It was all very confusing.

Roxanne would have liked to have some books around that could answer her questions, but, unlike Mrs. Barbour, her master had no use for books and preferred to spend his free time gambling, hunting, and drinking. Roxanne's opportunities to read were limited to the rare newspaper that found its way into Mr. Barbour's house.

There were some lawbooks in the house, and one other type of book that Barbour kept under lock and key in a cabinet in his bedroom. On one occasion, Roxanne had found the cabinet unlocked and had looked inside. At first, she had been excited to discover a cache of books, but her excitement had turned to unease when she saw that the books contained illustrations of men and women engaged in activities that she had seen practiced in the dark in the slave quarters of Barbour's plantation before she'd been moved to the house. Some of the activities also reminded her of the goings-on of barnyard animals.

Roxanne's perusal of these pictures had aroused her. She found these new feelings confusing and frightening. Did looking at the illustrations arouse similar stirrings in Mr. Barbour? Since her breasts had begun to grow and her body had started to change shape, there had been times when her master had looked at her strangely. On one occasion, Mr. Barbour had surprised her while she was bathing and had stood overly long at the door, eyeing her queerly. On another occasion, she had turned suddenly before leaving the parlor and had caught Barbour staring at her, then flushing red and glancing away quickly. There was something unhealthy in the way he looked at her.

Roxanne shifted in the heat. Remembering the illustrations made her start to feel the way she felt while looking at them in Mr. Barbour's bedroom. Her hand strayed between her legs, and her fingertips touched her thigh. A current shot through her body, and she moaned. It was an animal moan, and it made her think again of what Mr. Goodfellow had said. Was it true? Was she somehow closer to the animal than the human? Did these feelings prove Goodfellow's point? Roxanne closed her eyes and fought the urge to let her fingers creep upward. She was not an animal; she was a human being, no matter what Caleb Barbour might think.

CHAPTER 11

Milling crowds stirred the dust on the sun-baked streets of Portland into a swirling brown cloud that drifted upward toward the red, white, and blue banner that stretched across First Street. Matthew pressed his handkerchief to his mouth to keep from choking as he hurried along the plank sidewalk toward the waterfront and the strains of a rousing march. Most of the cheering throng was massed along the wharves, but some young men had climbed to the rooftops to get a better view. Sailing vessels, their masts furled, and steamers, their whistles blasting and their smokestacks ejecting plumes of smoke, jammed the Willamette River. At the center of this furor was the steamer *Pacific*, upon whose deck stood the Oregon Pony.

Matthew crossed the street, dodging a wagon and almost tripping over one of the gnarled and blackened stumps that were still in the ground years after Portland's founding. Then the city had been known as Little Stump Town, and its single street ran from forest to forest, unpaved and ungraded, with potholes deep enough to drown a good-size child during the long rainy season, and only trails made by woodsmen leading through the stumps and logs out into the forest. No one called the city Little Stump Town anymore. This thriving waterfront community was the seat of the newly created Multnomah County and the center of every-thing moving up and down the Willamette and Columbia Rivers, which met at the town. Coastal steamers docked near Stewart's Willamette Theater, which had been built exclusively for dramatic productions. There were three daily papers delivered to subscrib-ers for twenty-five cents a week. In addition to livery stables, a public school, saloons, butcher shops, and grocery stores, the town boasted a bookstore, a private academy, a candy factory, and other establishments one expected to find in an up-and-coming metropolis. Today, most of these businesses were closed to cele-brate the arrival of the Oregon Pony.

A grandstand decked out in patriotic bunting had been con-structed opposite the spot on the river where the *Pacific* was docked. Seated in the stands were several dignitaries, including Benjamin Gillette, who was the president of the Oregon Railway and Navigation Company; Multnomah County district attorney W. B. Thornton, who was heavily invested in the company; and Jedidiah Tyler. Matthew found a place on the edge of the crowd as the mayor concluded a long-winded introduction of Joe Lane, the former United States senator from Oregon.

The Democrats had held their presidential nominating con-vention in Charleston, South Carolina, a month before the Repub-licans nominated Abraham Lincoln in Chicago. The delegations of eight cotton states withdrew after the convention rejected a plank that would have guaranteed slavery in the territories. With-out these delegates no candidate was able to win the two-thirds majority required for the party's nomination, so the convention adjourned to Baltimore and chose the fiery orator Stephen A.

Douglas as the official nominee of the Democratic Party. The seceders held a rival convention, nominating James Buchanan's vice president, John C. Breckinridge of Kentucky, as its presidential candidate and Joe Lane as his running mate.

A great cheer erupted from the crowd when Lane was introduced. He smiled and waved. There was another blast of steamer whistles and a flourish from the band.

"Ladies and gentlemen, this is an historic day for Oregon, the West, and our nation," Lane shouted when relative quiet returned. "In this, our second year of statehood, we are about to witness a first—the Oregon Pony! This steam locomotive, built by the Vulcan Iron Works in San Francisco, is the first ever constructed on the Pacific Coast, and it will be the first to run in our state. But," Lane said, pausing for effect, "I promise you it will not be the last."

Lane waited for the shouts and applause to die down. Then he pointed to the occupants of the viewing stand.

"Three years ago, the farsighted men sitting on this platform conceived the idea of building a railroad in this state. Someday soon, the Oregon Pony will run on tracks that will eventually stretch to the Atlantic Ocean. Today, we take the first step in fulfilling that dream."

Hats flew in the air, the band blared, and the crowd cheered as the transfer of the locomotive from the deck of the *Pacific* to the dock began. People started moving from the grandstand to the spot where District Attorney Thornton's portly wife, Abigail, would christen the Oregon Pony. After the christening, Lane, Thornton, and Gillette planned to ride in the cab with an engineer down a short stretch of specially laid track to the railroad bridge that was being built across the Willamette. After the ceremony, the locomotive would be ferried across to the other side of the river where they were laying the line.

As the crowd swept Matthew toward the Pony, he spotted a young man with a slight build who stood five feet seven inches above the ground and sported bright red hair that contrasted sharply with his pale, freckled skin. At twenty-two, Orville Mason was Oregon's youngest attorney. He had been given an eastern education by his father, the Reverend Ezekiel Mason, and his Harvard law degree made him an oddity in a state where most attorneys read law while serving as an apprentice to a member of the bar, and the only requirements for practicing law were a high school education, the ability to pass the supreme court's test of knowledge, and membership in the male sex.

An outspoken supporter of Abraham Lincoln, Orville had been a delegate to the nominating convention of the six-year-old Republican Party and was gaining notoriety in politics. Recently, he had been instrumental in destroying Joe Lane's presidential aspirations.

Early in the year, many had seen Lane, a Northern man with Southern principles, as the only candidate who could unite the Democratic Party, but a combination of Douglas Democrats and Republicans in the Oregon legislature had thwarted Lane's bid to be reelected to the United States Senate. Orville Mason had worked hard behind the scenes to bring about Lane's defeat, which had destroyed his viability as a presidential candidate. But his vice-presidential candidacy as a pro-slavery Democrat worried Oregon Republicans, who knew Lane had many supporters in his home state.

Some of the people standing next to Orville stepped aside, and Matthew noticed that Mason was talking to a young woman. He cut through the crowd to his friend's side and laid a hand on his shoulder.

"I never thought I'd catch you within a mile of Senator Lane," Matthew said.

"Joe's not so bad. It's his politics that stink. Besides, I'm not here to listen to that windbag. I'm here to witness the end of civilization."

"You have no sense of history, Orville," said the young woman, who Matthew guessed to be about eighteen. She was slender and dressed in a sky-blue frock outlined by white lace that tucked in to highlight her narrow waist. Above the waist, the material billowed out, hinting at the full breasts concealed by the soft fabric. A white bonnet decorated with yellow flowers covered her golden hair.

"It's not history I'm worried about," Orville joshed. "Those metal monsters belch black smoke that darkens the countryside and ruins every fabric on which it alights. I have also heard that they travel at speeds so great the passengers risk heart failure."

The attractive young woman was so serious about the subject of locomotion that she did not realize that Orville was teasing her.

"The smoke is true enough," she said, "but you simply shut your window. And I can assure you that no medical problem is presented by the speed. In fact, it is their speed that recommends them as a means of transportation. Think of how quickly you'll be able to get to Washington when Mr. Lincoln appoints you to the United States Supreme Court."

"I shall take a slow boat on that day, and live to serve my country."

The woman turned to Matthew. "I hope you're not as narrow-minded as Mr. Mason, Mr. . . . ?"

"Pardon me," Orville said. "I assumed you knew each other. Heather, allow me to present my good friend and fellow attorney, Matthew Penny. Matthew, this is Heather Gillette."

Before Matthew could respond, Francis Gibney materialized out of the crowd. "Miss Gillette, your father wants you to join him at the christening."

"You two must accompany me," Heather said, hooking Orville's arm with her right and Matthew's with her left. Before Matthew could say anything, she was steering them along the path Francis Gibney was clearing.

THE OREGON PONY was stenciled in grand gold letters on the shiny black carapace of Oregon's first locomotive. Miniature American flags decorated the cowcatcher. In the cab, waiting for Abigail Thornton to christen the Pony, was Joshua Coffee, an engineer sent from San Francisco to train an Oregonian in the secrets of locomotion. Mr. Coffee had tried to talk the well-dressed gentlemen out of their planned ride to the railroad bridge, but they would hear none of it.

"I was afraid you'd miss the ceremony," Benjamin Gillette said to his daughter. Then he spotted Matthew. "Glad to see you again, Penny. Will you be at the reception?"

Before Matthew could answer they were interrupted by the sound of a champagne bottle shattering, an explosion of cheers, and the shrill of steamer whistles.

"See you tonight," Benjamin said as Thornton and Lane dragged him toward the tender. Heather followed her father. Matthew held back for a moment.

"What reception is Gillette talking about?" he asked Orville.

"It's at his mansion. They're celebrating the off-loading of the Pony. Are you a friend of Ben's?"

"No, an adversary, actually. I won a lawsuit against him in Phoenix a few weeks ago."

"Ah, the infamous duel."

Matthew blushed. "That's been greatly exaggerated."

"Well, you must have made an impression on Gillette if you whipped him and he's still inviting you."

"How do you know Gillette's daughter?" Matthew asked, regretting the question as soon as he'd asked it. Rachel had been dead little more than two years, and he castigated himself for having an interest in any woman.

"The Gillettes attend my father's church. Heather just returned from Boston, where she finished her schooling. She was bringing me up to date on my old stomping ground when our debate over the merits of locomotion sidetracked us."

Lane, Thornton, and Gillette climbed into the tender just as Matthew and Orville reached the spot where Heather was standing. Gillette waved at his daughter, and she waved back. Then Mr. Coffee blew the whistle, and the crowd went wild as the locomotive started chugging slowly down the track. The crowd flowed along, shouting encouragement. Heather laughed and cheered like everyone else. The mood was contagious, and Matthew found himself joining in the revelry.

All went well for the first quarter mile. Then, without warning, the engine started spitting water and smoke out of her stack in a regular stream. Dirty water and cinders rained down on the occupants of the tender. Gillette, the district attorney, and Senator Lane tried to duck, but there was no place to hide in the cab. By the time they arrived at the end of the line, their white shirts were black and soggy and their beaming faces were streaked with grime.

"I do believe they're the dirtiest bunch I've ever seen," shouted Heather, who was laughing so hard she could not stand up straight.

"Thornton's such a stuffed shirt," roared Matthew. "Look at him try to maintain his dignity."

"Oh, my," Heather giggled. Then they both started laughing again.

The Pony halted at the railroad bridge, and Benjamin Gillette jumped down, waving his plug hat above his head.

"Your father seems none the worse for wear," Matthew observed.

"He's a boy at heart, and boys love to get dirty. And now, if you'll excuse me, I must get Father home and dried out before he catches his death of cold. I'll see you at seven."

CHAPTER 12

The two Yankee settlers who'd flipped a coin to decide if their proposed town would be called Boston or Portland had situated it in the most idyllic setting imaginable. On clear days a man could look east across a vast expanse of emerald green and feast his eyes on the Cascades, where snow-covered Mount Hood, Mount Adams, and Mount St. Helens pointed toward heaven. On the west side of the river, forest backed up onto two high hills. Gillette House was a solitary gem set in the deep green of the northwest hill. Building anything in that rugged forest was a major undertaking, and the mansion's isolation was a testament to the wealth and power of its owner.

Gillette House could be reached only by a corduroy road that wound upward from the outskirts of town and ended at a curved driveway where carriages discharged those fortunate enough to receive an invitation to feast in the oak-paneled elegance of the dining room or dance in the crystal-lit ballroom. Gillette, who pioneered the use of brick in his bank, broke with convention again by using brick to construct part of the ground floor, but the rest of the mansion was built of solid, horizontal board, painted dark blue to contrast with the white borders of the gables.

The mansion's upper stories projected past those below, and a three-story tower, capped by a conical roof, dominated the north-west side of the house. Broad bay windows on the east side pro-vided a view of the city, the river, and the mountains. The house was situated on the edge of a meadow, and the wide back porch, shaded by a gable, overlooked a garden in which bloomed every conceivable variety of rose. Beyond the rose garden, trails led into the thick evergreen forest.

The sun was still shining, and a piney odor drifted out of the woods as Matthew rode up from the town at a lazy pace. He had pressed a white shirt, and his black silk cravat was neatly tied. A swallowtail coat, light-colored vest, and striped trousers com-pleted the ensemble. When Matthew rode into the large front yard, several prominent citizens in fancy dress were ascending the broad steps to the front porch. He skirted their carriages and secured his horse to a hitching post.

This was the first time Matthew had been invited into the home of anyone of distinction in Portland, and he found the pros-pect of mingling with high society daunting. After dismounting, he pulled his coat down nervously and adjusted his britches before climbing the porch steps.

The chandelier that illuminated the foyer of the mansion made the fixture in Harry Chambers's inn look insignificant. Oil paint-ings decorated the brocaded wall of the stairwell. Matthew fol-lowed the curve of the polished wood banister to the second-floor landing and found himself in a ballroom where skirts swirled, glasses of golden champagne picked up the crystal light of many more chandeliers, and laughter competed with the strains of a waltz. And there, framed in the sunlight that shone through one of the ceiling-high windows was Heather Gillette. Clothed in a white satin gown, her golden hair done up and her elegant neck graced by a diamond necklace, she was chatting amiably with a small group of her father's friends and acquaintances.

Matthew felt guilty about the excitement he felt when he saw Heather. He was still very much in love with his wife. Death didn't put an end to love; it only made a great love more poignant. But Matthew was still a young man, and there had been occasions when he had felt an attraction to a woman he'd seen or met. Whenever this happened, he felt disloyal to Rachel's memory. To date, it had been easy to avoid attachments because no woman had come close to Rachel's combination of warmth, intelligence, and beauty. But something about Heather Gillette created a great conflict in Matthew, and he'd found himself thinking about Benjamin's daughter a lot since parting from her.

Matthew worked his way through the dancing couples, watching Heather every step of the way and failing to notice Caleb Barbour, who turned from the group surrounding Benjamin Gillette.

"What are you doing here, Penny?" Barbour blurted out.

"He's my father's guest," answered Heather, who had not heard about the incident in Phoenix and was shocked by the intensity of Barbour's anger.

"I hope we're not rehashing old business," Benjamin cautioned his attorney.

"I would assume Mr. Penny hasn't much business since he's stooped to representing niggers against men of his own race," Barbour answered.

"That we're of the same race is a source of deep embarrassment to me, sir," Matthew said.

"Enough, gentlemen," Gillette said forcefully. "We're here to celebrate an historical event, not to talk business."

"Do you dance, Mr. Penny?" Heather asked.

"Not well," answered Matthew, who was still staring angrily at Barbour.

"We'll see," Heather said as she took his hand and led him toward the dance floor and away from Barbour.

"Why is Mr. Barbour so angry?" Heather asked as soon as there was a barrier of dancers between them and Benjamin's attorney.

"Caleb brought two slaves with him when he moved here from Georgia, a father and daughter. The father learned that slavery is banned in Oregon and insisted on his freedom. Barbour ran him off his property, but he's keeping the child as a servant. I've sued on the father's behalf to make Barbour give her up."

"Father is letting me write articles for *The Spokesman*," Heather said, naming a newspaper that Gillette owned. "Your lawsuit will make a great story."

To Matthew's relief, Heather's fascination with Worthy's case made her forget about dancing, and he went into detail about Worthy's plight to distract himself from the feelings Gillette's daughter was evoking.

"Surely Barbour won't win," Heather said when he finished.

"If Worthy was white, I would be very confident. But it will be difficult for a judge to side with a Negro. And Barbour will fight to the bitter end, if for no other reason than to torture Mr. Brown for daring to stand up to him."

"I detest Barbour. I can't understand why Father keeps him on."

"He's a good lawyer."

"But you're better. At least, that's what Orville Mason says. Oh, my, you're blushing, Mr. Penny."

Heather laughed, and Matthew's blush deepened.

"I'm glad you came," Heather told him. "Orville said you might not."

"I couldn't pass up an opportunity to see Gillette House," he said, though this was only a partial reason for his acceptance of Benjamin Gillette's invitation.

"You've never been here before?"

"Your father and I travel in different circles."

"Would you like me to show you the grounds while it's still light?"

"I'd enjoy that."

The music stopped, and Heather led Matthew away from the dance floor, almost colliding with Sharon Hill at the entrance to the ballroom.

"Good evening, Mr. Penny. How nice to see you again. Has Mr. Lukens recovered?" she asked with fake solicitousness.

"He was well enough to leave Portland," Matthew answered stiffly.

"Tell him I bear him no ill will, if you see him again, won't you?" Hill said. Then she headed across the crowded ballroom in Benjamin Gillette's direction without another word to the young couple.

"Who is that woman?" Heather asked as she watched Hill walk toward the crowd surrounding her father.

"Sharon Hill."

"You seem to dislike her."

"I think Sharon Hill is very dangerous," Matthew said. Then he told Heather about Clyde Lukens's criminal case and his suspicion that Hill had stolen Lukens's money and lied for revenge.

"If she's just arrived in town, I wonder how she came by an invitation to our reception."

"She knows your father. He gave her a ride in his carriage when he returned to Portland from court."

A frown shaped Heather's brow for a moment. Then her eyes met Matthew's, and the frown became a smile.

"Come, I'll give you a tour of the grounds. But we have to hurry or we'll lose the light."

Matthew followed Heather downstairs and along a narrow hallway that ended at a door near the kitchen. Outside, the smell of roses was overpowering, and the splashes of red, yellow, pink, and a myriad of other colors delighted Matthew's eye. Heather hooked her arm in his as she had that afternoon, and they walked through the grounds in silence until they arrived at a gazebo on the edge of the forest. There were benches along the latticework wall and a view of the mountains. They sat down, and Matthew felt awkward. He had not been alone with a woman in a long time.

"This is my favorite place," Heather said. "I read here every afternoon when the weather permits."

"What do you like to read?"

"I'm addicted to Shakespeare, I'm afraid."

Matthew smiled. "He's a favorite of mine, too."

"You know, I have it on good authority that Charles and Ellen

Kean have been enticed to perform *The Merchant of Venice* at Stewart's Willamette."

"The Keans of London?"

"They're on an international tour," Heather answered.

"But how?"

"It was all spur of the moment. They're in San Francisco. John Potter, who manages Stewart's Willamette, convinced them to come north."

The Keans were among the most esteemed actors in Britain and were touring Australia, North America, and Jamaica, to rave reviews. Stewart's Willamette had never had anyone like them on its boards. Their *Merchant of Venice* would be the cultural event of the decade.

"Would you like to see it, Mr. Penny? We have a box."

Matthew hesitated. There was no question he wanted to see the Keans' performance, and he was thrilled by the thought of spending an evening at the theater with Heather Gillette, but what would it say about his feelings for Rachel?

"I'm sure my father wouldn't mind," Heather went on, and Matthew wondered if he wasn't making too much of the invitation. It was only an invitation to an evening at the theater, not a love affair.

"This is very kind of you," he heard himself say. "I accept."

WITH HEATHER BY HIS SIDE, the hours at the reception had flown by. At one point, it had dawned on him that he was actually happy. The feeling departed as rapidly as it had come to him, banished by uneasiness and guilt, but it had been there, and that gave Matthew hope.

Matthew was reluctant to go home when the party wound down, but the guests began leaving, and Heather had started to yawn. It was dark and cool when Matthew crossed the yard to his horse. He'd just untied the reins when he sensed someone behind him. The incident with Caleb Barbour had made him nervous, and he whirled around faster than he would have under other circumstances. To his relief, it was Francis Gibney who stood before him.

"A word, Mr. Penny?"

"Certainly."

"Just some advice. You've had two run-ins with Caleb Barbour, and there's this lawsuit."

"Yes?"

"Barbour is a man who should be taken seriously. He won't come at you himself unless the odds are heavily in his favor, but he's not above having others do his dirty work."

"Are you saying that you know of a plot by Barbour to harm me?"

"No, nothing like that. But he's been Mr. Gillette's lawyer for a while, and I've seen the way he works. Do you go armed, Mr. Penny?"

"Not normally."

"Then change your ways and learn to shoot. And now, if you'll excuse me, I've got to return Miss Hill to town."

Gillette's bodyguard walked away, and Matthew thought about his warning. If Gibney was right, he would have to be alert at all times. That was no way to live, but he would not run from a man like Barbour, and he would not betray the trust of Worthy Brown by resigning from his case.

Matthew sighed. Coming west had been nothing like he'd

imagined. Losing Rachel had broken his heart, and he'd continued on to Oregon because he knew that he would be reminded of her every day if he went back to Ohio. Matthew had hoped that it would be easier to work through his grief in new surroundings. That hadn't happened, and his law practice had not been much of a success. Now there was Barbour. He wished that life were not so full of the unexpected. All he really wanted was peace, but it looked as if that state of bliss would have to wait. His new priority was learning to shoot a pistol with great accuracy.

CHAPTER 13

Sharon Hill closed her eyes and rested her head against the back of her seat. The carriage Benjamin Gillette had provided for her rocked gently as Francis Gibney guided it down the hill to the Evergreen Hotel. This evening had been interesting. Gillette had not been overtly affectionate in public, but he had introduced her to some of his crowd. They were all powerful and well connected, and she felt that she had charmed the men. How much she'd succeeded with the women was another question. A few had been cold to her. Some, she suspected, were suspicious. A few had been cordial.

And then there had been her encounter with Justice Tyler. He had been leaving just as she arrived.

"I saw you on the grandstand, this afternoon," she had said, "but I wasn't able to get over to say hello. I'm glad I've run into you again. Ever since Phoenix, I've wanted to tell you how impressed I was with the way you ran your court."

"I did my job and nothing more," was his stiff reply, and she sensed that he was uneasy around her.

"And the way you handled the mob. That, too, was impressive."

"They were good men who were misled by their passions. That we are a nation of laws is a concept that's new to many in the West.

Most men will follow the law when they know what it is and that it's there for them," Tyler had said, sounding like a man giving a lecture on civics to a group of students.

"Would most men obey the law without strong men to enforce it?"

"Perhaps not, but I would hope so."

"But are there not outlaws?" Hill asked. "Men whose nature makes it impossible for them to conform their conduct to the rules of society? And doesn't the existence of these outlaws create a need for men like you?"

"Unfortunately, that is so," Tyler admitted.

Sharon Hill had smiled wickedly. "Have you ever broken the law, Judge?"

Tyler had seemed to loosen up, and he'd smiled back. "If I have, I would be foolish to admit it."

"Then you've sinned?"

Tyler's smile had widened. "Ah, Miss Hill, you have me there. I know of no man who hasn't committed some sin, but a man may sin without violating the law."

Tyler had just begun to relax when Ben had come along and the judge had left. Hill sensed in Tyler a ruthlessness and drive that matched her own. And he had been so nervous around her, a sure sign that he was attracted to her. It didn't matter anyway. Tyler was interesting, but Gillette was rumored to be worth millions and he was the prize.

The carriage halted, and Hill opened her eyes. Francis Gibney stepped down and offered his hand. She accepted it but felt no warmth when they touched.

"Thank you, Francis," she said as he helped her out.

Gibney eyed her coolly but didn't reply. He was one of the few men Sharon Hill feared. Gibney was impervious to her charms and made no effort to conceal his contempt for her when his boss was not around. Though she had no reason to believe that he was interfering with her plans for Gillette, she suspected that he would be a formidable opponent if he decided to intervene.

Hill crossed the lobby and climbed the stairs to the suite Benjamin was renting for her. A maid had lit the gaslights when she'd turned down the covers of the oversize bed. As soon as she closed the door, Hill went to her dressing table. She was in the act of removing her jewelry when someone knocked loudly.

The knock was too belligerent for one of the hotel staff. Sharon looked through the peephole and found an intoxicated Caleb Barbour swaying back and forth in the hall. Barbour pounded on her door again. Hill opened it, and Barbour staggered in. She closed the door quickly.

"What are you doing here?" she asked.

"I wanted to see you."

"You're drunk, and it's late."

"Then why did you let me in?" Barbour asked with a self-satisfied smirk.

"Let me make one thing clear, Caleb. I let you in to lessen the chance of a scandal. If someone were to see you at my door in your condition, they might not understand."

"You know I find you very attractive," Barbour said, his speech slurred.

"I repeat, you're drunk, and it's late. I know you'd never come here if you were clearheaded. What would Ben say if he found out that you forced your way into my room in this condition? He's already upset with the way you handled that case in Phoenix."

Hill's mention of Phoenix hit Barbour like a bucket of cold water. Anger cut through some of the effects of the liquor he'd imbibed.

"That bastard Penny," he muttered.

"His accusations were vile, but they forced Ben to settle, and he didn't want to lose that case. He's told me so."

"Did he say anything about me?" Barbour asked, suddenly concerned.

Hill forced herself to look ill at ease. "I don't want you to worry."

"What did he say?"

"Just that he was upset. He wondered if you'd given him good advice when you told him that he could get out of the contract with Farber. I really don't know any more, Caleb."

"But you'd tell me if you knew?"

"Why should I tell you anything Ben tells me?"

"Because I know what you want to do, and I can help you."

"I don't know what you mean."

"You want to get your hooks in him." Barbour cast a sly look in Hill's direction. "Maybe you even imagine yourself as Mrs. Benjamin Gillette."

"Why should that be your concern?"

"You know he'll never marry you."

"Whether he does or not is none of your business."

"It could be if I told you a way to achieve your ends."

"And how would I do that?"

Barbour ran his eyes down Hill's body. "There's nothing free in this world, Sharon. Everything has a price."

"I think you should leave."

"If I leave, you'll never learn a surefire way to make Gillette's fortune your own."

"And how would I do that?"

"Gillette is taking you to San Francisco. Did you know that in California a marriage can be consummated by contract? I know an attorney in San Francisco who will draw up a contract of marriage between you and Ben and forge Gillette's signature by copying the signature on a document I have in my possession."

"What use would a forged contract of marriage be if Ben denies he entered into it?"

"Gillette couldn't deny anything if he was dead. And if Ben was dead, I could be counted on to verify the signature on the contract . . . for a price."

Hill laughed. "I can assure you that Ben is as healthy as an ox. Assuming I agreed to your plan, there's no way we could count on his dying anytime soon. He could last another twenty years. Then what good would the contract be?"

"I've made some inquiries, Sharon. It seems that a pimp named Quimby died under mysterious circumstances shortly before your appearance in Phoenix. I also learned of the equally mysterious disappearance of a woman fitting your description who was living with Quimby and was rumored to be one of his working girls."

It took every ounce of Hill's self-control to keep from reacting.

"I don't know anyone named Quimby," she answered coolly.

"I'm sure you don't. But the woman who did may know how to

make a man's death appear to be from natural causes. If a woman like that owned a contract of marriage with Benjamin Gillette and the affections of Gillette's attorney, she would stand an excellent chance of being recognized as the rightful heir to his fortune."

"You've mentioned this lawyer several times, but you've yet to mention his name."

Caleb moved toward her. "If you're nice to me, I might tell you."

CHAPTER 14

Caleb Barbour slammed open the front door of his house, awakening Roxanne, who cowered in her room. When the door opened like that, it usually meant that her master was mean drunk. And when Barbour was mean drunk, it was often Roxanne who paid.

Roxanne heard the heavy tread of Barbour's boots in the entryway and prayed that he would pass out. The beatings had gotten worse since her father had been chased off. She still ached from the pain Barbour had inflicted the day the papers in her father's lawsuit had been served. She hadn't said a word about the beatings to Worthy because she was afraid of what he might do.

Barbour's heavy steps paused at the stairs. *Please, God, let him go to bed*, she prayed.

"Roxanne! Damn it, nigger, where are you?"

Barbour was so drunk he'd forgotten that she was locked in. Roxanne bit her lip and started to shake. Moments later, the key turned in the lock. Barbour wrenched open the door and stood in the hall, swaying.

"Get out here."

Roxanne forced her feet to move. Barbour stood still and forced Roxanne to walk forward until she was close enough to smell the liquor on his breath and his body's sour odor. She stopped when they were almost touching and cast her eyes down. They stayed in that position for several seconds. Then Barbour walked into the parlor and collapsed into a chair.

"Get over here and take off my boots."

"Yes, suh," Roxanne said as she scurried over as fast as she could. Barbour raised a leg, and Roxanne knelt in front of him. She'd been sleeping in a loose shift, and the fabric pulled away from her body, revealing the tops of her breasts. Even though her concentration was on Barbour's boot, Roxanne knew that he was looking down her nightdress. She tried to block out the thought and focus on the boot. She gripped it and pulled. It was hard to take off, and she failed in her first attempt.

"Are you useless? Can't you do something as simple as this?" Barbour shouted.

"I'm sorry, suh. I'll get it."

Roxanne's hands were trembling when she gripped the boot again. This time she got it halfway off, but it caught on Barbour's heel. Barbour lashed out with his other foot and kicked her in the ribs. Pain shot through her side, and she sprawled on the floor for a second before rolling over to get out of Barbour's range.

"That's right, roll over like a dog," Barbour shouted as he wrenched off the first boot and flung it at Roxanne's head. She raised her hand quickly and deflected the boot, then huddled on the floor waiting to see what Barbour would do next.

"Get this boot," Barbour said, and she was up like a shot. Fear gave her the strength to pull off the second boot on her first attempt. Barbour looked down at her, and she clutched the muddy boot to her chest, fighting back the tears that she knew would inflame him.

Barbour stood unsteadily. He swayed above her and raised his hand to strike her. Then, as suddenly as his rage had come, it departed, and he lost interest in tormenting her. He brought his hand to his forehead and rubbed it. Roxanne tensed, preparing for more violence, but Barbour appeared to have forgotten that she was lying at his feet. The next moment he was weaving up the stairs to his bedroom.

Roxanne lay on the parlor floor curled around the boot until she heard Barbour's bedroom door close. Then she collapsed from relief and sobbed. When she'd shed enough tears, Roxanne took the boots into the kitchen and shined them, knowing that there would be hell to pay if the boots were not clean in the morning. Somewhere in the middle of her chore it dawned on Roxanne that Barbour had forgotten to lock her in her room. The back door was a few feet away. Barbour was probably passed out. If she ran for it now, she would be miles away by morning.

But where would she go? He would send the sheriff after her. They'd come with dogs. She'd seen that happen in Georgia. And she didn't want to think about the beating she would receive once she'd been returned to Barbour's custody.

No, freedom wasn't for her, not for someone whose skin color left her no place to hide. Roxanne returned to her task, sobbing silently as she scraped the mud from her master's boots before shining them so brightly that she could see her tearstained face reflected in the soft leather.

CHAPTER 15

Matthew's mount whinnied when he pulled back on the reins in front of Worthy Brown's log cabin. After dismounting, he rearranged the sack coat he had taken to wearing since Francis Gibney warned him about Caleb Barbour. He'd used part of the attorney fee in the *Farber* case to purchase the coat and two revolvers. The coat hung below his knees and had deep pockets in which the barrels could lie. Matthew had practiced firing the pistols through them, which made the pockets useless for anything but mayhem. The coat was heavy for the season, but it kept the dust off his clothes and provided Matthew with a sense of security.

After receiving Caleb Barbour's assurance that he would set the Browns free, Worthy had built his one-room home in a wooded glade near a fast-moving stream. When he heard Matthew's horse, he looked up from the wood he was chopping. He was stripped to the waist, and his corded muscles were streaked with sweat. Matthew's eyes were drawn to the scars etched into the former slave's chest. When Worthy turned to lay his ax on the woodpile, Matthew saw more scars crisscrossing his back.

"What brings you out here, Mr. Penny?" Worthy asked warily as he wiped his hands on his pant legs.

"Mr. Barbour filed his return to our petition. I want to read it to you and hear what you have to say."

"Is it bad?"

"It's neither good nor bad. It's merely a court document that Barbour had to file. Our petition accuses him of holding Roxanne illegally. If he didn't disagree, we'd win without a fight."

"I see," Brown said. He sounded dejected.

"Mr. Brown," Matthew said firmly, "I'm going to do everything I can to get Roxanne back."

"I know," Brown answered quickly. "It's just . . . I guess I was hoping Mr. Barbour would just give Roxanne back once he saw I had a lawyer."

Matthew dismounted and took a legal document out of his saddlebag. His chestnut mare lowered her head and began grazing next to the front door.

"Why don't we go around back, where it's cooler," Worthy said. Matthew shucked his heavy coat and draped it over the saddle. Then he followed Worthy past well-tended rows of tomatoes, cabbage, beans, carrots, and lettuce.

"Those look good," Matthew remarked.

"I'll give you some 'fore you leave. Try the tomatoes with a touch of salt."

"I'll look forward to that."

They walked down to the stream. Worthy had built a bench and placed it under the shade of an overhanging tree. Matthew drank a handful of water then pulled a handkerchief from his pocket and wiped his hands and brow.

"I don't see how you can work so hard in the heat of the day."

Worthy laughed ruefully. "I been farming since I was owned by Major Whitman, and I been working in the heat of the day seems like forever. Besides, I don't mind the heat. It reminds me of home."

"Georgia?"

"Africa."

"What's Africa like?"

"Speaking now, Africa is mostly a dream. I'm not sure anymore what's real and what my imagination's painted in."

"How old were you when . . . ?"

"When I was stolen away?" Worthy sat on the grass and rested his back against a tree trunk while Matthew took the bench. "Seventeen, I believe, but that's guessing, too. I do recall living near Bambuk-Bure, where the traders came across the desert from Timbuktu to trade for gold. My father sold the traders goats. One day the raiders of al-Hajj Umar Tall attacked our village. My parents were killed. I never saw my sister again. I was captured and chained with the other slaves. They took us to the coast."

Worthy laughed humorlessly. "I'll tell you a funny story. In the harbor I saw a great ship belching smoke from its stacks. I fought like a wild dog then. My people had heard that the white men ate the slaves they captured. We didn't know about steam engines. I thought the slaves were roasting in the ship's ovens.

"You won't believe me," Worthy said with a wry smile, "but I was greatly relieved when they shackled me to my bunk instead of throwing me in the fire. But I didn't truly believe I wouldn't be eaten until I was sold to Major Whitman and he put me in the fields."

"I've heard the journey across the ocean is hard."

Worthy sobered. "Mr. Penny, that ocean voyage must be what the damned suffer when they arrive in hell. Hundreds of stinking bodies packed together in the hold of that ship. We was put in narrow bunks with hardly room enough to raise our heads. They lowered food down and we fought over it like animals. I reckon they feared we'd try to kill them if they come down, but the truth was none of us had the strength. I know I used up mine just trying to stay alive."

"I'm sorry," Matthew said.

Worthy's laugh startled him. "Ain't no reason for you to be sorry, Mr. Penny. Weren't your doing. Now, why don't you read me that paper you brung?"

Worthy's story had depressed Matthew, but he was glad he'd heard it. The abstract arguments against slavery made more sense now that he knew Worthy Brown, and Caleb Barbour's treatment of the Negro was more hideous in the context of Worthy's miserable past.

"Now, remember, this is just what Barbour says. It's not necessarily true. The judge will listen to the evidence both sides present in court and decide what happened based on the evidence, not on what we and Barbour say in the court papers."

Matthew waited to make sure Worthy understood what he'd just said. As soon as Worthy nodded, Matthew began reading Barbour's return to the petition for a writ of habeas corpus.

"'Caleb Barbour, the respondent in said writ, makes the following return thereto, to wit: that he has the body of the said child described in the writ in his care and possession and under his control, to wit: in the county of Multnomah in the state of Oregon.

" 'That the petitioner and father of said child is of the African or Negro race and was a slave of, and owned by, the respondent for many years in the state of Georgia, where the right to hold slaves exists by the law of that state. That the said Roxanne was born in the state of Georgia as a slave and was also the property of this respondent.

" 'That in the year 1856, this respondent brought said slaves to the territory of Oregon as his servants and property.

" 'That in the year 1857, Oregon passed a constitution which, by its provisions, prohibited slavery. In that year, and for some time following, petitioner requested his freedom from respondent, and, in the year 1859, an agreement was entered into between petitioner and respondent to the effect following, to wit:

" 'That the petitioner would work for respondent for one year as a free person, but without pay, respondent to provide room and board for petitioner at no cost to him. And that this respondent was to keep Roxanne and to hold her until she came of age according to the laws of the territory, now state, of Oregon, to wit: eighteen years of age for a female. And that respondent was to hold Roxanne not as a slave, but as his ward.

" 'That this respondent has kept the child at a heavy expense while she was young and her service was of little or no value and now that she has arrived at an age when her services will be of some benefit, the respondent insists that he has the right to retain said child as his ward during her minority, as part compensation and remuneration for the expenditures made by him on her behalf.

"'That this respondent was advised, after it became settled that the people would not be permitted to hold slaves in Oregon, to take petitioner and his child back to Georgia and there sell them, but refrained from doing so because of said agreement between petitioner and respondent, which respondent had reason to believe petitioner would abide by.

"'Furthermore, respondent insists that it is not only his legal and equitable right to retain said child in his possession, but also that it would be far better for said child to be retained by him than to be placed in the hands of petitioner, who is poor and ignorant and unfit to have care and custody and bringing up of said child.

"'And this respondent further says that the said child has always been well and kindly treated and used by respondent, but that said petitioner is somewhat harsh and cruel to the child.

"'And this respondent further says he holds said child by no other authority than set forth above.'"

By the time Matthew finished reading Barbour's answer, Worthy's muscles were bunched and his mouth was set in a grim line.

"Those words are lies, Mr. Penny. I was never cruel or harsh to Roxanne. Never. She is my life. And I never made any agreement to give Roxanne to that man.

"And as for being poor, well, that you can see. But there is plenty of folks has got kids and is poor, and they ain't unfit."

"The judge won't hold your poverty against you, Worthy, and I'm certain that Barbour alleged that you were cruel to Roxanne to put us on the defensive. What does concern me is the allegation that you agreed to let Barbour keep Roxanne as his ward in exchange for his promise that he wouldn't take the two of you back to Georgia and sell you as slaves. If you did make a contract like that, it could complicate matters."

"Mr. Penny, I never discussed that child staying with Mr. Barbour. And as far as going back to Georgia, Mr. Barbour always threatened to take us back when I brought up our freedom, but I never paid him no mind. He ran away from Georgia on account of his debts. I knew he wasn't going back there. The only true thing in that paper is that I agreed to work for our freedom."

Matthew sat silently, thinking. A bird sang and leaves rustled when another bird took flight. Matthew stood.

"You're certain you've left nothing out?"

"That's all I can think of, Mr. Penny. Mr. Barbour is a wicked man, and he's keeping Roxanne to punish me."

"Well, that's it, then. I'll draw up an affidavit for you to swear to, setting out your answer to his allegations. Then we'll get the case set for the next term of court in September."

"You mean I might not have Roxanne back until September?"

"Worthy, I want to be honest with you. There is no guarantee you'll get her back then. The law is very slow at times. Even if we win, there can be appeals that can stretch the case out for months. You shouldn't expect this matter to be decided quickly."

Worthy looked furious for a second, then his rage departed as suddenly as it had appeared and he sighed.

"I'll try to be patient. It's just hard knowing Roxanne's with that man."

"I know it is, and I'm going to try my hardest to get her back. But you have to be prepared for the worst."

THEY TALKED A LITTLE LONGER, then Worthy put some vegetables from his garden in Matthew's saddlebags and the lawyer went on his way.

Worthy watched Matthew disappear around a bend in the trail. He wanted to believe that Matthew would save Roxanne, but there were times when his belief in the possibility of justice wavered. He'd not had much justice since the raiders came to Bambuk-Bure, and it was hard to believe that his luck would change now.

CHAPTER 16

The weather changed for the worse a week before the Keans' Saturday evening performance of *The Merchant of Venice*. The rain, which drove the denizens of Portland to seek shelter, made Matthew realize that he didn't own any means of transport suitable for squiring a young lady of Heather's class to the theater. That problem was solved after Sunday services at Ezekiel Mason's church when Heather invited Matthew to dine at the mansion before the theater and ride into town with her and her father.

On the evening of the show, Matthew was so nervous that he nicked himself shaving. As he rode up the hill, he worried that the Gillettes would notice he was wearing the same clothes he'd worn to the reception for the Oregon Pony, his only nice outfit other than the funereal black suit he wore to court. He also worried about his feelings for Heather Gillette and how he could have them if he still loved Rachel.

When Matthew visited Worthy Brown at his cabin, Worthy had told Matthew that the passage of time had transformed Africa into a dream in which he could no longer distinguish reality from what his imagination had painted in. Was Rachel becoming less substantial with each passing day? There were moments when he had to struggle to recall her scent after a bath or the exact contours of her face. This made him sad.

Even if his memories of Rachel might be fading, Matthew knew that he would always love her. One thing he had learned after Rachel passed was that there was no truth in the part of his marriage vow that read, "Till death do us part." Rachel's death had forced Matthew to think about the biggest of questions, and he had decided that death did not part people who truly loved each other. A person was not only a body. The body was only a vessel that contained a person's soul. The way a person looked did not define her. It was her personality that made Rachel different from every other person on Earth. And that personality—her soul—would live as long as those who remembered Rachel existed.

If death had not parted Rachel's soul from Matthew and he was still passionately in love with her, would it be fair to court Heather, no matter how strong his feelings for her? Was it possible to love two women equally?

And there was another problem. Heather had rekindled feelings in Matthew he thought were dead, but Matthew wondered if he was foolish to pursue her. There were two inescapable facts he had to confront; he was poor, and Heather Gillette was the daughter of the wealthiest man in Oregon.

DURING DINNER, HEATHER TALKED NONSTOP about the interview for *The Spokesman* she'd conducted with the Keans. Benjamin Gillette smiled proudly during Heather's excited recitation of her discussions of Shakespeare, the theater, and the arts with the famous thespians. By dinner's end, Matthew was completely relaxed. He had worried that Benjamin might be upset that Matthew had accepted his daughter's invitation to the theater, but Benjamin seemed pleased to be in his company. When Heather left the men to make her final preparations for their evening out, he offered Matthew brandy and a cigar.

A brief return to summer's balmy weather had surprised Portland, and Ben led Matthew outside to the front porch. Matthew sipped his brandy and contemplated the snowy face of Mount Hood, which was turning a shade of rose in the rays of the setting sun. Benjamin blew a stream of smoke into the air.

"What's come of that matter with Caleb?" Gillette asked.

The question surprised Matthew. Then he realized that it shouldn't have. After all, Barbour was Gillette's attorney.

"He's shown no inclination to return Mr. Brown's daughter, so we'll have to go to court."

"How do you fancy your chances?" Gillette asked as Francis Gibney brought the carriage to a halt at the bottom of the porch steps.

"I think it will be a hard case, but I believe I'm on the right side of it."

Gillette nodded as the front door opened and Heather bustled out, all smiles, her excitement a delight to the two men who waited for her.

PORTLAND'S NIGHTTIME STREETS WERE ALWAYS crowded, but the throng in front of Stewart's Willamette was unusually large. Gaslight shone down on the hoi polloi, who crowded around the entrance to the theater eager for a glimpse of the elegantly dressed ladies and gentlemen lucky enough to have a ticket for the performance. Francis drove the carriage to the curb, using it as a barrier to protect his passengers from the mob. Matthew helped Heather down. She looked stunning in blue satin, her slender neck graced by South Sea pearls the color and shape of a full moon.

The lobby was even more claustrophobic than the street, and Matthew was grateful for Benjamin's bulk, which, coupled with his prestige, cleared a path through the crowd. They were almost through the lobby when Orville Mason hailed them.

"Have you ever seen anything more thrilling?" Heather asked him.

Matthew suspected that Heather was swept away by the excitement of the moment and her visit with the actors, since she must have had some experiences in San Francisco and Boston that rivaled the Keans' premiere.

"Not in Portland," Orville answered.

"Everybody is here," Heather said after a quick perusal of the theatergoers.

A bell signaled the ticket holders to take their seats, and Orville looked for his parents. Heather grabbed Matthew and pulled him after her father.

THE PERFORMANCE WAS MAGNIFICENT. AFTERWARD, Mr. and Mrs. Thomas Eldridge, prominent patrons of the Portland art scene, hosted an elegant affair at their mansion so Portland's elite could meet the Keans. Matthew shielded Heather as they pushed through the crush of bodies in the entry hall. Ahead was a grand room from which issued the music of a string quartet that could barely be heard over the hum of conversation. At one end of the room, the Keans held court near a massive fireplace. Matthew was about to follow Heather inside when Benjamin Gillette grabbed his biceps.

"Matthew, I've some business to attend to in town, so I won't be returning to Gillette House tonight. Francis will take you and Heather back. He'll return here as soon as he's dropped me off and wait until you're ready."

Gillette walked off, and Matthew took two flutes filled with champagne from a silver tray carried by a waiter in livery. As he handed Heather a glass, he told her Benjamin's plans. Heather looked troubled.

"What's wrong?" Matthew asked.

"It's nothing."

"Tell me."

"I think he's seeing that woman, again."

"What woman?"

"Sharon Hill. They were observed dining at the Evergreen, and Papa is taking her with him when he goes to San Francisco on business. I'm not supposed to know, but Francis let it slip." Her shoulders sagged. "I know Papa is a grown man and mother's been dead for some years. I just worry about him, especially after what you told me about Phoenix."

"Your father is very savvy. I'm sure he'll be fine."

"I suppose so, but I don't like it."

"Don't let Sharon Hill spoil the evening," Matthew counseled.

"You're right. Papa can take care of himself. Now, come with me."

Heather took Matthew by the hand and led him toward the Keans, who were surrounded by a crowd of their admirers. Ellen Kean spotted Heather and pulled her into their inner circle. By the time Heather left the party it was clear that her heady experience with the actors and the effect of the champagne she'd imbibed had left her too elated to worry about her father and Sharon Hill.

HEATHER CHATTERED AWAY WHILE FRANCIS drove their carriage through the noisy, gaslit streets of Portland, but she became quiet and thoughtful during the rest of the ride to Gillette House. As soon as Matthew helped her out of the carriage, Francis drove away. When the carriage was out of sight, Heather closed her eyes and breathed in the aroma of roses that drifted up from plantings that edged the turnaround in front of the porch.

"What a magical evening," Heather said dreamily. "I'm too excited to sleep, and the night is so pleasant. Will you walk with me to the gazebo?"

She hooked an arm in one of Matthew's. As they strolled along the path that led around the side of the house and into the garden, their hips touched, and Matthew was painfully aware that only the fabric of his shirt and jacket lay between him and Heather's bare arm.

When they were inside the gazebo, Matthew sat beside Heather. It was too dark to see her face clearly. Then the moon came out from behind a cloud, and he caught her staring at him. He wanted to hold her. From the way she was looking at him, he knew she would not resist. Then they were in each other's arms. The moment their lips touched, Matthew was overwhelmed by guilt and he pulled back.

"What's wrong?" Heather asked.

"There's nothing wrong. It's just that . . . Heather, I was married."

"I know. Orville told me," she answered cautiously.

"She died. You need to know that I loved her very much."

"You don't have to say anything else. I understand."

"No, you don't," Matthew said firmly. "I like you. When we're together, it feels . . . I don't know . . . right. But you need to know that I'm still in love with Rachel and I always will be, no matter what feelings develop between us."

Heather didn't answer for a moment. Then she looked at him steadily. "How did Rachel . . . ? What happened to her?"

"She drowned. We were on our way to Oregon from Ohio. There was a river we had to ford. She was riding with a pregnant friend so she could comfort her during the crossing. The wagon was washed away. It was the only wagon that didn't cross safely."

Matthew choked up when he remembered Rachel's waving at him just before the wagon entered the river. Heather touched Matthew's cheek. Her hand was warm and comforting, and he did not draw away.

"I would never ask you to forget someone you loved so much," she said.

Matthew didn't know what to say. His heart was beating hard enough to frighten him. Until this moment, it had seemed impossible that he would ever be happy again.

THE REST OF MATTHEW'S SHORT STAY in the gazebo was chaste, and he took his leave after promising to see Heather the next day at church. She waved from the front door, and it wasn't until it had closed and she was no longer in sight that Matthew realized that the temperature had dropped and the night air had turned cold. His sack coat was in his saddlebags. He put it on and stuffed his revolvers into the pockets before untying his horse and riding back to town. He let the horse walk slowly, content to prolong the trip so he could think through what had just happened.

Until he kissed Heather, Matthew had not realized how much he missed a woman's touch. Making love with Rachel had always been wonderful, even if they were tired or intercourse was hurried, because he had been with Rachel. More important than the act of sex was the touching and holding, the warmth of Rachel's body and the comfort she provided. Being in Heather's arms reminded Matthew of how much he missed just holding hands with Rachel. Now there was the possibility that he could find that closeness with Heather and be happy again.

So absorbed was Matthew by these thoughts that he didn't notice the two men until they were almost upon him.

Tall firs blocked the moon, casting the trail in shadows, and the men were wearing dark clothing that helped them blend into the night. The nearest man swung a club at Matthew. His horse reared. Instinct lifted Matthew's arm and bent him away from the strike. He took the blow on his forearm as he toppled out of the saddle, falling hard, his arms flailing as the stars whipped past his eyes. The fall stunned him, but his startled mount backed and moved sideways, stopping his attackers from getting to him. While his assailants tried to maneuver around his horse, Matthew regained his wind and his senses. By the time his mount was steady enough for one man to run around it, Matthew's hands were grasping his pistols.

Matthew had gotten to the point where he could hit a man-size target from a good distance. But those targets had been stationary, and they hadn't been trying to kill him. Matthew squeezed the triggers of both weapons as soon as his assailant rounded the horse's rump. Both shots missed at six feet, but the explosions had the desired effect. The attacker froze for a second then raced into the woods. Matthew looked under his horse and saw a second pair of legs in pursuit of the first. He forced himself to his feet and pointed both pistols at the trees behind which the men had disappeared. He fired two more shots; then he waited until his fear abated and his arms grew heavy before lowering the guns.

Matthew's arm burned where the attacker's club had connected, and his legs and back hurt from the fall. The gunshots had startled Matthew's horse and it had run off. He limped down the road after her, turning his guns on the trees at the slightest sound. The horse was grazing in a clearing a quarter mile on. Matthew considered himself lucky that he didn't have to walk back to town and luckier still that he was alive to ride back.

CHAPTER 17

The Reverend Ezekial Mason had built the First Congregational Church on a high hill to serve as a beacon for those in need of enlightenment. Its belfry had served as young Orville Mason's window on the world. Perched like an eagle in his aerie, Orville had peered down from his tower at the wake of stern-wheelers paddling up the Willamette and steamers chugging toward the mouth of the Columbia and wondered where they were bound.

Ezekial and Amelia Mason gave their son his wings and an education at Harvard, where the intellectual curiosity the tall, rawboned minister and his wife had fostered in their only child served Orville well. Orville loved Harvard, but he grew homesick. As soon as he graduated, he returned to the West, where the winding rivers, iron mountains, and verdant forests left no doubt about man's insignificance and God's majesty.

When Matthew rode into the churchyard on Sunday morning, he heard Orville talking to several parishioners about the upcoming election.

"Bell will not be a factor," Orville stated with confidence in response to the question about the chances of John Bell of Tennessee, the presidential nominee of the Constitutional Union Party. "With four parties competing for the presidency, Bell's only hope is to win enough electoral votes to send the election into the House of Representatives, but that's not going to happen."

Like Orville, most Oregonians had firmly held opinions about the upcoming election, and everyone was expressing their opinion because the issues being debated in the newest state in the Union were of a magnitude never seen before. Slavery and secession dominated the editorial pages of Portland's papers, the street-corner arguments of the rabble and the drawing room discussions of the well-to-do.

Matthew's arm was still sore where the club had connected and his back and legs continued to ache. The discomfort had made it difficult to sleep, but pain was not the only reason he had not been able to rest. When he closed his eyes, thoughts of Rachel and Heather alternated with speculation about the origins of the attack. Had he been the victim of a random robbery attempt or the object of Caleb Barbour's wrath?

When Matthew entered the church, he saw Heather and her father standing near their pews in the front row. The thought of meeting Benjamin made Matthew more nervous than the attack. His assailants were gone. The father of the woman he'd kissed in the gazebo was only a few feet away.

Matthew steeled himself and walked down the aisle. Heather broke into a wide grin when she spotted him. Ben turned to see why his daughter was smiling.

"Have you recovered from the events of last evening?" Gillette asked Matthew.

Matthew assumed that Ben didn't know he'd been attacked, and he hoped that Heather had kept their kiss in the gazebo secret, so he guessed that Ben was referring to the Keans' performance.

"I doubt I'll ever see *The Merchant of Venice* performed better," Matthew answered.

"I agree," Ben said. "It was magnificent."

With Heather's father near, Heather and Matthew confined their conversation to the Keans and Shakespeare. When the service ended, the congregation walked across an open space to the social hall, where the wives had laid out a sumptuous feast. Heather and Matthew managed to slip away from her father and find a spot on the side of the church where they could talk unobserved. Matthew didn't want to worry Heather, so he didn't mention the attack.

"I didn't get much sleep last night," Heather said.

"I didn't, either."

"Are you upset with me because I kissed you?" Heather asked.

Matthew saw her concern. He took her hand in his and smiled.

"You have no idea how much that kiss meant to me." Matthew paused. "Even so, Heather, I'm still grieving for Rachel. I don't want to rush into anything."

Heather couldn't help looking disappointed.

"You mean a lot to me," Matthew said, "and I don't want to hurt you."

"I understand," she said. "Do you still want to see me or . . . ?"

Matthew squeezed her hand and looked directly into her eyes. "Yes, Heather, I do want to see you."

She smiled.

"Now let's go to the social," Matthew said, "or tongues will start wagging."

CHAPTER 18

Monday morning, Matthew tried to work on Worthy Brown's case, but his mind kept wandering back and forth between the attack and Heather. He was staring into space, wondering when he would see her again, when someone knocked on his office door. Matthew picked up a pistol and peeked through the curtains. When he saw that his caller was Francis Gibney, he breathed a sigh of relief and put down the gun.

"Good day to you, Mr. Penny." Gibney said as soon as the door opened.

"What can I do for you, Francis?"

"You can come to Mr. Gillette's office. He requests the pleasure of your company, if you've got a few minutes to spare."

Matthew wondered if Gillette was going to warn him away from Heather, but Gibney seemed too cheerful to be the emissary of an outraged father.

"I could use a break," Matthew said as he grabbed his sack coat.

"I don't think you'll be needing those," Gibney commented when Matthew put the revolvers in his coat pockets.

"You couldn't be more wrong. I owe you a debt of thanks for instructing me on the need to go armed. Two men attacked me when I rode home from Gillette House after the theater. I scared them off by shooting at them. I could have been badly injured if you hadn't told me to start carrying a gun."

Gibney frowned. "Can you identify these men?"

"No. It happened very fast, and it was dark. If they walked in right now, I wouldn't know them."

"Let's hope it was only someone fixing to rob anyone who came by, though the road to Gillette House in the dead of the night would be an odd place to wait."

Gibney thought for a moment. Then he said, "Maybe you should carry those pistols, Mr. Penny."

BENJAMIN GILLETTE'S BANK WAS THE first brick building in Portland. His office was on the third floor. An oil painting depicting a deer grazing near a shadowy mountain lake hung in a gilt frame over a satin-covered sofa on the north side of the room. A marquetry cabinet and several glass-fronted bookshelves filled with hand-tooled, leather-bound volumes occupied the east wall. The window behind Benjamin had a view of the Willamette. When Matthew walked in, Gillette motioned him into a high-backed chair on the other side of his ornately carved desk.

"Thank you for coming," Gillette said as he drew out a cigar from a teak box inlaid with ivory. He snipped off the end and lit it.

"Join me?" he asked.

"Thank you, sir."

"It's Ben, and you'll have to get used to calling me that if we're going to do business together."

Gillette noticed Matthew's puzzled look and took delight in his consternation.

"Let me get to the point. I'm a businessman. Business made me wealthy. To become as wealthy as I have, a man has to twist the law on occasion, but I pride myself on never having broken it, and I don't condone lawlessness on the part of those who work for me."

Gillette smiled. "I like you, son. You've got spunk, and I appreciate the way you handled the case in Phoenix. You could have made me look bad, but you did what was best for your client. That's smart business."

Gillette worked his cigar for a moment. Then he pointed it at Matthew.

"I'll tell you something else. This business with the child bothers me. When Heather told me Caleb was keeping that child just to spite his servant . . . Well, it seems to me a white man has no business playing a nigger like that.

"Then there's that bribe. Francis has had a chat with Otis Pike. He admitted Caleb paid him to fix the case. He was surprised I didn't know." Gillette aimed a stream of smoke at the ceiling. He looked grim. "That really bothers me. I won't hold with bribery of a juror, and I won't have my reputation damaged by someone who will.

"I've tolerated Barbour because he's an excellent attorney, but I believe you go him one better, and I heartily approve of your character. Heather approves of you, too, which I assume you know." If Gillette saw Matthew turn red, he made no comment. "That carries weight with me. I'm going to get rid of Barbour, and I'd like to retain you as my lawyer. What do you think of that?"

Matthew was stunned. A lawyer who represented Benjamin Gillette would do very well for himself, but Matthew wondered if he had what it took to represent Gillette's diverse interests. Matthew's conflict could be read on his face.

"There's no need to make up your mind right now," Gillette said. "Think on my offer. I'm going to San Francisco on business. I'll wait for your decision until I get back. Caleb is out, no matter what you decide."

"I really appreciate the offer, Mr. Gillette."

"Ben. Use the week to check me out." Gillette grinned. "Heather can give me a reference. Why don't you have a chat with her?"

Matthew blushed again, but Gillette pretended not to notice. When the door closed behind Matthew, he burst out laughing.

"What do you think?" Gillette asked Francis, who'd watched from the sofa.

"He's a good lad. Plenty of spunk, as you said. He needed it Saturday night."

"Oh?"

"Two men jumped him when he was returning to town from your house. He fought them off."

Benjamin looked upset. "Do you think Caleb was behind it?"

"Hard to say. Penny can't identify the men, and they didn't say anything."

"See what you can find out."

Gibney nodded, and Gillette sighed.

"Bring Caleb here so I can get this nasty business over with."

"Good riddance, if you ask me."

Gillette nodded. Then he crushed out his cigar.

CHAPTER 19

In Phoenix, the "courthouse" was a field shaded by an ancient oak tree. In Portland, a large, open loft on the third floor of the Coleman Barrel Company was rented when the circuit rider came to town. Thick, unpainted timbers supported the roof; sawdust covered the floor; dust motes floated in the light filtering through the cracks in the walls. The crates and barrels that usually covered the floor had been stacked against the walls so the space could accommodate a crowd larger than usual. The spectators, waiting for a glimpse of the nigger who was crazy enough to sue a white man, filled several rows of wooden benches. Among them was Heather Gillette.

Brown v. Barbour was second on the docket behind a criminal case that Orville Mason was defending. Matthew, anticipating the unruly crowd, had Worthy Brown wait in his office. The criminal case took up the morning and part of the afternoon. When the jury reported that it had a verdict, Matthew walked to his office and got his client.

Matthew wore his black broadcloth suit, a white shirt, a black string tie, and polished boots. He was nervous as he escorted Worthy past the jeers and belligerent stares of the men who lined the stairway leading up to the makeshift courtroom. Worthy, wearing the same clothes he'd worn to Matthew's office, walked with his back straight, his head held high, and his eyes straight ahead. There might have been violence had it not been for the entertainment promised by the ex-slave's suit, which captured the imagination of even the most brutal of the spectators. When they reached the loft, Orville Mason was accepting a congratulatory handshake from a grateful client and the district attorney, W. B. Thornton, was walking away, red-faced with anger.

"Looks like you won," Matthew said.

Orville ignored the compliment and glanced at the hostile gallery.

"I wish you the best on this."

"Thanks," Matthew said as he began laying out his lawbooks and court papers.

Orville walked to the back of the loft in search of a seat. Heather motioned him to a spot beside her just as Caleb Barbour started working his way through the crowd. Barbour looked poised and confident and gave no indication that he'd been dead drunk for most of the weekend. When he reached the front of the room, he ignored Matthew and Worthy Brown, but he nodded to the bench.

"Good afternoon, Your Honor."

"Mr. Barbour," Justice Tyler responded tersely.

There was a commotion in the back of the loft, and Matthew turned in time to see Barbour's law clerk, a skinny, bespectacled youth, dragging a reluctant Roxanne Brown into court. This was the first time Matthew had seen the subject of this notorious lawsuit. He knew that Roxanne meant the world to her father, but she appeared to be perfectly ordinary. She was wearing a cheerful red-and-yellow head tie and a new blue dress. Matthew's first impression was that Barbour was taking good care of his charge, but when he looked closer, he detected fear in Roxanne's eyes and tension in her hunched shoulders.

When Roxanne spotted her father, she started toward him. Barbour's clerk gripped her by the upper arm and pulled her back as if she were a recalcitrant child. Worthy started to rise, but Matthew laid a hand on his forearm.

"Your Honor," Barbour said, "I've complied with the writ by producing my ward, but I see no beneficial purpose in having her remain." He cast a glance at Worthy, who stared back angrily. "In fact, Your Honor, the child's presence seems to be stirring up Mr. Penny's client. I suggest my clerk be permitted to take Miss Brown to my office so as not to subject her young mind to the confusion these proceedings may engender in one not capable of fully understanding them."

"Mr. Penny?" Tyler inquired.

Matthew glanced at the spectators before leaning over to his client. "I don't like this crowd, Mr. Brown. If it gets out of hand, Roxanne will be safer in Barbour's office."

Worthy wanted to see his daughter, but he recognized the wisdom of Matthew's recommendation.

"Mr. Brown and I have no objection to Miss Brown being spared the rigors of this proceeding," Matthew informed the judge.

"Very well. Mr. Barbour, have your clerk take Miss Brown to your office, but be prepared to return her here if I so order."

The clerk yanked on Roxanne's arm. Her composure broke, and she looked as if she was going to speak. Worthy shook his head sadly. Roxanne lowered her head to hide her tears as the clerk led her through the gauntlet of the spectators' cruel comments.

"Let's proceed, gentlemen," the judge said when Roxanne was out of sight.

"If the court please," Barbour said pleasantly, "I have a preliminary matter I'd like to raise."

Barbour handed a document to the bailiff and a copy to Matthew.

"This is a motion to dismiss. I believe this suit is prohibited by the Oregon Constitution."

Matthew felt sick after reading the document. Barbour picked up a copy of the state constitution.

"I read from Article I, Section 35: 'No free negro, or mulatto, not residing in this state at the time of the adoption of this constitution, shall come, reside, or be within this state, or hold any real estate, or make any contracts, or maintain any suit therein . . .' I repeat, ' . . . or maintain any suit therein . . .'

"Your Honor, in the affidavit in support of this petition for a writ of habeas corpus, petitioner swears under oath that he is a free man. The court can take judicial notice that he is of the Negro race. The constitution forbids free Negroes from bringing lawsuits in our state. That is my argument."

"Mr. Penny?" the judge inquired.

"May I have a moment? Mr. Barbour never gave me notice that he was going to raise this issue. This is the first time I've seen this motion."

Matthew read the motion slowly, growing more despondent with each paragraph. Barbour smiled at Matthew's distress. He planned to prove to Benjamin Gillette that he was twice the lawyer Matthew was by humiliating Gillette's new attorney in court.

Matthew rose to his feet. "The constitution only bars free Negroes *not residing in Oregon when the Constitution was adopted* from filing lawsuits. Mr. Barbour brought Mr. Brown to Oregon prior to the adoption of the constitution. Mr. Brown was residing in Oregon when the constitution was adopted. He is exempt from the prohibitions of Article I, Section 35."

"Not so," Barbour answered. "It is true that the petitioner resided in Oregon before the constitution was adopted, but not as a free person. He was my slave. He didn't gain his freedom until after the adoption of the constitution."

"What do you say to that, Mr. Penny?" the judge asked.

"Oregon has a history of forbidding slavery, Your Honor. The provisional government prohibited slavery in 1843, and the territorial government did the same in 1848. I would argue that Mr. Brown ceased to be a slave the moment he crossed the border of the Oregon Territory and was a free man when our constitution was adopted. The fact that Mr. Barbour considered him a slave is irrelevant."

Tyler scowled. "Gentlemen, it is clear to me that this issue is too complex to be hashed out in a courtroom during a hearing. Mr. Penny should have been given notice so he could prepare a response to your argument, Mr. Barbour. I'm going to adjourn this case until the next term of court, two months hence. That will give both sides an opportunity to brief the issue. We'll recess for fifteen minutes. Then I'll take the case of *Asher v. Deerfield.*"

"But, Your Honor," Matthew said, "if this case is postponed, my client will be without his child for two more months."

"The issue I must decide is whether Mr. Brown has a right to sue Mr. Barbour. I won't make that decision without adequate research and thought. Have I made myself clear?"

"Yes, Your Honor," Matthew answered, choking back his anger.

"Mr. Penny . . ." Worthy started as soon as Tyler left the bench.

"Not here, Mr. Brown," Matthew cautioned. "I'll answer your questions at my office. Let's get you through this pack of smiling jackals."

"Mr. Penny, I want to know what this means *now*."

Matthew felt sick at heart, but he forced himself to sound determined.

"Barbour has made a clever legal argument, which I believe to be flawed. When next we argue, I'm certain I can convince Judge Tyler that there's no merit to it."

"But that will not be for two months?"

"Unfortunately."

"And Roxanne must stay with Mr. Barbour until then?" Worthy asked as he turned toward the smirking barrister.

"Yes."

"And at that time, I may be told that I have no right to sue him because I am a Negro?"

"That may be true, but I doubt it. I'm certain there's no merit in Barbour's argument."

Worthy drew himself up to his full height and glared at Caleb Barbour with such hatred that the force of his emotions chased the smirk from the attorney's lips.

"You take good care of my Roxanne," Worthy said menacingly.

"Or what?" Barbour responded with false bravado, fearful of the damage to his already-tarnished reputation if a Negro backed him down.

"I'll make myself clear, Mr. Barbour. I ain't your slave no more. I'm a free man. The day when I had to ask your permission to breathe is over. If any harm comes to my Roxanne, I'll kill you, plain and simple, and take the consequences."

Barbour turned pale, and Matthew gripped Worthy's arm.

"Mr. Brown," Matthew said, "this will do you no good. Come to my office, please. We'll discuss this calmly."

Worthy shook off Matthew's hand, but his knotted fists uncurled. Then he threw back his shoulders and walked proudly from the courtroom.

"My, my," Barbour said, his courage returning now that Worthy was gone. "Your nigger's got himself a temper."

Matthew held his tongue and gathered up his lawbooks as the litigants in the next case moved between him and Barbour. Heather and Orville Mason closed in behind Matthew as he rushed after his client.

"That was tough luck," Orville said as they descended the stairs.

"I should have seen this coming," Matthew replied bitterly as he pushed through the door to the street. A wagon rolled by and raised a billowing cloud of dust. Matthew choked and turned his head. When the dust settled, he searched the street for Worthy Brown but couldn't find him.

"The poor man," Heather said.

"He put his faith in me, and I let him down."

"Nonsense," Orville said. "Barbour's ploy is clever, but I'm sure there's a way around it. Let me help you find it."

"Thank you, Orville, but—"

"No 'buts,'" Orville answered with a smile. "I can't abide the idea that Worthy Brown can be deprived of his child simply because he's not white. And, knowing Caleb, I'm certain he's doing this for sport."

"I'll leave you to your work, gentlemen," Heather said. "I must write this story for *The Spokesman*. Please come see me tonight, Matthew."

Heather walked off toward the offices of the newspaper, and the two attorneys headed for Matthew's office. Hope was beginning to edge away the depression that had overwhelmed Matthew in court. Orville Mason was the smartest lawyer in Oregon, and he had been deeply involved in drafting Oregon's Constitution. He would know the intent of the crafters of Article I, Section 35 intimately. If there was a way around Barbour's argument, Orville Mason would find it.

CHAPTER 20

C ourt recessed when Jedidiah Tyler rendered his decision in the last docketed case. The judge was exhausted and wanted nothing more than a quiet evening at home. The sky was threatening by the time Tyler opened the front door of his modest two-story house on the outskirts of downtown, several blocks from the river. There was a white picket fence around his well-tended yard. The house was yellow with white trim, a surprising choice of colors for a man as somber as the judge. Aside from Mrs. McCall, his housekeeper and cook, few people entered the jurist's sanctuary.

The house was dark. Tyler lit the oil lamp in his bedroom then sat on the bed. He was so tired. Lately, everything seemed to take an extra effort. After taking off his jacket, tie, and boots, Tyler opened his shirt at the throat. There was a mirror across from the bed. He examined his face. Lines of age were beginning to show. Gray tinged his temples.

Tyler picked up the lamp and wandered down the hall to his study. He was aware of the silence in the house, a sign of the emptiness of his life. Tyler's study was the only room beside the bedroom where he spent much time. Lawbooks filled the shelves, and legal papers covered his desk. The law was Tyler's passion. On the frontier, where everything was new, it pulsated with life. His dedication to his art had been repaid when he was elevated to the highest legal position in his adopted state. He had achieved everything he could have dreamed of in his profession. Why then did his books and papers seem so lifeless tonight? Why did the legal issues he was charged with resolving seem like petty squabbles between petty men, instead of matters of importance?

Sharon Hill, a small voice whispered. Justice Tyler's world had changed during that moment in Phoenix when he saw her in the crowd, but there was no profit in wanting someone he could never have. Benjamin Gillette wanted Sharon Hill, and what Gillette desired his wealth would always secure for him.

Tyler placed the lamp on the edge of his desk and stared into the shadows in the corner of his study. What did he have, a room full of books and a black robe? Before he attained his current position in society, he had imagined that his elevation to the court would fulfill his greatest wish. Now that he'd achieved his goal, he was still consumed by a desire for something more. *Sharon Hill*, a voice whispered, Sharon Hill. He was bewitched by her.

Tyler considered himself a man of influence, one who was respected and even feared. But he did not have power. Wealth brought power with it. When Gillette said something must be done, it was done. To go against Gillette was to risk ruin. A woman as beautiful as Sharon Hill would be drawn to power and wealth. Ben could offer Gillette House, whose very location bespoke Gillette's place in the hierarchy of society. He could offer Hill wealth beyond the dreams of all but the chosen few. Tyler could offer Sharon a comfortable home and an adequate salary. It did not require deep thought to determine where Hill would come down if presented with a choice between diamonds, silk, and a position in society second to none and his own modest home and equally modest income.

Tyler closed his eyes and tried to beat down the thoughts that besieged him. Envy was a sin, and he was most definitely a sinner because he envied Benjamin Gillette's wealth, which had ensnared the woman who dominated his thoughts and his dreams.

CHAPTER 21

Worthy Brown left the courtroom filled with rage. The pain of the lash was nothing compared to the torment Justice Tyler's ruling caused him. How could a decent man let someone like Caleb Barbour keep hold of his sweet child for even a moment? Roxanne never mentioned it, but Worthy suspected that Barbour beat her. While the thought of Roxanne in pain tore him apart, there was something that frightened Worthy more. Roxanne was maturing, and there was no other woman in Barbour's house. Worthy had seen the way Barbour eyed Roxanne, and the thought of what might happen to her made him sick.

Worthy walked the five miles to his cabin without seeing an inch of the dusty road. His hatred of Caleb Barbour and the system that kept Roxanne from him was an animal that gnawed at him. His anger stretched his muscles so taut that he felt they might rip free from his bones. As he trudged along, Worthy thought about all the things Roxanne meant to him. Polly was dead. He owned nothing but the clothes on his back and his small cabin. His future was over. Roxanne was his hope. She had a chance to grow up free, and Worthy meant to see that she got that chance, but how would he do it? He had put his faith in the law, and it had failed him. Matthew Penny meant well, but Caleb Barbour had outwitted him. Worthy could not read the words in Barbour's motion, but he had read the emotions on Matthew's face. His lawyer had looked defeated, and Worthy had no faith in his ability to turn the case around.

It was late afternoon when Worthy reached his cabin. The walk from town had not diluted his anger and he still had no plan, so he put away his shoes, stripped off his shirt, and did what he always did when he needed to figure out a knotty problem. Worthy took his ax to the woodpile and channeled his hate through it. At first, the logs at his feet exploded, the sound of his blows echoing like pistol shots as chips and splinters flew through the air like bullets. An hour later, Worthy could barely lift the ax. Moments after he made a decision he let it slip through his sweat slicked fingers.

As a slave, Worthy had no choice but to bear every indignity imposed on him. But he was free now. When night fell, Worthy would go to Caleb Barbour's home. When he left, Roxanne would be with him.

CHAPTER 22

Earlier in the day, the drapes had been drawn across the bay windows in Benjamin Gillette's living room to keep the glare of the sun out of the high-ceilinged room, but storm clouds had done a better job than the drapes. Soon after Matthew settled next to Heather on a silk upholstered couch, rain smashed down, rattling the windowpanes, and a darkness that matched Matthew's mood filled the room.

"Orville believes that the case will not go well for Worthy," he said despondently.

"It can't be hopeless."

"Oh, no, in the end we may prevail, but when will the end come? That's the problem. The question is close and one of interpretation. Barbour will appeal if he loses. And there may be a federal question, which will bring the case into the federal courts for more hearings and delays and appeals so that it could be years before there's a resolution."

"And all that time, Roxanne will be at Barbour's mercy," Heather said.

"I'm afraid so."

"Oh, Matthew, it's so unfair."

"Yes, but that's the way the law works," Matthew answered

bitterly. "Damn Barbour. He's just doing this to make Worthy suffer."

"He may also want to get back at you because my father sacked him so he could offer you Barbour's position."

"There's that, too."

Heather stood and began to pace. "There must be a way to make Barbour give up Roxanne."

"We can appeal to his conscience," Matthew said with a harsh laugh.

"That's it!" Heather shouted.

"I was joking. Barbour doesn't have a conscience."

"But he does have debts."

"What are you getting at?"

"Without my father's retainer, Barbour will be strapped for cash. The way he spends, he'll need every penny he can lay his hands on. What would happen if you approached him privately and offered to pay for Roxanne's freedom?"

Matthew considered Heather's plan. Then he shook his head. "It might work if I could raise the cash, but Worthy has no money, and I'm sure I haven't enough to pay the type of ransom Barbour will demand."

"I, on the other hand, am quite rich," Heather said, smiling broadly.

"Would your father give Worthy the money?"

"I don't know, but I would."

"I couldn't let you do that," Matthew said.

Heather stared steadily at Matthew. "We must rescue Roxanne from Caleb. And the cost is no concern to me. I have money of my own, and it is considerable."

"You're certain you want to do this?"

"You've seen how Worthy suffers, and you saw the fear in his daughter's eyes. How could I not be certain?"

"Then I'll go to Barbour and find out if he'll settle this matter for money." Matthew stood up.

"Come back when you're done," Heather said as she stood with him. "I don't want to wait until morning to find out what happened."

Matthew squeezed her hand. "I'll be back soon."

Heather walked to the front door. When Matthew ran to his horse, he hunched his shoulders and pulled down on his hat brim in an attempt to shield himself from cascading drops the size of small stones. As soon as he was mounted, he turned in his saddle and waved. Heather waved back.

This vision of Heather bathed in the glow of the crystal chandelier in the entryway would stay with him during the terrible times that followed.

CHAPTER 23

The morning of the hearing, Caleb Barbour had been very nice to Roxanne, and that frightened her more than the threat of a beating. Mr. Barbour had told her to cook the same breakfast for herself that she was cooking for him. She was used to porridge with bread and water, so eggs and steak were a treat. After breakfast, he'd told her to bathe. When she was clean, he'd given her a new dress and a new head tie to wear to court. That's when Roxanne realized that her master wanted everyone to think she was well cared for. Roxanne thought about tearing the dress to pieces, but she was afraid of what Barbour would do to her, and she didn't believe that anything she did would help. She had tried to imagine her father victorious and the family reunited, but her imagination had failed her. Barbour was white, the judge was white, and everyone who mattered but Roxanne and her father were white. They were going to lose.

Barbour's gray, two-story house stood in a copse of cottonwoods, a mile outside the city limit. In the morning, they had driven to town in his buckboard with Roxanne seated beside him. On the return trip, she rode in the back on the hardwood slats. When they arrived, Barbour ordered Roxanne to give him her dress and fix him a meal. She'd changed into a dress she wore for housework and went into the kitchen. Barbour's victory had made him jubilant, and he drank through dinner. Roxanne thought her master was studying her every time she was near him. On one occasion, as she set a plate before him, his hand stroked her arm. The touch made her sick, and she hurried out when Barbour released her.

After dinner, Barbour commanded Roxanne to prepare a bath. She set a fire under a tub she filled with water she drew from the well each day for Barbour's bath. As she waited for the water to boil, Roxanne prayed that Barbour would go to sleep after he bathed.

When the water was hot enough, Roxanne filled a pail to the brim. The pail was heavy, and Roxanne had to use both hands and bend her back to get it up the stairs to the second floor. The house was dark and quiet, and the only sound other than her heavy breathing was the sound of rain beating against the roof and windows. Barbour's bedroom was at the end of the hall. Roxanne's dread increased with every step she took down the shadowy corridor. She set the pail down in front of the door so she could open it. Some of the hot water sloshed over the rim and scalded her foot. Roxanne bit back a cry and squeezed her eyes shut. When the pain ebbed, she turned the knob.

The door opened into the bedroom and revealed a four-poster bed with the fresh sheets she'd put on that morning. A deep metal washtub was sitting by the window. Caleb Barbour was sprawled in a chair near the tub. A whiskey bottle stood on the rug within easy reach. His shirt was undone at the top and his shirttail was out of his pants. His elegant boots had been pitched across the room, coming to rest beside the chiffonier. A flickering oil lamp left most of the room in shadow.

Roxanne kept her head down to avoid eye contact when she lugged the pail across the room. Barbour sat motionless as she emptied it into the tub. When she leaned over, her dress rode up her slim legs and molded to the curve of her buttocks. Roxanne heard Barbour's breathing grow shallow. The splash of water against metal was the only other sound in the room. Roxanne could feel Barbour's eyes on her, and she left the room quickly to fetch a second pail. She trembled as she descended the stairs.

Roxanne barely felt the weight of the water as she climbed the stairs a second time. She was so distracted that she stumbled on a runner and burned herself again. Roxanne had left the door partly open. She turned her back to it when she pushed it open so she wouldn't be facing Barbour when she entered. From the corner of her eye, she could see him sitting in the chair. The steam from the tub fogged the window. When she bent to fill the tub again, she heard Barbour's chair scrape along the wooden floor.

"Pretty Roxanne," Barbour said softly. A fist clenched in Roxanne's chest. She straightened slowly the way she would in the presence of a rabid dog she did not want to alarm. Her legs shook, and she struggled for breath. When she turned, Barbour was standing inches from her, swaying slightly.

"I'll be right back, Mr. Barbour. The tub gonna take one more pail."

Barbour reached out slowly and touched her cheek. His hand was coarse. Roxanne drew back.

"One more pail," she repeated. If she got out of the room, she could hide until he passed out.

"Shhh," Barbour said soothingly. "There's no need for another pail. The bath is for you, and there's plenty of water in the tub."

"For me? Oh, thank you, suh, but I cleaned myself this morning before court, remember?"

"It's just a bath, Roxanne," he continued as if he hadn't heard her. Then he reached out and undid the top button of her dress.

"No, Mr. Barbour, you don't want to do this," she begged. Barbour undid two more buttons, and she began to sob. When the buttons were undone, Barbour stepped back, and she saw his eyes caress her body. She bit her lip. The dress hung loosely from her slender frame, still covering her breasts but exposing her stomach and the place where her legs met. She kept them clamped together and moved her hands over her groin.

"Take off the dress," Barbour commanded.

"Please," Roxanne begged once more.

"You can't bathe in your dress, Roxanne," Barbour responded with a dry laugh. "You'll get it all wet."

Barbour walked behind her and slid the dress off her shoulders. It glided down her arms and crumpled to the floor, leaving Roxanne naked. She bolted for the door, but Barbour gripped her wrist and wrenched her backward into his arms. Roxanne's scream was muffled by a sweaty palm. Her feet left the ground and flailed for a moment before she was tipped over and thrown to the floor. Barbour followed her down, crushing the breath out of her.

Barbour rested for a moment, breathing heavily. Then he pushed himself up so he could see Roxanne's breasts and flat stomach. His eyes moved to the patch of black curly hair between her legs. He seemed paralyzed for a moment. Then he got to work on his pants. With a burst of energy, Roxanne scuttled backward like a crab. She couldn't see where she was going, and her head smacked into a leg of the bed, stunning her.

Barbour's pants were down around his knees, but he crawled forward and was on her before she could recover. He gripped her knees to pry them apart. Years of hard work had made Roxanne strong. She struggled to keep her knees together while she fought his hands. Barbour struck her in the face with his fist, breaking her nose. The force of the blow uncoiled her body, and Barbour wedged himself between her legs. Roxanne was dazed. Suns burst behind her closed eyelids, and she repeated over and over a simple prayer she knew by heart.

Barbour labored over her in a frenzy, sucking and biting her breasts and slapping her when he found her dry and rough. Roxanne was dazed when he entered her, but pain cleared her head as he thrust back and forth. She gritted her teeth in agony until Barbour collapsed on top of her, breathing heavily for a moment before rolling onto the floor. Roxanne stayed as quiet as a mouse, her eyes closed, too terrified even to cry. Her head ached where it had struck the bedpost, her eyes and lips were swollen from Barbour's blows, and she felt as if a razor had been drawn between her legs.

When Barbour struggled to his feet, she risked opening her eyes. His back was to Roxanne, whom he'd forgotten now that he had no further use for her. He groped for his pants. When they were around his ankles, Roxanne sprang up and streaked for the door. As she fled, her hip struck the bed, moving it sideways into the end table and knocking the oil lamp to the floor. Barbour's eyes fixed on Roxanne, and he failed to notice the flames that licked at the bedroom rug.

Roxanne's terror made her unconscious of her nakedness. She bolted down the stairs and raced into the night. As she leaped from the porch, she ran by Matthew's horse, spooking it.

CHAPTER 24

Matthew Penny rode from Gillette House through a downpour so heavy that he could not let his attention wander from the trail that led to Barbour's yard. The rainstorm was so distracting that Matthew didn't notice Roxanne until she raced in front of his mount. The horse reared. Matthew pulled back on the reins and stared openmouthed as the naked girl streaked into the woods. He almost had his horse under control when the front door slammed open and Caleb Barbour, half dressed and looking like a wild man, leaped off of the porch and pounded after Roxanne.

Matthew dismounted in one smooth motion and planted himself in Barbour's path. The men went down in a heap with Matthew underneath. Barbour planted his knee in Matthew's chest and tried to stand. Matthew grabbed his leg and threw him to the ground. Both men gained their feet and faced each other in a crouch, fists up.

"Penny!"

"What's going on here?"

"Get off my land."

"Not without an explanation. What did you do to that girl?"

"That's none of your concern. Didn't you learn that in court today?"

"Did you molest that girl?"

"The nigger's my property, or did you forget that? A man can do what he wants with what he owns."

"Roxanne Brown is a human being."

"She's a nigger, and she's mine because you couldn't beat me in court. When Gillette gets back and finds out how easily I bested you, he'll realize he's made a mistake. You'll be out, Penny, back representing penniless farmers and niggers—the only clients you'll be able to get."

"Is this what it's all about, Benjamin Gillette's business? Caleb, I had nothing to do with Ben letting you go. Don't take out your anger at Ben and me on this helpless girl. Let me take her away, and I'll make it worth your while. I'll pay you. Let's get out of this rain and settle this lawsuit. Name your price."

"My price?" Barbour jeered. "You're offering to buy Roxanne? I can't sell you a human being, Penny. That's slave trading."

"Not sell her. I'll compensate you for the money you've expended in raising her. It will be a straight business deal."

"Roxanne's not for sale. I like her . . . company. The nights are getting cold, and I'll need to keep warm."

"You bastard," Matthew breathed between clenched teeth.

"A whore's a whore, Penny, whether she's a nigger slave or the boss's daughter."

Matthew roared as he lunged forward. Barbour flung up his hands, but Matthew's fists smashed through them, beating Barbour back through the muddy yard and toward the porch. The bottom step caught Barbour's heels and his feet flew up, tilting his body backward. Matthew heard a sickening crack when Barbour's head struck the pointed corner of the top step. Matthew's momentum carried him over Barbour's limp body and onto the porch. He rolled, then rose, fists at the ready, waiting for Barbour to stand and resume the fight. When Barbour didn't move, Matthew dropped beside him, listening for a heartbeat and feeling for a pulse. There was no heartbeat and no pulse and no reaction to the raindrops that pelted his face and body.

Matthew rocked back in shock. He was a murderer. He'd struck Barbour dead in a rage, without legal justification. It was he who had attacked. Barbour had made no aggressive move before Matthew launched his assault. Matthew had not been defending himself or Roxanne, who was safely away when the blows were struck. Matthew had hit Caleb Barbour in a rage because Barbour had insulted Heather Gillette.

Glass exploded in a second-story window. Matthew looked up and saw flames. He threw his arm across his face as hot glass showered down. A flaming board fell across Barbour's face and set the flesh on fire. The explosion acted like a slap in the face. He remembered Roxanne's desperate flight. She was out there in the dark, naked and terrified. Matthew leaped onto his horse and raced after her.

Roxanne had made no attempt to hide her trail. Matthew tied his horse to a tree near the spot where she'd crashed into the dense woods. The mare neighed with fright, the smell of smoke in her nostrils and the flames reflecting in her panicked eyes. Matthew knew he had to act fast before she tore free of the makeshift hitching post in her zeal to escape the fire. He wasted no time shouting after the fleeing girl. Instead, he rushed through the thick underbrush, ignoring the low limbs that slashed at his face and tore at him. He heard the snap of branches as Roxanne fought her way through the woods and redoubled his efforts until he was in sight of the frightened girl. Blood streaked her flanks. Her arms swung this way and that as she batted aside branches and pushed through the brush.

"Roxanne," Matthew cried.

The girl turned her head, her eyes wide with terror.

"I'm Matthew Penny, your father's lawyer."

The words made no impression on Roxanne, but her momentary halt gave Matthew a chance to reach her. She lashed out, fighting with a fury born of desperation and insanity. Matthew grabbed her in a bear hug. Her body was slippery from the rain, and he had to fight to hold her. She lowered her head and bit him. The sharp pain forced Matthew to loosen his grip, and Roxanne broke away. He tackled her, and they fell to the ground.

"I don't want to hurt you," he cried, but Roxanne was in no condition to understand him.

"Oh, Christ," Matthew thought as he steeled himself to do the only thing that made sense. He felt awful when he hit Roxanne. She went limp and slumped to the ground. Her flesh had been torn in dozens of places, her nose was bleeding, and her lip was split. Matthew took off his coat and put her arms through it. Then he carried the unconscious girl to the road. His mount was barely tethered to the tree. Her eyes bulged with terror as she stared toward the burning house. Matthew hoisted Roxanne onto the horse in front of him and rode toward Gillette House.

There was no need to lay on the whip. Fear drove his mount

full tilt. As he raced through the dark, the rain let up and Matthew remembered Barbour's lifeless form stretched across the porch steps. He wept bitter tears for all he'd lost in that moment of animal rage. His hopes for a life with Heather had been dashed the moment Barbour died. All he could look forward to now was imprisonment or the hangman's noose.

Heather was waiting expectantly in the study at the front of the house. When Matthew's horse raced into the front yard mounted by Matthew and a partially clothed Roxanne, Heather shouted for the houseman then rushed out the front door.

"What happened?" she cried when she saw Roxanne's condition.

"Barbour's dead. His house is on fire," Matthew answered as he helped Roxanne down. Her breathing was labored, and her eyes were now wide with shock; the cuts and bruises all over her body continued to ooze blood.

"Go for Dr. Sharp," Heather told the houseman, who was walking onto the porch followed by a maid as Matthew carried Roxanne inside. "Then tell Marshal Lappeus that Caleb Barbour's house is on fire and Barbour is dead."

Heather followed Matthew inside. "Get this child some clothing," she told a maid as she directed Matthew to a guest bedroom.

Matthew laid Roxanne on the bed, making sure that his jacket covered her. Heather lit a lamp before rushing out of the room. There was a straight-back chair in a corner of the room and Matthew dropped onto it. Adrenaline had kept him going since he rode into Barbour's yard, but he'd depleted his supply. His shoulders sagged, and he held his head in his hands. What was he going to tell Heather when she asked him what had happened?

Heather and a maid came in with clothing and bedding. Heather held the light over Roxanne and pulled aside Matthew's coat. Her face showed her shock when she saw the cuts and bruises that covered Roxanne's body.

"Who did this?"

"Caleb Barbour," Matthew answered in an exhausted monotone.

"Why is she unclothed?" Heather demanded, outraged by the answer that suggested itself.

Matthew shook his head wearily.

"Fetch soap and hot water," Heather told the maid. As soon as she left, Heather knelt beside Matthew.

"Are you hurt?"

"No."

"What happened?"

"Please, not now. I'm exhausted."

Matthew closed his eyes and rested his head on the back of the chair, hoping to forestall the inevitable.

"Was . . . Did Worthy Brown . . . ?"

Matthew opened his eyes, confused by the question.

"Did Mr. Brown kill Barbour?" Heather asked.

It had not occurred to Matthew that Worthy would be a suspect until Heather spoke his name. It now dawned on Matthew that Worthy's name would be the first that came to mind when Barbour's body was discovered.

Matthew started for the door and Heather grabbed his arm.

"Where are you going?"

"I have to go back to Barbour's place to talk to Marshal Lappeus.

There could be a lynch mob. Worthy threatened to kill Barbour in front of the whole courtroom. Everyone heard him. He'll need my help."

Matthew ran out of the room just as the maid returned. Worthy was in danger, but Matthew had more than the ex-slave's safety in mind as he ran out of Gillette House. As long as he wasn't with Heather he could postpone telling her that he had murdered Caleb Barbour.

CHAPTER 25

Worthy Brown left for Caleb Barbour's house shortly after the rain stopped. He brought no weapon. Worthy only wanted his daughter back. He hated Barbour, but he had no wish to hurt him unless it was necessary. It wasn't difficult to find his way through the woods in the dark. Worthy had made this trip from his cabin many times. When he traded the forest path for a country road that connected Barbour's house to a neighboring farm he noticed a splash of scarlet above the treetops. As soon as he understood what he was seeing, Worthy broke into a run. When he burst into Barbour's front yard he saw the body sprawled across the porch steps and rushed toward the corpse. Pieces of burning debris had blistered its face, but the scorched flesh vaguely resembled Caleb Barbour.

"Roxanne," Worthy shouted. The creaking of timbers and the crackling fire answered him. He called his daughter's name as he jumped onto the porch and headed for the front door. The heat and the flames forced him back. A section of the roof started to go. Worthy jumped backward into the yard and heard the sound of horses riding hard.

"It's the nigger," someone shouted as men galloped toward him. One of the riders spotted the corpse stretched out on the porch steps.

"That's Barbour. He killed Caleb Barbour," the man cried out.

Some of the men drifted over to view the rain-soaked, half-burned corpse. Then the men around the corpse turned their horses and rode toward Worthy. He tried to run, but the riders surrounded him. Then a lasso encircled him, and he was pulled up on his toes.

Worthy didn't see the man who broke his ribs with the point of his boot, but he heard the rib snap. Another blow numbed his shoulder. He wanted to protect his head, but the lasso pinioned his arms to his side, and he could only writhe in pain.

"Stop!" Matthew Penny yelled as he drove his horse into the crowd. The men scattered, and Matthew leaped to the ground beside Worthy. He slashed the rope with his knife.

"Get back," Matthew shouted as he brandished his knife.

"He killed Barbour," someone shouted.

"Get the nigger lover," shouted another.

A pistol butt came down on Matthew's head, and the pain blinded him.

"The nigger," someone shouted. Matthew saw Worthy running for his life through a red haze. Then he saw Marshal Lappeus and several other riders charging into the yard. He started to tell them that Worthy was innocent, but before he could speak a rifle butt connected with his skull and he crumpled to the ground.

PART THREE

WORTHY BROWN'S CHOICE

CHAPTER 26

Matthew opened his eyes, but he couldn't focus. When he turned his head toward the light, slivers of pain pierced his pupils. After he'd rested a bit, he raised his eyelids slowly, letting the sunlight in a little at a time. It still hurt, but it didn't sting as it had before. Without the pain from the light to distract him, he could feel his head throb. He closed his eyes again and drifted off to sleep.

The next time Matthew woke up Heather was sitting next to his bed. She wore a plain gray dress, her brow was creased with worry, and her face was free of makeup, but he thought that she had never looked lovelier.

"Matthew," Heather said when she noticed his eyes were open. He wanted to say something, but it took too much effort to speak, so he just stared.

Heather touched Matthew's cheek. "Are you okay? Do you know where you are?"

Matthew could hear the worry in her voice. He tried to say her name, but his throat was so dry that he could only croak. Heather disappeared, returning a moment later with a cup of water. She tipped his head up to make drinking easier and held the rim of the cup to his lips.

"Only sip a little. Dr. Sharp says you must drink slowly at first."

Matthew had difficulty swallowing. He coughed up the first mouthful but succeeded with the next.

"Good. That's better," Heather said.

Drinking a few mouthfuls exhausted Matthew. He lay back on his pillow and rested his eyes, but he managed to stay awake.

"Where am I?" he asked.

"In a guest room in my house."

It suddenly dawned on Matthew that he had no idea why he would be in a guest room in Gillette House or how he'd gotten injured. His inability to remember was unsettling.

"How long have I been here?"

"Two days."

"Two days?" Matthew repeated.

"You've been unconscious most of the time."

"What happened to me?" he asked.

"Don't you know?"

Matthew started to shake his head but stopped when a bolt of pain shot through it.

"You rescued Roxanne Brown. Do you remember that?"

Matthew knew who Roxanne was, but his only memory of her was from court.

"I can't . . . I don't remember."

"Caleb Barbour attacked Roxanne. You saved her and brought her here."

"How was I injured?"

"Worthy Brown killed Barbour. Some men were beating him.

You tried to stop them, and you were knocked out. Marshal Lappeus rescued you."

"Worthy killed Barbour?"

"He's in jail."

Matthew sensed that something wasn't right, but he didn't have the energy to figure out what was bothering him, and he was too tired to ask another question. He closed his eyes.

"I'd like to rest now, if that's okay."

Matthew heard Heather leave the room. The short conversation had exhausted him, but nagging questions kept him awake. Roxanne hurt by Barbour, Barbour dead, and Worthy Brown in jail for Barbour's murder. It made sense but . . . But what? The answer was just out of reach when he fell asleep.

THE NEXT MORNING a light rain fell. It stopped around eleven, and the day was sunny by the early afternoon. Dr. Sharp had told Heather that fresh air would be good for Matthew. With Heather at his elbow, he made his way into the garden along a path strewn with fallen leaves. Even though the walk was short, it exhausted him and he had to rest in the gazebo to get his wind back. When Matthew regained his strength, they set out along the garden paths again.

"How is Roxanne managing?" Matthew asked after a while.

"Her mental state is poor. She has no interest in food, and her sleep is troubled. The maid tells me she has nightmares."

"Does she know that Worthy's been arrested for Barbour's murder?"

"Marshal Lappeus talked to her to try to find out what happened. He told her about her father."

"What did Roxanne tell him?"

"Not much. She was very frightened when he interviewed her. The marshal gave up when he saw how much his questions upset her."

"Has she told you anything else?"

"I haven't asked. She deserves peace and forgetfulness."

Matthew and Heather rounded the side of the house. Heather was talking about Dr. Sharp's diagnosis when the steps that led to the front porch came into view. For an instant, Caleb Barbour stretched across them, blood pooling under his head. Matthew froze. He didn't remember seeing Barbour's dead body, but the memory or hallucination or whatever it was seemed so real.

"What's wrong?" Heather asked.

"Nothing," he lied. "I just feel faint. Maybe we should go inside."

CHAPTER 27

On their third day in San Francisco, Benjamin Gillette told Sharon Hill that he had a business meeting that would take up most of the day. He apologized for abandoning her and gave her money with which to enjoy herself until the evening, when he promised her a dinner she would not forget. Hill placed the bills in her purse, knowing that they would stay there until the afternoon. This morning she would not be visiting the charming boutiques and jewelry stores of the West Coast's greatest metropolis. She would be going to a part of San Francisco that no one described as charming.

In the late 1840s, Latin American whores, intent on mining the forty-niners, pitched their tents near the foot of Broadway and Pacific. Around the whores there soon settled hundreds of convicts shipped by the British from penal colonies in Sydney, Australia, and Tasmania. It wasn't long before the area bounded by Broadway, the waterfront, Powell Street, and Commercial was known as the Barbary Coast, a wicked place where respectable San Franciscans did not go and even the police entered only in pairs and never at night.

Sharon Hill knew the Barbary Coast intimately and had chosen a well-worn, plain brown dress for her outing so as not to draw the attention of the thieves, tramps, and cutthroats who called the coast home. For safety's sake, she also carried her derringer and a knife, though there was less chance she'd need them in the light of day, when many of the neighborhood blackguards were sleeping or passed out drunk. Hill's destination was the Dancing Bear, a thoroughly disreputable saloon owned by an equally disreputable attorney.

The ground floor of the Dancing Bear smelled of smoke, stale beer, and vomit. Two prostitutes, looking pasty and aged without their makeup or the protection afforded by dim lighting, sat at a table near the bar. A rich nob was sleeping it off at a corner table, doubtless stripped of the coin he'd carried when he'd entered sober and eager the night before. Hill paid them no attention as she crossed the room and climbed the stairs. There were many rooms on the second-floor in which the whores entertained. Hill passed them by and stopped in front of the farthest door, which bore the words BERNARD R. HOXIE, COUNSELOR-AT-LAW.

After a sharp knock, the door was opened by an armed and violent-looking thug whose presence was made necessary by the nature of Hoxie's extra-legal endeavors.

"Yeah?" he asked, with no pretense of civility.

"Would you please tell Mr. Hoxie that Sharon Hill, a friend of attorney Caleb Barbour of Portland, is here to speak to him about a legal matter?"

"Let her in, Macy," intoned a deep, rumbling voice from within the room.

The bodyguard stepped aside. Though it was daytime, the

curtains were drawn. Lamplight shone dimly, illuminating some but not all of an office crammed with legal papers, lawbooks, and locked filing cabinets. Dominating the clutter was Bernard Hoxie, a fat man of epic proportions.

"Bring a chair for the young woman, Macy," Bernard Hoxie commanded.

Macy placed a straight-back, wooden chair in front of Hoxie's desk, and Hill sat down.

"Forgive me for not standing," Hoxie said.

Sharon smiled.

"So, you say you're a friend of Mr. Barbour, and you're here on a legal matter?"

Hill nodded. "One requiring discretion and your unique talents."

Hoxie looked at his visitor's attire. It was plain and unpromising. "I'm expensive, Miss Hill."

"Don't let the clothes fool you. I couldn't very well walk through the Barbary Coast looking like the queen of England, could I?"

"Go ahead."

"I need a marriage contract prepared, one that will hold up in court, should that become necessary."

"Why are you asking me? Any lawyer can prepare a marriage contract."

From her purse, Hill withdrew a letter bearing Benjamin Gillette's signature.

"The marriage contract has to have this signature on it, and it has to be prepared by an attorney who's willing to swear, under oath, in a court of law, that the contract was signed in his presence by both parties. Are you up to that?"

Hoxie leaned back and folded his hands across his ample stomach. He studied Hill long enough to make her uncomfortable. Then he sat up as far as he was able.

"For the right price, I might be," Hoxie said.

CHAPTER 28

M atthew's health was improving; he no longer needed to lean on Heather's arm during the walks that had become their daily routine. This morning, the rain had stopped, the sun was shining, and the air was cool and crisp. Being with Matthew every day made Heather happy, but she sensed that something was bothering him.

"What's troubling you?" she asked.

"I didn't sleep well again."

"Did you have another nightmare?"

Matthew nodded. "I was in Barbour's yard, and there was a wall of flame that went from the ground to the sky. It was terrifying, and Roxanne raced toward me. She had her arms spread out." Matthew raised his to demonstrate. "Her eyes were wide with horror, and she was screaming."

This was not the first nightmare he had recounted to Heather. On two occasions he had talked loudly enough in his sleep to bring her to his room.

"What did Roxanne say?" Heather asked.

"I think she was just screaming. If she said something to me, I can't recall what it was."

"You're just remembering what happened when you rescued

Roxanne. She must have been in a panic. She'd been beaten and violated. She was escaping from a burning house."

"What you say makes sense, but . . ." He shook his head. "It just seems that there's more to it . . . something happened that I can't remember that would explain the dreams."

"They're just dreams, and dreams are often nonsensical. You've been through a brutal and frightening experience. You saved Roxanne from fire and violence, and you were beaten unconscious trying to protect Mr. Brown. That would unsettle anyone."

"You're probably right." Matthew said. "Let's not talk about my dreams anymore." He looked up at the sky. Clouds were gathering in the distance. "I don't think this weather will last for long. Let's enjoy the day."

Matthew took Heather's hand, and his mood changed for the better. When they had begun these therapeutic walks, Matthew had needed to lean heavily on Heather for support. When he could make do without her help, they had walked side by side without touching. But yesterday, midway through their stroll, Matthew had reached for Heather's hand, and she let him take it. That simple act had signaled a change in their relationship. Neither had spoken about it, but the heat from Heather's hand filled Matthew with joy and made him feel the way he used to feel with Rachel.

While they ambled through the garden, Heather did most of the talking, and her enthusiasm made Matthew smile. Heather was so positive, so upbeat, that Matthew found it hard to be depressed in her presence, despite the pain from his injuries and his concern for Worthy Brown. As they neared the woods, Heather talked about a story she was writing for the paper. Then she switched to a discussion of a dish she was thinking of asking the cook to make for dinner.

Matthew let his mind wander when they entered a path that led into the forest, and a thought occurred to him. Over the past few days, bits and pieces of his attempt to rescue Worthy had come back to him. Most of his memories were fuzzy, but he had a vivid memory of seeing Barbour's badly burned corpse sprawled along the front porch steps when he'd raced into the front yard where Brown was being assaulted. He'd also had another vision while out walking with Heather in which Barbour was dead but his flesh had not been ravaged by the fire.

Matthew stopped so suddenly that Heather asked again if something was bothering him. Matthew lied and said he felt fatigued. While they walked back to the house, Matthew worked out the only possible scenario that fit the facts. He had to have seen Barbour's corpse on two separate occasions.

In Matthew's nightmare, Roxanne had run out of a burning house. Matthew knew that Barbour had made it out of his house because his body was found on the porch. If his house was on fire, Barbour would have run out, too, and he would have run out before or shortly after Roxanne. How did his body get burned? There was only one possible answer. The roof that overhung the porch had caught fire and collapsed. If Barbour's body was stretched out on the steps, he would have caught on fire.

Matthew concluded that he must have seen the unburned corpse when he rescued Roxanne and the burned corpse when he returned for Worthy. Who had slain Barbour if Worthy was not present when Matthew rescued Roxanne? As soon as he asked the question, Matthew's memory of the events at Barbour's house returned.

Roxanne pulled the curtain back a fraction of an inch so she could spy on Miss Heather and Mr. Penny as they walked in the garden. Her shoulder was pressed against the wall so she wouldn't be seen if the couple looked up. She didn't want anyone to see her. She didn't want anyone to be in the same room with her. She felt soiled by the thing Caleb Barbour had done to her. She felt unfit to be in the presence of decent people.

When Matthew and Heather disappeared from view, Roxanne sat down in the wicker chair next to her bed. Miss Heather treated her so well, but how would she act if she knew what Roxanne had done with Mr. Barbour? She hadn't wanted to do that thing; she had fought as hard as she could, but that didn't change what had happened. And now her father might hang because of her.

Roxanne remembered the night her master came home drunk and made her shine his boots. She could have run away that night, but fear had paralyzed her. She deserved what Mr. Barbour had done to her. It was her punishment. She had known what would happen if she stayed in Mr. Barbour's house; she'd seen the books in Mr. Barbour's room and the way he looked at her. She knew and she'd stayed, and now her father would pay the price of her cowardice.

CHAPTER 29

Worthy Brown and Kevin O'Toole, who'd been convicted of murdering a man named Flynn, were the city jail's only occupants. The paucity of prisoners had nothing to do with Portland's crime rate. The jail was a disgrace. There were numerous cracks in the hewn-timber roof and walls, and the narrow passage up the center of the building had an earthen floor. Wind blew constantly through the chinks. During Oregon's long rainy season, the floor turned to mud. If the roof had been repaired, the marshal would have used one of the rooms in the jail as officers' quarters, but the city council refused to allocate funds for this purpose, so Marshal Lappeus refused to post his men in the jail when the rains came. This didn't mean there were unattended prisoners in the jail. Scarcely a day went by without an arrest for drunkenness or some minor offense, but during the rainy season, insignificant rogues and scoundrels were released because of the marshal's extreme reluctance to confine them in Portland's shoddily constructed dungeon. An exception had been made for the two murder suspects, who could not be set free or left unattended, and the marshal had assigned guards to watch the prisoners.

On the morning Matthew visited the jail, a wall of rolling black clouds hid the snowcapped mountains of the Cascade Range from view and erased the sun. Then rain fell with a vengeance, turning the dusty streets of Portland into a bog. Some merchants had laid planks across the swampy thoroughfares in hopes of encouraging trade, but most of the city's residents had enough sense to stay out of the rain. Two men nursing coffees in a café on First Street watched sympathetically when Matthew, mud-spattered, distracted, and bedraggled, fought past their window, one hand on the brim of his hat and bent low into the wind like a sailor standing watch in a gale.

Matthew had to shout at the top of his lungs and rap three times on the jail door to be heard above the torrential downpour. When Amos Strayer opened up, Matthew saw a chair, an oil lamp. and a Bible in the only dry spot near the outer wall. There were beads of water on Strayer's beard and poncho.

"Sorry I took so long, Mr. Penny. I couldn't hear you."

"Don't apologize, Amos. Just let me in. I'm drowning."

The guard stepped aside, and Matthew squeezed by.

"What's that?" Strayer asked, suspiciously eyeing the bundle Matthew withdrew from under his slicker.

"A blanket and a change of clothes for Mr. Brown. I cleared it with the marshal."

"I don't know—"

"You want me to make Jim run across the street in this rain to clear this up? He'll have you patrolling outside until the skies clear. Not that it'd make much difference," Matthew said, just as a huge drop bounced off the brim of his hat.

Strayer smiled. "You made your point. Prisoner's in the last cell."

Matthew followed Strayer to the end of the muddy corridor, stepping carefully to avoid the largest puddles. The deputy opened a square peephole in the center of a thick wooden door and peered inside. The prisoner was curled up in his bunk on the moldy straw that served as a mattress, but he was not asleep.

"Stay where you are, boy," Strayer commanded, "you got a visitor."

Strayer opened the door, and Worthy lifted his head, staring at the lawyer with dull eyes. Strayer locked the door behind Matthew.

"Holler when you want out," the deputy said before returning to his post.

Matthew's nostril's flared involuntarily when they were assailed by the dank, repulsive odor of decay that permeated the cell. Worthy shivered under the thin blanket he'd wrapped around his shoulders. When he sat up, he seemed less substantial than the muscular giant Matthew had seen chopping wood when he'd visited Worthy's cabin.

Matthew shook off the water from his hat and revealed the dressing that covered the wound on his head and the yellow-black bruises around his eyes. Worthy's jaw was still swollen, and he moved slowly as he tried to find a comfortable upright position.

"We're a sorry-looking pair," Matthew said with a tired grin.

"I been better."

"How are they treating you?"

Worthy shrugged. "Mostly, they leave me alone."

Matthew suddenly remembered the bundle. "I brought you a blanket and a change of clothes. Thought you might need them."

"Thank you," Worthy said as he stowed the package in a dry corner of his bunk.

"I would have come sooner, but I was pretty beat up."

"I understand." Worthy hesitated. Then he took a deep breath. "How's Roxanne?"

"She's staying at Gillette House with Heather. Heather's a rock. She's with her all the time."

"How is my girl?" Worthy persisted.

"She's quiet, Worthy. What Barbour did to her . . . She's bearing up, but it's been hard. Heather thinks she's getting better every day."

Worthy nodded, but he seemed to draw inside himself. Matthew thought about the best way to bring up the reason for his visit.

"Worthy, about your charges . . . ," he said.

Worthy looked up. Matthew sat on the bunk beside him and looked away, unable to meet Worthy's eye.

"I know you didn't kill Caleb Barbour," Matthew said. "I did."

"You?"

"Barbour . . . attacked Roxanne." He couldn't bring himself to say the word *rape* in Worthy's presence. "After he'd . . . had her, she got away. I rode up just as she ran out of the house. She was naked, Worthy, and that bastard was pursuing her."

Matthew was having trouble breathing. He grabbed his pant legs to stop his hands from shaking. When he turned to Worthy, there were tears in his eyes.

"I didn't have to kill him. It just happened. I could have taken Roxanne away."

Matthew paused to catch his breath. "I would have told the marshal or District Attorney Thornton, but I didn't remember what happened until two days ago. I was too weak to see you until today. I'm sorry you were beaten and put in this place. You'll be out soon. I'm going to see Mr. Thornton after I leave. I just wanted a chance to tell you what happened before they lock me up."

Worthy digested what Matthew had told him. Then he nodded his head a few times like a man who'd made an important decision.

"They ain't locking you up," Worthy said firmly.

"They'll have to. I murdered a man in cold blood."

"You saved my Roxanne. I ain't gonna let harm come to you."

"There's nothing you can do."

"That's where you're wrong, Mr. Penny. I'm an old man. Ain't no one gonna miss me when I die, 'cept Roxanne. But you are a young man, a good man. You have your life in front of you."

It slowly dawned on Matthew where Worthy was going. He shook his head vigorously.

"You're not going to take the blame for something I did."

"Ain't your say. Everyone believes I killed Mr. Barbour, and I would have if I was in that yard when Roxanne came out of that house. It was God put you there to save Roxanne, and it was God put me in this cell so you can be free to do his work."

"Worthy, they'll hang you."

"I know, but don't you see, all I ever wanted was for Roxanne to be free. Now I got that, I'm ready for what comes."

"You're being ridiculous. I can't let you die for me. Believe me, it would be no gift. Barbour was scum, but even his death is an unbearable burden. Imagine what it will be like for me to have your death on my conscience. I couldn't live with that. What kind of man do you think I'd be if I let you do this?"

"Mr. Penny, I'm free, and free men decide what to do with their lives," Worthy answered calmly. "That's the difference between being free and being a slave. You talk about living with yourself if I take the blame for killing Caleb Barbour. Imagine how I'll feel knowing our troubles destroyed your life?"

Matthew argued with Worthy a little longer, but it soon became clear that he had no chance of changing Worthy's mind this morning. Matthew stood and hollered for Amos Strayer.

"I'm going now. You think about what I said. I appreciate what you're trying to do for me, but it's not the right thing."

"Thank you for the blanket and clothing," Worthy answered, avoiding further discussion of who would take responsibility for Caleb Barbour's death. "Tell Roxanne I love her and think about her all the time, and thank Miss Heather for her kindness."

CHAPTER 30

A group of miserable stevedores huddled together on the shore as the steamer *Argentine* slipped sideways toward its mooring. Sheets of rain had made the gentle slope that led down to the water treacherous. Boards covered the ground to give the drenched dockhands some purchase when they unloaded the *Argentine*'s cargo.

The driver stopped Benjamin Gillette's coach as close to the dock as possible and scrambled down from his seat. He was wrapped in a poncho and wearing a wide-brimmed hat, but they were of little use in this downpour.

"I'm going down to the dock, Miss Gillette," he shouted into the coach before trudging toward the steamer with a large umbrella. Heather could barely hear him over the rain, which rattled on the roof like a cascade of iron nails. She strained for a glimpse of her father through the rain-streaked window, but the downpour was keeping the passengers inside the lounge.

The steamer's whistle blared as its gangplank was lowered to the landing. Moments later, Francis Gibney preceded Benjamin Gillette and Sharon Hill onto the deck. The driver held the umbrella over the heads of Benjamin and his mistress and they rushed over the gangplank toward the coach. Heather opened the door. Her father and Hill ducked inside while the driver returned to the ship to help Francis with the luggage.

"You shouldn't have come out in this weather," Benjamin told his daughter.

"I had to. Something terrible happened while you were gone, and I wanted to tell you right away. Caleb Barbour is dead. He was murdered."

Benjamin and Sharon Hill looked shocked, but for different reasons.

"Who . . . ?" Benjamin asked.

"Worthy Brown."

"The man who was suing Barbour for his child?" Benjamin exclaimed.

"The slave?" Sharon Hill said.

"Barbour *raped* his daughter," Heather said.

"My God!" Benjamin whispered.

Heather told her father how Matthew had rescued Roxanne from Barbour and informed him about the injuries Matthew had suffered when he tried to protect Worthy.

"Is Matthew all right?" Benjamin asked.

"He stayed at Gillette House for the first few days, until he felt well enough to move back to his place. It's Roxanne I'm worried about. She's recovered physically, but she's so quiet. Everything seems to frighten her."

"Poor girl. I knew there was something wrong with Caleb, but raping a child . . ." Benjamin shook his head in disgust.

The coach shook as Francis strapped the luggage to the roof then climbed up next to the driver.

"I've put Roxanne in one of the guest rooms," Heather said. "I hope that's all right."

"Of course."

The coach began to move. Heather glanced at the street and saw Matthew Penny, his shoulders hunched and his head down, lost in thought as he struggled through the rain and wind. Benjamin said something to her, but Heather was only paying partial attention. Something was wrong with Matthew. They had become close while he was recuperating. The reserve he had shown when they were first together had disappeared. He had been relaxed with her, and she was certain that he had feelings for her. Then everything had changed.

Heather had wanted Matthew to spend a few more days recuperating before moving back to his apartment, and she assumed he would agree if only so they could spend more time together. Suddenly, however, Matthew had been anxious to leave. Why had he wanted to get away from her? And why did he look so troubled just now? Heather wished that she knew.

CHAPTER 31

Matthew sat in his rocker, which he'd brought in from the landing when the rainy season started. He had been drinking, and his thoughts were slow and muddy. He looked around him. There was so little in this room. There had been so little in his life since Rachel died. When Rachel was alive, his world had been full of vivid colors. After his intense grieving had ended, Matthew was shocked to find that his day-to-day life was just like it had been when Rachel was alive, with one big exception: everything around him appeared in shades of gray. Then he'd met Heather and he had dared to hope that he could be happy again. What wonders would life have held for him if he hadn't murdered Caleb Barbour?

Matthew contemplated his bleak future and the one ray of hope in it. He could still have everything if he let Worthy Brown take the blame for Barbour's murder. That was what he'd realized during the walk from the jail to his office in the unrelenting rain. No one but Worthy knew who had murdered Barbour. Not even Roxanne, who probably thought that Barbour had been alive when Matthew carried her to Gillette House. If Matthew said nothing, he could have Heather, the wealth her father's business would bring him, and a life. But what kind of life would it be if Worthy Brown had to die for him to live it?

Then again, didn't Worthy want to make the sacrifice? Hadn't he told Matthew that he was willing to die to save him? What Worthy said made sense. He was a man with no future, while Matthew had the whole world in front of him. If Worthy had been there when Roxanne ran into the yard, Worthy would have killed Barbour. There was no question about that.

Matthew buried his head in his hands, appalled that he could even think such thoughts. What would Rachel say to him if he told her what he was thinking? Worthy was a human being, a good man who had suffered terribly his whole life. That Matthew would consider letting Worthy die for him proved he was not worth the sacrifice.

No, in the morning, he would tell W. B. Thornton the truth, even though he was terrified of what would happen when he visited the district attorney. In the morning, he would do what was right.

CHAPTER 32

Sharon Hill begged off having dinner with Benjamin, claiming exhaustion and pointing out that Heather hadn't seen him since they had left for San Francisco. She was relieved when Gillette agreed to drop her at her hotel. Putting up a facade twenty-four hours a day was tiring. And the news of Barbour's death was devastating. Her plan could not succeed if Caleb was not alive to testify that the signature affixed to the marriage contract was that of Benjamin Gillette.

When they arrived at the Evergreen Hotel, Francis brought her luggage to her room. Later, while luxuriating in a warm bath, Hill tried to think of a way to use the contract, which was hidden in her valise, but she was too hungry to think clearly. After the bath, she dressed and headed downstairs to the restaurant. When she neared the dining room, she saw Jed Tyler talking to the maître d'.

"How nice to see you again, Justice Tyler."

Tyler turned. A look of surprise then pleasure suffused his features when he saw that it was Sharon Hill who had spoken.

"Do you dine here often?" she inquired.

"Not often," he replied, "but on occasion. I've just returned from riding the circuit, and I have a craving for a good steak."

"That sounds delicious."

"Would you care to join me?"

"If it's not an imposition."

"To the contrary. I would be grateful for your company. Riding the circuit is a lonely business."

The maître d' seated the couple, and they ordered chowder, porterhouse steaks, and wine.

"I can tell from your accent that you are originally from the East," Hill said when the waiter left.

Tyler smiled. "A good guess."

"New York?"

Tyler laughed. "Yes."

"Were you raised there?"

"I was."

"What made you travel so far from home."

"My brother. It is he who should be sitting here, talking to you."

"Oh?"

"David is obsessed with the West. He reads every article written about it, and he was always dragging Muriel and me to these stuffy, overheated halls to hear ministers or veterans of the Oregon Trail or Indian fighters talk about the opportunities awaiting men of action in San Francisco and the Oregon Territory."

"Muriel?"

"David's wife."

"Ah. But he stayed in New York?"

"David is a dreamer. He's not a man of action. But his dreams infected me, and I decided to live them."

"What did your family think about your decision to move three thousand miles away from them?"

"David supported me but my father was very upset. He foresaw great things for me in the New York Bar, followed by an advantageous marriage and a prestigious place in New York society. I found the life he'd planned for me tedious and unbearable. Father would always point to David as an example of how life should be lived, never noticing that David felt trapped and stayed put only because he loves Muriel so much. She would never agree to leave New York and her society friends."

"Did your father come around eventually?"

"No, he made it clear that I would receive no help from him if I left."

"It must have been devastating to be rejected by your father."

"At first, it made me very sad. I wanted him to see what I saw, to support me. But, in the end, it was liberating. It left me with nothing to fall back on and forced me to rely solely on my wits."

"Was it simply boredom that made you move to Oregon?"

"No, Miss Hill. I was always a loner. I never fit in. I had one interest, one love—law. I believed that the West was wild and unformed, a place where a new social order was developing, and I wanted to help shape it."

"And have you?"

Tyler nodded. "I believe I've had an impact on our state, I believe I've left my mark."

"Was there ever a time when you questioned your decision to leave New York?"

"Never."

"And did you find the West to be as wild as you imagined it?"

Tyler smiled.

"What's so funny?" Hill asked.

"Your question made me remember *The King of Prussia*. It was the steamer on which I booked my passage west in 1851. A pretentious name that was unsuitable for such a sorry vessel. The accommodations were deplorable, but I never thought about them. Every moment was an adventure. I remember when we off-loaded at Chagres, a pitiful little town on the Isthmus of Panama. I and the other California-bound passengers were poled upriver to Cruces in small boats by Indians. Indians! David would have given anything to meet an Indian.

"From Cruces, we rode mules over the mountains, where there were other steamers waiting to take us to San Francisco. The scene there amazed me. I found thousands of people waiting for passage near the docks. Some passengers in steerage sold their tickets for $750 and took their chances on finding something cheaper."

"Was San Francisco what you expected?"

"It was more than that. You've lived there, you know how it is. The streets were filled with Americans from every state in the Union, Chileans, Frenchmen, Kanakas from the Sandwich Islands, Russians and Chinese, and the crowds rushing through the streets never seemed to rest."

"Why didn't you stay in San Francisco?"

"There were too many lawyers. I reckoned that my chances of making something of myself would improve if I moved north. And that's how I came to settle here. I stepped off the boat with all my worldly goods and saw an OFFICE FOR RENT sign in the window of Gillette's Mercantile Emporium."

"Benjamin Gillette?"

Tyler nodded. "It was one of Ben's first enterprises. We struck a deal—work for rent—and my fortunes rose with his. But I never liked the daily practice of law. When Ira Corbett fell off his horse while riding circuit and broke his neck I used every marker I had to secure my spot on the Supreme Court. The day I joined the court was the happiest day of my life."

It would be natural for Tyler to turn the conversation to her life, a subject she wished to avoid, and Hill was relieved when the food came. She was exhausted and she wasn't sure she could keep her lies straight. During dinner, Hill deflected questions about her life before Phoenix and steered the conversation to their food, the life of a judge, Caleb Barbour's murder, and other topics that saw her safely through the meal. The waiter was clearing their plates when the grandfather clock in a corner of the dining room chimed.

"My goodness," Hill exclaimed, "I had no idea it was so late. I'm exhausted and you must be, too."

The judge stifled a yawn. Then smiled. "I am done in."

"Thank you for the dinner and the entertaining conversation."

"The pleasure is mine. I enjoyed your company."

"Perhaps we can dine again sometime."

"I'd like that," Tyler said.

CHAPTER 33

By most measures, W. B. Thornton was a success. Before his election to the position of Multnomah County district attorney, he had built up a respectable practice representing the shipping companies whose trade had made Portland a booming port city. He lived in an elegant Italianate mansard residence with Abigail, his plump, adoring wife, and their three children. He was an intimate of the rich and powerful in Portland society and a shareholder in the Oregon Railway and Navigation Company, which he hoped would soon make him wealthy. And, of course, he held a position of power and had aspirations for gaining more. But he never really felt secure, and he frequently worried about the way others saw him.

To improve his self-image, Wilbur Bartholomew Thornton had dealt away his first and middle names because he thought they sounded effeminate, so he was now W. B. Thornton. To seem older, he had cultivated a paunch and had grown the full beard that covered his baby face. He also consulted his pocket watch frequently in order to appear contemplative.

As there was no courthouse in the county, Thornton conducted public business from his law office, which was near the docks on Front Street. Thornton was busy with an insurance claim when

Matthew Penny appeared in his waiting room. Thornton cultivated those with influence in Portland society, and there were
rumors that Matthew might soon join that group by becoming
Benjamin Gillette's attorney, so he told his secretary to show the
young man in.

"Good to see you up and about, Penny," the DA said as he
studied the fading evidence of Matthew's beating.

"Thank you," Matthew answered after taking a seat across the
desk from the prosecutor.

"I heard that you were badly injured."

"I was laid up for several days."

"Well, it looks like the worst is over. So what may I do for you?
I assume this is about Brown."

"Yes."

"I'll be going for an indictment the next time we convene a
grand jury. Will you be representing him?"

Matthew swallowed hard. "No, sir, I will not."

"I see. Then why are you here?"

"I . . ." Matthew paused. His heart was beating rapidly, and he
felt short of breath. "There has been a mistake. Mr. Brown did not
kill Caleb Barbour."

Thornton cast an incredulous look at Matthew. "Then who
did?"

"I . . . I believe I am responsible."

Thornton stared at Matthew as if he had not understood him.

"Believe? Are you saying that you are unsure?"

"No, I killed Barbour. I struck him, and he hit his head and
died."

Thornton leaned back in his chair. His expression told Matthew that he was having a hard time crediting what he had just heard.

"Mr. Penny, Caleb Barbour was murdered over a week ago. If you killed him, why have you waited so long to make this confession?"

"I didn't remember what I had done. When I was struck on the head, I lost my memory."

"And you have suddenly recalled that you perpetrated this horrible crime?"

Matthew looked down at his hat, which rested on his lap.

"My memory did not return all at once. At first, I had nightmares. I saw Roxanne Brown running from the flames. I had a sudden vision of Mr. Barbour sprawled across his front porch steps, dead, his head bleeding, but the body was not burned."

"Barbour's corpse was badly burned."

"Yes. That's what made me realize what must have happened. Barbour's body had been badly burned by the time Marshal Lappeus arrived on the scene but not in my vision. The only way I could reconcile my vision with the condition of the body was if I'd seen Barbour's corpse twice with time intervening."

"Even if you saw the body twice, what makes you think that Brown did not strike the fatal blow?"

"That's not how I remember it now."

Thornton leaned forward. "Look, Penny, I don't know why you've come here, but if you are taking the blame for Brown's cowardly act out of some . . ." Thornton waved his hand in the air, at a loss for words.

"Frankly, I don't know what has possessed you. I know you're an abolitionist. Maybe this confession was prompted by pro-Negro sentiments. But this case had nothing to do with slavery or race. It is about murder, plain and simple, and it's clear that Brown killed Caleb Barbour. He hated his former master for keeping his daughter from him. He threatened to kill Barbour on the very day Barbour was murdered. He was caught red-handed at the scene of the crime."

"But I did kill Barbour. I'm sure of it."

"Your certainty is a product of nightmares and visions, not fact. Go home, Penny. Get a good night's sleep or, better yet, see Dr. Sharp. I think you're still suffering the effects of that blow to the head."

Matthew saw that he would not be able to convince Thornton, so he stood up.

"Thank you for your time," he said before turning toward the door.

"Brown will hang, Penny," the DA said. "In time, you will see that his punishment was just."

MATTHEW WAS IN TURMOIL AS he walked back to his office. He was certain that he had murdered Caleb Barbour, but Thornton would not accept his confession. It took him only a few moments to realize why. W. B. Thornton was a political opportunist. A conviction in this murder case would make him wildly popular, and it would be so much easier to prosecute a Negro for the murder than to bring a white man to trial for the crime.

But even if Thornton was not politically ambitious, Matthew

could see why he would be reluctant to accept a confession that had come so long after the crime and was inspired by visions and nightmares. Yet Matthew was convinced his memory was real. The problem was convincing someone who mattered that he was a murderer. If he could not, Worthy would die, and Matthew would live with Brown's death on his conscience.

CHAPTER 34

A small barred window at the top of Worthy's cell let in light and chill air. Worthy was wearing all of his clothing and had a blanket wrapped around his shoulders. He looked ill.

"I brought you some food," Matthew said, placing a pot of hot soup, thick with meat and vegetables, on the edge of Worthy's bunk.

"Thank you," Worthy said.

Matthew took the cover off the pot and handed Worthy a large wooden spoon. Worthy lowered his face over the pot and let the steam warm him. After a moment, he dipped the spoon into the soup. When he raised the spoon, his hand shook and some of the soup spilled. Worthy waited a moment before bringing the spoon to his lips. He took a long, slow sip. Matthew remembered how vigorous Worthy had looked chopping wood, and it pained him to see how difficult it now was for Worthy to complete this simple task.

"This is good."

"You need to keep up your strength."

Matthew gathered his courage while Worthy drank more soup.

"I went to District Attorney Thornton and confessed," Matthew said.

Worthy paused, his spoon halfway to his lips. "What did he say?"

"He didn't believe me."

"That's good, because I killed Mr. Barbour."

"That's not true, Worthy."

"It's a fact," Worthy replied calmly. "Ain't no one can change a fact."

"I know what you think you're doing, and I appreciate it, but this is insane. Roxanne needs you."

Worthy ignored Matthew and took another spoonful of soup.

"Damn it, Worthy, you'll be hanged."

Worthy looked completely at peace, and Matthew knew that no argument would change his mind.

"I hoped you'd give up this foolish idea, but I knew you might not, so I have a question for you. If you could go free without anyone knowing that I murdered Barbour, you'd want that, wouldn't you?"

Worthy stopped eating, and Matthew saw that he had the former slave's attention.

"This doesn't have to be all or nothing. You could win your case at trial."

"Go on."

"It isn't always illegal to take a life. There are times when killing is justified. Say you catch someone stealing your cattle. You tell them to stop but they pull a gun. You can legally shoot the rustler in self-defense."

Matthew paused. When Worthy nodded to let Matthew know that he was following him, the lawyer continued.

"Now, let's say it's Roxanne who sees the thief and he tries to shoot her. You can shoot to kill in that situation to protect a third party who is in danger."

Matthew paused again. He leaned close to Worthy and lowered his voice. "If Caleb Barbour was beating Roxanne when you came on the scene, you would have been within your rights as her father to protect her."

Worthy looked down at the dirt floor. It was so quiet Matthew heard the wind whistling through cracks in the wall. After a moment Worthy looked up. "You're saying I should lie?"

"For God's sake, you'll be lying if you say you killed Barbour. Why not say it was in self-defense and give yourself a chance to live?"

"Ain't no white jury gonna free me."

"Barbour wasn't respected, Worthy. People know what happened in Phoenix, and they know about your lawsuit. Caleb was a coward. He backed down from our duel, he bribed those jurors, and keeping a child from a parent—even a Negro child—doesn't sit well with most folks. A lawyer like Orville Mason can make a jury see Caleb Barbour for what he was. If you agree to say you killed Barbour in self-defense, we'll work on your story until it's perfect. Then I'll ask Orville to represent you. With him on your side, you'll have a fighting chance."

"I want to ponder this some, but I won't go to court unless you are my lawyer."

Matthew shook his head vigorously. "No, I'm too involved. I'd botch the case."

Worthy looked directly at Matthew. His voice was calm and steady.

"Only you. Otherwise, I'll plead guilty."

"This won't work. It's unethical for a lawyer to testify for a client."

"What would you testify about?"

"I . . . Well, I'll tell the jury what happened, only I'll tell it as if you were there instead of me. I'll say I rode up and I saw Roxanne running from Barbour's house. She was naked and he was running after her. Then I'll say I saw you step between Barbour and Roxanne to protect her. Barbour tried to knock you down so he could get at your daughter, but you hit him and he fell against the steps. We'll call Roxanne. She'll back up your story. After she tells the jury how Barbour raped her, Orville will have a good chance to win an acquittal."

As Matthew talked, Worthy grew more distant. When he was done, Worthy's face showed no emotion.

"What do you think?" Matthew asked eagerly.

"If you say you saw me kill Barbour after confessing to Mr. Thornton, he's going to ask you about that, and you'll come off sounding like a liar either way. But like you said, you won't be allowed to testify if you are my lawyer. That's why I want you representing me instead of Mr. Mason.

"And I'll never make Roxanne sit in front of a courtroom full of people and tell what . . . what that man done to her. If I go through with your plan, I'll do it myself. I ain't dragging Roxanne or anyone else into it."

"You have to have witnesses or no one will believe you," Matthew said desperately.

"That's the chance I'll take."

"Damn it, Worthy. This plan can work. We'd both . . . You'd be free. You're being stubborn for no good reason. Let me get Orville to represent you."

Worthy didn't answer. Matthew was exasperated. He took a deep breath and calmed down.

"I respect you. You're a good man, and I know why you're taking this position, but it's a foolish position that will do more harm than good in the end. You'll realize I'm right after you've had some time to think. I'll come back in a few days. In the meantime, consider what I've said. Roxanne is free, too. She should have her say about what she wants to do."

"Thank you for the soup, Mr. Penny."

"You're welcome, Mr. Brown," Matthew said out loud, while he silently added, *and may God bless you.*

CHAPTER 35

During her first week at Gillette House, Roxanne Brown had stayed in bed staring listlessly at the trees on the hillside outside her window. Roxanne's body healed, but her mental wounds disabled her. Heather tried to coax her out of her room, but Roxanne wouldn't leave her sanctuary. Heather grew desperate. She heard Roxanne moan in the night and saw the tears that appeared for no apparent reason. She was determined to rescue Roxanne before she became so indifferent to life that she was lost to despair.

One day, Heather stood in Roxanne's doorway and ordered the invalid out of bed.

"There's work to be done in the kitchen," Heather had proclaimed. "Your days of lying abed and contributing nothing to this household are over."

Heather felt terrible as she led the terrified young woman downstairs, but she vowed to stay strong.

At first, the cook had been pleased to have a helper, but she was soon voicing concerns to her mistress. The girl was a good worker, but she never spoke unless spoken to, her responses were terse and vague, and she never smiled. Heather assigned Roxanne other chores on the theory that the more Roxanne was occupied with work, the less time she would have to worry about her troubles.

Roxanne's favorite place in Gillette House was the library. With the help of Mrs. Barbour, who was amused by her precocious slave, she had puzzled out the meaning of the lines and circles in the books that her mistress read on the veranda of the Big House in Georgia. Mrs. Barbour had warned Roxanne about letting her husband know that she could read because he punished slaves who had the temerity to try to educate themselves. Roxanne had fewer opportunities to read after Mrs. Barbour died, but the Gillette library with its surfeit of treasures rekindled her interest. And there was one particular book she found irresistible. It rested on the end table next to a big easy chair where Heather had left it. It was bound in rich maroon leather that smelled wonderful and felt luxurious. The title was embossed in gold on the spine, and the tops and bottoms of the pages were tipped with gold. It was the most beautiful book Roxanne had ever seen.

One of Roxanne's chores was dusting, and she cast covetous glances at the book as she worked her way around the library. Heather and Mr. Gillette were in town, the cook was busy with dinner, and the other servants were working in other parts of the house. No one would know if she took a peek at that book. Soon her feather duster was flying over the shelves and racing across the furniture. When the room was spotless, Roxanne opened the library door an inch and listened carefully for a sound that would warn her that someone was near. When she was certain that she was safe, Roxanne lay down the duster, wiped her hands on her dress, settled into the armchair, and picked up the book, handling it with the care of a mother holding her newborn for the first time.

One of Benjamin's business associates had sent the book from

London, where it was all the rage. Roxanne sounded out the writing on the cover page. The name Charles Dickens meant nothing to Roxanne, but the title, *A Tale of Two Cities*, promised adventure. Next, Roxanne sounded out "Book the First, Recalled to Life," speaking the words aloud.

The title of the first part of the book gave her pause. How could someone be recalled to life? Once you were dead, you were dead, unless you were one of the African spirits her father had told her about. Roxanne was certain the book was about white people who didn't believe in wood spirits and water spirits. Of course, there was Jesus, who had died and been recalled to life. She wondered if the book was about Jesus, and she turned to the first page of text to find out.

"'It was the best of times, it was the worst of times,'" Roxanne read. This, too, was confusing. How could a day be very good and very bad? Roxanne was so involved with solving this puzzle that she didn't hear the door to the library open.

"Roxanne?" called Heather, who was surprised to find the young girl sitting with a book in her lap.

Roxanne leaped from the chair like a startled deer and watched in horror as the beautiful book hit the floor with a resounding thud.

"Oh no, oh no," she moaned, horrified that the book might be damaged.

"What were you doing?" Heather demanded.

"Nothing, Miss Heather. I was just dusting. I . . . I was dusting that book."

"Then why are you acting like a thief?"

Roxanne's eyes grew wide with horror. "I wasn't stealing. I would never steal your books."

Heather instantly regretted her choice of words when she saw the terror in the young girl's eyes.

"I shouldn't have said that," Heather apologized. "I just meant that you jumped like a guilty person might, but I know you're no thief. I just want to know what's going on."

Heather bent down and picked up the book. "Were you reading this?"

"Oh no, Miss Heather. I can't read. It ain't allowed."

"What are you talking about? Where is reading not allowed?"

Roxanne looked trapped. A possible reason for her fear occurred to Heather.

"Did Mr. Barbour forbid you to read when you were a slave in Georgia?"

Roxanne nodded.

"But you can read. I heard you."

Roxanne was paralyzed. She'd remembered the horrible screams of the slaves Barbour had whipped and saw in her mind their backs flayed raw.

Heather held out the book to Roxanne. "You're not a slave anymore. You're a free woman. And you're not in Georgia. You have as much right to read as I do."

Roxanne swallowed. *Was this a trick?*

"Can you do sums?" Heather asked.

"A few," Roxanne whispered, chancing Heather's wrath and praying she was not confessing to a crime that would end in a beating.

"And you can read a little?"

"A little."

"Would you like me to teach you mathematics?"

Roxanne let her head bob an inch.

"And reading?"

"Yes, ma'am, but I do know some of that."

"Then my job will be easier, won't it?" Heather responded.

HEATHER SPENT A GOOD PART of their dinner telling her father about Roxanne and *A Tale of Two Cities*. Benjamin listened politely, but Heather thought he was distracted. When he finished, Benjamin walked into the foyer and grabbed his coat.

"Where are you going?" Heather asked.

"Into town."

Her father sounded defensive, and Heather was certain she knew why.

"Are you going to visit that woman?"

"I don't know why you dislike Miss Hill. You really haven't given her a chance."

"Matthew told me what happened in Phoenix. He believes Miss Hill lied at the trial."

"Then he is the only one. The verdict of the jury was unanimous."

"What if Matthew is right? You know so little about her."

"I know all I need to," Benjamin insisted stubbornly.

"That's not true. If you were considering a business partnership, you would investigate the other party thoroughly. You'd never merge with another company without looking at its books and speaking to others who did business with it. Someone with your wealth should never leap blindly into a relationship."

"This is really not your business," Benjamin answered angrily before grabbing his hat and walking out of the house.

CHAPTER 36

On a blustery November Sunday, Reverend Mason stood in the doorway of his church chatting with his parishioners before shooing them next door to the assembly hall. Two days ago, news of Abraham Lincoln's victory had been telegraphed to Oregon. The reverend was pleased by the election results but sobered by events on the other side of the continent. His service had started with a prayer for the president-elect and ended with a sermon condemning secession and preaching abolition.

A narrow alley separated the assembly hall from the church. By the time Orville entered the meetinghouse, many of the adults were warming their hands at the potbellied stove in the center of the hall while they talked politics and caught up on the latest gossip. The children made a beeline for the pies, ham, corn, and other edibles the wives had set out on a long table next to the wall. Orville looked forward to joining in the political discussions, but he decided to get a piece of pumpkin pie before it was gobbled up. A gentle touch on his forearm stopped him as he was reaching for his slice.

Heather Gillette was carrying a fur muff for her hands and wearing one of the tiny bonnets that were the current rage. Her cheeks were apple red from the cold, and the crimson color contrasted nicely with the blond ringlets that strayed from beneath the bonnet.

"Congratulations on Mr. Lincoln's victory," Heather said.

"Thank you."

"There is talk that you may be offered a federal judgeship."

"Is this an inquiry from a friend or from *The Spokesman*'s intrepid reporter?"

"Both."

Orville laughed. "The rumor mills always grind after an election, but I'd be an ingrate to desert your father so soon after taking on his legal work."

Heather looked like she wanted to say something, but she hesitated. Orville waited for her to gather her thoughts.

"Do you consider yourself Matthew Penny's friend?" Heather asked.

"I do."

"I'm worried about him. He's changed since Caleb Barbour was murdered. Did you know that father asked Matthew to be his attorney before he offered the position to you?"

"Yes. Ben told me Matthew sent him a letter turning down the offer. He claimed that he didn't feel up to the task and recommended me because I have more business experience."

"We both know that Matthew could have handled the job."

"Maybe he hasn't fully recovered from his injuries," Orville said.

"Something else is troubling him."

"Representing a client who may be hanged is a heavy burden."

"There's more to it than that." Heather looked frustrated. "I can't explain it in words. I just know something's wrong. Have you talked to him recently?"

"No, and now that I think about it, I have had the impression that Matthew has been avoiding me. When I've seen him on the street or in court, he's seemed uncomfortable, and he's made excuses to break away if I suggested a meal or just getting together to discuss Mr. Brown's case."

"About Mr. Brown's case, I'm not a lawyer but . . . Orville, the night Barbour died, Matthew brought Roxanne to my house. She had been beaten, and she was in a state of shock, and . . ." Heather colored. "I'm certain she had been violated."

"Yes?"

"If you were defending Mr. Brown, wouldn't you want to call Roxanne as a witness?"

"Probably."

"Matthew has made no attempt to talk to her."

"That is odd."

"All of his behavior for the past weeks has been odd," Heather said. "At first, when he was recuperating at my house, he wasn't withdrawn. He was injured, of course, and he slept a lot, but we went on walks together and he was at ease when we talked. I'm sure he was happy. Then everything changed suddenly, and I'm certain that the change has something to do with Caleb Barbour's murder.

"Orville, can you talk to Matthew? Can you try to find out what's troubling him?"

"I can try," Orville promised.

Heather hesitated. "There's something else I want you to do."

"Concerning Matthew?"

"No. This concerns my father and that woman, Sharon Hill."

CHAPTER 37

M atthew woke up to the stench of a body he had not bathed in days. His face was covered by stubble. There were dark circles under his eyes and his skin had the texture of thin, yellowed paper. He did not look well. He did not feel well, either.

Worthy Brown's case was a wagon wheel sunk firmly in mud and he could think of no way to pull it out. Matthew had tried reason with Worthy, he had begged, he had played on Brown's heartstrings by using Roxanne as an argument, but Worthy would not be moved. The only future Matthew could see for the ex-slave dangled from the end of a hangman's noose. Matthew's future was equally clear. If Brown hanged, Matthew would drag guilt and regret behind him like an anchor for the rest of his life.

Matthew's body odor had grown strong enough to repulse him, so he forced himself to bathe and shave before going to the café across the street for breakfast. He was hunched over the remnants of his meal, sunk in his thoughts, when the grating sound of a chair leg drawn across naked boards made him raise his head.

"May I join you?" Orville Mason asked as he sat opposite his friend.

"Please," Matthew said, though in truth he did not want company.

"I need your help," Orville said, "but you must keep what I tell you confidential."

Matthew nodded, grateful for anything that would distract him from his troubles.

"Tell me about the case you handled in Phoenix for the salesman," Orville said.

"Why do you need to know about that?"

"Ben is spending a lot of time with Sharon Hill, and Heather is worried."

"She should be. Hill is bad business."

"Why do you say that?"

Matthew told Orville about Hill's accusations and the consequences for Clyde Lukens.

"You believe Lukens?" Orville asked when Matthew finished.

"I don't trust Hill, and Lukens is pathetic. I don't think he'd be brave enough to sneak into an occupied room in the middle of the night."

"If you're right, the situation is serious. I'm going to follow some leads and see what turns up."

"Good. I like Ben. I'd hate to see him hurt."

"I feel the same way," Orville said. "So how is Worthy's case going?"

"Okay," Matthew said, his tone guarded.

"I assume you'll call Mr. Brown's daughter at the trial."

"Why do you say that?"

"To prove Barbour molested her. You are going to argue defense of another, aren't you?"

"I haven't decided."

"Have you talked to Roxanne about what happened before you rescued her?"

"Why is my case of interest to you?" Matthew answered defensively.

"I'd like to help if I can. Barbour was despicable, and what he did to Mr. Brown and his daughter was inexcusable. You can count on me to do anything I can to see that justice is done."

"Thank you," Matthew said, but his tone let Orville know that he would probably not hear from Matthew.

"Are you okay?" Orville asked.

"Why do you ask?"

"You look exhausted."

"I've just been working hard."

"You're sure there's nothing else?"

"I'm fine," Matthew said as he stood. "I've got to get back to my office."

Matthew put some money on the table and walked away. As he crossed the street, he could feel Orville's eyes boring into his back. Were Orville's questions about Worthy's case simple curiosity, or did Orville sense that something about the case was not right? Orville was very smart. Did he suspect that Matthew had killed Caleb Barbour? What a relief it would be if Orville proved that Matthew was responsible and Worthy went free, but there was no way Orville could prove his suspicions were true, assuming that he even had any. Matthew accepted the fact that no one could help him. This battle of wills was between him and Worthy Brown, and Matthew was being defeated soundly.

CHAPTER 38

The mind of Roxanne Brown opened like a budding flower. Heather tutored her in reading, writing, and mathematics then exposed her to history and geography when she saw how easily Roxanne absorbed any subject put before her. Little by little, the excitement and distraction engendered by her education helped banish the terror that had imprisoned Roxanne, but it did not make a dent in the pain caused by her father's imprisonment.

During one of their walks, Roxanne gathered her courage and asked Heather if she could arrange a visit to her father. Heather had dreaded that question because she had already broached the subject with Marshal Lappeus, who had told her that only attorneys and clergyman could visit the prisoner in the jail. Roxanne's shoulders and spirits had sagged at the bad news, but her mathematics lessons had taught her that there were solutions to even the most knotty problems.

One morning, Roxanne put on a pair of boots and a heavy coat and trudged down the winding road from Gillette House to the jail. It was a cold winter day, and the walk was several miles on a pathway turned into swamp by heavy rains. Roxanne turned up her coat collar, stuffed her hands in her pockets, and bent into the wind. She didn't pass many people on the road down from Gillette

House, but Portland's population had swollen to three thousand souls by 1860, and she began to encounter its inhabitants as soon as she drew near the residential area that had sprung up on the edge of the city. A Negro girl was an oddity on the streets of Portland, but Roxanne was also the central figure in two of Portland's most talked about trials. Even well-mannered passersby could be forgiven for staring. Those who were less refined directed cruel comments at her. Roxanne was focused on her mission and was oblivious to many of the comments, but some of the barbs struck home. Her fear and embarrassment increased with each insult, but nothing would deter her from carrying out her plan.

Marshal Lappeus had told Heather that Roxanne could not visit her father inside the jail. He had said nothing about talking to him from outside, so Roxanne walked behind the jail to the muddy lot that Worthy's cell window overlooked.

"Daddy," she called out.

Worthy was spending more and more time lying on his bed, his mind drifting as he tried to dream away his time in jail. At first, he believed his daughter's voice was a figment of his imagination, but a lump formed in Worthy's throat when it dawned on him that Roxanne was really outside. He climbed onto the edge of his bed on wobbly legs and gripped the bars on the window to steady himself. He had never fully recovered from his beating, and the conditions of his incarceration had further weakened him. Worthy started to say something when he remembered Amos Strayer.

"You shouldn't be here," he whispered.

"The marshal told Miss Heather I couldn't go inside the jail. He didn't say anything about outside."

"If Deputy Strayer sees you, he might arrest you."

"If he tells me to go, I'll go. Let's just talk now. We . . . we might not get another chance."

"You talk and I'll listen," Worthy whispered. "That way, there's less chance the deputy will know you're outside."

ROXANNE TOLD HER FATHER ABOUT her life at Gillette House, and Worthy's chest swelled as she reeled off her accomplishments. He would be leaving this world soon, but he would be leaving behind a wonderful young girl who was growing into an accomplished young woman. Life would be hard for a Negro child in this world where color meant so much, but Roxanne could read and do sums—skills Worthy had never dreamed of mastering. The world was changing, and Roxanne gave him hope.

The day grew long, and Roxanne said good-bye because she had to return to Gillette House to finish her chores. Worthy lay down on his bed and tried to picture Roxanne in ten years. A big smile spread across his face as he imagined a fine young woman with a husband and children like his Polly had been, only free. Maybe Roxanne's family would live on their own farm. There was a husband and wife in Portland—free Negroes—who owned a store. That was a wonder. Roxanne was smart. Maybe she and her husband would own a store some day.

Worthy could not imagine much more than that for a girl, but what if one of Roxanne's children was a boy. Would he grow up to be a doctor or a lawyer? Wouldn't that be something? A grandson he could call doctor!

Worthy sobered. If that did happen, he would never know

about it. He would never know any of the truth about his daughter's future past his hanging, and he was going to hang. Worthy's heart seized up, tears clouded his eyes, and he cried for all the things he would never know: the wedding he would not attend, the grandchildren he would never get to hold.

Worthy's face grew hot with sorrow, and he let go for the first time since he had been imprisoned. Seeing Roxanne had done this to him; but seeing her so happy made the pain worthwhile, and knowing in his heart that Roxanne would be all right was worth any sacrifice.

CHAPTER 39

In the weeks preceding Christmas, Roxanne's duties kept her from town. On the first day she was able to break away from Gillette House, she was stunned to find a crowd surrounding a wooden scaffold that had been erected in the field behind the jail. Roxanne listened to the excited chatter of the crowd and soon learned that the noose had been prepared for Kevin O'Toole, the jail's other inmate.

O'Toole had shot a man named Flynn through the meat of his arm, wounding him. Flynn had gone to his room to lie down and recover while O'Toole brooded in the saloon where the shooting had occurred. That evening, as Flynn lay sleeping, O'Toole had crept into Flynn's room and cut his throat.

Roxanne stood on the edge of the crowd as O'Toole walked from the jail to meet his fate, reading scripture the whole way. The crowd grew silent as he was led up the wooden steps to the plank platform. Roxanne's imagination substituted her father for the condemned man, and her heart beat rapidly.

"You got anything to say to these people?" Marshal Lappeus asked O'Toole.

"I do," O'Toole answered, his voice catching.

"Then say your piece."

O'Toole looked out at the crowd. He was tall, and his time in the lockup had given him a skeletal appearance that made him look far older than his twenty-two years. He'd combed his long brown hair to look his best on his last day. There were shadows under his muddy brown eyes. When he spoke, his voice shook.

"I did kill Jake Flynn, and I'm sorry I done it. But I had my reasons, and I want you to know it wasn't from pure cussedness. I knew Jake, and he knew me. Some three months before I killed him we had a quarrel over cards where Jake stabbed me with a knife and would have killed me if my friends didn't stop him. Ever since, I wanted revenge because that quarrel wasn't my fault. Also, Jake was threatening me whenever he could and said he would kill me, first chance he got.

"When I shot Flynn, he drew first, as God is my witness, but I was lucky and didn't get hit, whereas he got hit. I should have left it there, but I took to thinking on it and drinking. I knew if he didn't die, there'd be no end to it, as Flynn was a man who held a grudge.

"I see many young men in this crowd, and I want you to take a warning from this not to drink or gamble, neither, because we wouldn't have quarreled if we wasn't playing cards, and I wouldn't have killed him if liquor hadn't got the best of my judgment.

"I got to pay now, but I hope this will be a lesson, as I said. And I hope I go to heaven, as I've been a good churchgoer my whole life, when I had the chance, and I am truly sorry for what I done."

O'Toole stopped talking, and the marshal asked him if he was through.

"I guess," O'Toole answered in a subdued tone. "Except I see my friends below, and I want to wish them good-bye."

The marshal took the Bible from O'Toole's shaking hands, tied his hands behind his back, and covered the young man's face with a hood. The crowd had turned somber while listening to the condemned man's last words, and they were quiet when the marshal put the rope around his neck. Roxanne saw a few women dabbing at their eyes with handkerchiefs.

Marshal Lappeus positioned O'Toole over the trapdoor and stepped back. Then he pulled a lever, and the trap opened. O'Toole dropped through, his body jerked, the rope snapped, and he dropped to the ground. The crowd gasped. O'Toole, blinded by the hood, his hands bound, writhed on the ground shouting, "Jesus, save me. Jesus, save me."

O'Toole's friends rushed under the scaffold and pulled him out as the marshal and his deputies scrambled down from the gallows. The crowd began chanting, "Let him live," and surged forward to surround the cowboy, who sagged in the arms of his companions, weeping and praying.

Marshal Lappeus, a deeply religious man, had been moved by O'Toole's words. It was only a few weeks before Christmas, and he could not discount the possibility that a higher power than the state of Oregon had overturned O'Toole's death sentence. Justice Tyler had imposed that sentence. Since he'd never encountered something like this, the marshal wished he could consult with Tyler, but the judge was riding the circuit, so Lappeus conferred with his deputies while gauging the mood of the crowd. After a short discussion, he decided to let O'Toole ride off with his companions on the condition that he promise never to set foot in Oregon again.

Roxanne had been stunned by O'Toole's miraculous escape from the grim reaper. Until the rope broke, Roxanne had accepted her father's fate. Now she wondered if the aborted hanging was a sign, and if there had been others as well.

One came immediately to mind. It had lain on the end table in Mr. Gillette's library. In *A Tale of Two Cities*, an act of heroism saves a condemned man. Why, she asked herself, had that particular book been left for her to find? And there was something else, another discovery she'd made in the library: a shiny, fully loaded Colt revolver in the lower drawer of Gillette's escritoire.

CHAPTER 40

F ather," Heather Gillette said. "There's someone you must meet and some things you must listen to, even though I know you won't want to hear them."

Benjamin Gillette was not expecting Heather or Orville Mason, and he had no idea of the identity of the nervous young man Mason had ushered into his office. The boy was dressed in a clean blue suit, a pressed white shirt, and a bow tie. His chubby face bore traces of acne, and Gillette guessed that he was still in his teens. On entering, the young man doffed his hat and stood at attention in front of Gillette's desk.

"What's this about, Heather?" Gillette asked, confused by the sudden intrusion.

"Orville will explain why we're here."

"Mr. Gillette, this is Emmett Bradford, a clerk at the Evergreen Hotel," Orville said. "Emmett, tell Mr. Gillette what you told me about Miss Hill's activities."

Gillette turned to Heather. He looked furious. "I told you Miss Hill was not your concern."

"I believe you will be glad that your daughter asked me to look into this matter, sir," Orville said. "Please hear us out."

Gillette looked as if he wanted to throw the intruders out of his office, but he loved Heather dearly and knew she had his best interests at heart.

"Very well," he said, making no effort to hide his displeasure. "But make this fast. I'm pressed for time."

"Go ahead," Orville told the boy. "You have nothing to fear."

Bradford shifted nervously from foot to foot. "Well, sir," he said, his voice shaking, "it's like I told Mr. Mason. Miss Hill has entertained Justice Tyler in our dining room."

Gillette looked past Bradford to his attorney. "I see nothing untoward about an occasional dinner, Orville."

"Tell him the rest," Orville told the clerk.

Bradford blushed, and his fingers worried the brim of his hat. Gillette looked puzzled.

"Go ahead," Orville urged gently.

"Well, sir," Bradford said, his eyes fixed on the pattern of the Persian rug that covered the office floor, "she . . . Miss Hill . . . she entertained Mr. Caleb Barbour in her room."

"Caleb?" Gillette repeated dully.

"Tell Mr. Gillette about the champagne."

Bradford swallowed. There were beads of sweat on his brow.

"Well, sir, one time I was asked to take a bottle of champagne to Miss Hill's suite, and Mr. Barbour was there."

"How were Mr. Barbour and Miss Hill dressed?" Orville asked.

"Mr. Barbour was in his shirtsleeves with his shirt open at the neck, and he was lounging on the couch in the sitting room."

"And Miss Hill?" Orville asked.

"I only saw her for a second. She was in another room. But I believe she was in a dressing gown."

Gillette's gaze dropped to his desktop, but Orville was certain that he was not seeing any item set upon it.

"Do you wish to ask Mr. Bradford any questions?" Orville asked.

"How many times did Mr. Barbour spend the night?" Gillette asked.

"I can't say for certain, sir. There were two times I know for sure he visited. When I brought up the champagne, he left close to dawn."

"And Justice Tyler, has he ever gone up to Miss Hill's room?"

"No, sir, not that I saw," Bradford answered quickly.

Gillette asked a few more questions, but his heart was not in the interrogation. Orville thanked Bradford and saw him out. Then he sat across from his client.

"There's more, Ben," Orville said softly. "I sent a telegram to Clyde Lukens's firm. They confirmed his version of the origins of the money found in his room in Phoenix. The firm gave him fifty dollars for expenses. A week before he arrived in Phoenix, he wired them that he had orders totaling approximately two hundred and fifty dollars."

Gillette exhaled sharply.

"And I've uncovered something that's more disturbing than everything I've just told you," Orville continued. "I had a sketch of Miss Hill made surreptitiously. I sent the sketch to a Harvard classmate who is practicing in San Francisco. He employed a gentleman who is comfortable circulating in the city's less reputable precincts to seek information about the woman in the drawing.

"I realize that a sketch is not an exact representation of a person's features, but I can attest that my artist created an excellent likeness. According to my friend, the woman in the sketch bears a striking resemblance to a prostitute who disappeared from the city shortly after her pimp—Warren Quimby—died under mysterious circumstances."

"Surely you don't think . . . ?" Gillette began, finding it impossible to complete the sentence.

"Absent an identification made by someone who knew the woman, I cannot form an opinion with any certainty," Orville said, "but I wanted you to know what I'd discovered. I suggest most strongly that you make further inquiries about Miss Hill's background, given what I've uncovered."

CHAPTER 41

James Lappeus owed his position as marshal to saloon power. In 1858, the electorate showed its opposition to ordinances regulating the sale of liquor by choosing Addison Starr, co-owner of Portland's first distillery, as mayor. In 1859, Lappeus, co-owner of the popular Oro Fino Saloon, was elected city marshal. Lappeus had been so big as a child that there was no one to bully him, so he grew up affable and secure. "Peace officer" was a perfect title for him because he would not tolerate anyone brash enough to disturb the serenity of his surroundings. Rowdy customers of the Oro Fino and obstreperous lawbreakers melted into docility when this smiling giant curled his thick fingers to form a ham-size fist.

Marshal Lappeus was on his way to the jail when he spotted Roxanne standing behind the jail in the rain. This wasn't the first time he had seen Worthy's daughter talking to her father. Duty demanded that he keep father and daughter apart, but each time he saw the slender girl speaking to the log wall of the lockup, another fragment was chipped from the stone wall that duty had erected around his heart.

The wide brim of Marshal Lappeus's hat kept the rain off him, but Roxanne had no head covering. It only took a few moments of watching rivulets of rain run down Roxanne's face to send the lawman trudging through the mud toward the young girl. Roxanne saw the marshal and froze in midsentence, certain that something bad was about to happen.

"Miss Brown," Lappeus said, "you shouldn't be out here in this rain. The cold and wet can make you sick. Would you like to visit with your father inside?"

Roxanne was too startled to speak and merely nodded.

"Then come with me, and I'll see you in," Lappeus said.

The *rat-a-tat-tat* of rain on the jail roof made it impossible for Worthy to hear what Lappeus had said to Roxanne, so he feared the worst. His heart began to pound when the marshal led her away. Several minutes later, Lappeus spoke through the opening in the cell door.

"Mr. Brown, I've brought your daughter to see you."

Roxanne had heard her father's voice many times since his incarceration, but she had not seen what the beating and languishing in the damp and cold of the jail had done to him. Her heart contracted with pity as soon as she entered the gloomy cell. Worthy had been iron and oak. The man who stood before her was stooped, gaunt, and old.

"Roxanne," Worthy said, his voice filled with wonder.

Roxanne crossed the space between them and was enfolded. The marshal locked the door and motioned Amos Strayer to follow him to the front of the jail to afford father and daughter privacy.

Worthy held Roxanne at arm's length. "I can't believe you're here."

"You're so thin, Daddy."

Worthy saw concern etched into his daughter's features. "I've been sick, child, but that ain't anything for you to worry about. Now that you're here, I feel a whole lot better."

"The next time I visit, I'll bring you food."

"I'd like that," Worthy said. "It looks like you been eating well."

"Miss Heather treats me like a sister."

"Knowing she's taking good care of you has eased my mind."

Roxanne leaned forward until her lips were almost touching his ear.

"I don't know how long the marshal is going to let me stay here, so I have to talk fast," she whispered. "You're not going to hang."

Worthy responded with a fatalistic laugh. "You know something I don't, child?"

"I know where a gun is," Roxanne replied evenly.

Worthy drew back, alarmed.

"If they convict you, I'm going to bring that gun with me, and we're going to leave this place."

"We're not doing any such thing. You come to this jail with a gun and a harebrained scheme to break me out, and you'll end up dead or in jail with me. Or, worse, you'll kill somebody and live your life with that on your conscience. It ain't happening."

"I know you're not hanging."

"Roxanne—"

"Hear me out."

Worthy decided to let Roxanne talk. When she was through, he'd explain why her plan wouldn't work.

"I've seen signs, Daddy. I can read them just like I read the white people's books. The signs all point to you being free. When

I bring the revolver, I'll make Mr. Strayer unlock your cell and we'll go."

"Where?" Worthy asked.

"Wherever we want. We're free people."

"If your plan works, we'll be fugitives. The law everywhere will be after us. Be reasonable, Roxanne. Who's going to hide two colored fugitives in these parts? How we going to blend in? I love you for wanting to risk everything to free me, but your plan won't work."

"Face facts, Daddy. If you're sentenced to hang, there's no way you could end up any worse."

"That's not true. If you were killed or ended up in jail trying to save me, it would be the end of me. I would rather spend eternity in hell than know you destroyed your life for me. The only thing that makes what's happening to me bearable is knowing you're safe and that good things are happening to you."

"I can't let you hang."

"I haven't been convicted yet."

"But you will be in a white man's court. I can free you. The signs I've seen are so clear."

"Roxanne, there ain't no such things as signs. That's juju mumbo jumbo."

"That's African religion, like you told me about."

"Those were children's stories. All that about the wood spirits and the river spirits, it's what I used to entertain you when you were little. Ain't none of it real."

"It's what you believed in Africa."

"And some good it done me. If the old gods are so powerful, how come so many Africans are slaves to white people?"

Roxanne sat up straight. "I read a book, Daddy. The one I told you about, the beautiful book all bound in leather."

"With the gold writing?"

Roxanne nodded. "It's called *A Tale of Two Cities*. There's a man in it. He dies in the end, but he dies in place of another man who's been sentenced to death. The man who is sentenced to death is saved. I've asked myself over and over why that book was left for me to find, and I believe God put it in my way to let me know you don't have to die."

CHAPTER 42

Angry winds and vicious rains had forced Heather to stay inside for three straight days. When the weather broke, Heather escaped into the garden to savor the fresh air. The sky was clear and a pale sun was shining. No clouds obscured her view of the snow-capped mountains, the river, and the verdant foothills. Heather took one of the trails that led into the forest. As she walked at a leisurely pace between the tight-packed evergreens, her thoughts turned to Matthew's odd behavior.

Heather had seen very little of Matthew since he had ended his convalescence at Gillette House. On the few occasions when they had met by chance, he had seemed nervous and distant. Heather wanted to believe that Matthew's odd behavior was a by-product of the pressure Worthy Brown's defense had laid on him, but she did not really believe that was the sole or even major cause.

Matthew's personality change had started while he was recuperating at Gillette House, but she could think of nothing that had happened during his stay that would have provoked it, and he had been completely normal before he rode to Barbour's home to offer to settle Brown's case for cash. That meant the precipitating cause had to have something to do with the events on the evening Caleb Barbour died.

It suddenly occurred to Heather that something had happened

that evening that made no sense. The more she thought about it, the more upset she became, because she did not like the place where logic was leading her. Heather had avoided discussing the rape and murder with Roxanne for fear of upsetting her, but she had no choice now.

Heather returned to the house and found Worthy's daughter in the kitchen shelling peas.

"Can you come with me, Roxanne?" she asked.

Roxanne wiped her hands on her apron and followed Heather to the den. Heather closed the door to ensure their privacy before sitting on the couch and motioning Roxanne to sit beside her.

"Do you trust me, Roxanne?"

Roxanne suddenly looked wary, but she nodded.

"If I asked you questions about what happened at Caleb Barbour's house on the evening Mr. Penny brought you here, would you give me truthful answers?"

Roxanne's eyes widened, her breathing grew shallow, and her body became rigid. She reminded Heather of a rabbit shaking in the shadow of a circling hawk.

"These questions . . . I wouldn't ask them to embarrass you. Your answers may help your father when he stands trial."

Roxanne did not move.

"Do you remember what happened to you in Mr. Barbour's house before Matthew brought you here?"

Roxanne's nod was almost imperceptible.

"Tell me what happened, Roxanne. It's important that I know."

Roxanne looked at the floor. When she spoke her voice was barely above a whisper.

"He . . . he touched me."

"Caleb Barbour touched you?"

Tears appeared in the corners of Roxanne's eyes. Heather watched them run down the girl's cheeks.

"Did he hurt you?" she asked gently.

Roxanne nodded.

"Did he force you to . . . Did he force himself on you?"

The tears were a flood now. Roxanne's shoulders folded in like broken wings, and her sobs shook her. Heather wrapped her arms around the quivering girl and held her. When Roxanne stopped sobbing, Heather eased Roxanne back against the couch.

"Did your father help you escape from Barbour?" Heather asked.

"No."

"Then how did you get away?"

"I ran outside."

"Was your father outside?"

"No, ma'am."

"Then who was there?"

BY LATE AFTERNOON, FOUL WEATHER had put in another appearance. The sky over Portland was slate-gray, and the cold cut Heather to the bone. The pedestrians she passed walked with hunched shoulders and grim faces. Heather hitched her buggy in front of the jail. When Amos Strayer opened the peephole on the second knock, he found Heather huddled against the wall, shielding herself from the wind. Strayer didn't like the idea of a woman entering the jail, but he couldn't leave Benjamin Gillette's daughter at the mercy of the elements. Heather rushed inside as soon as the door opened.

"What's this about, Miss Gillette?"

"I want to speak to Mr. Brown."

"I can't let you do that. Only his lawyer is allowed to talk to him. That's the marshal's order."

"I wouldn't ask unless it was important."

"I don't know, Miss Gillette. That Brown is a killer. There's no telling what he might try."

"Thank you for your concern, Mr. Strayer, but Mr. Brown should bear me no ill will. I've been taking care of his daughter since the night he was arrested."

"And there's still what Marshal Lappeus said."

"I won't be long with him, I promise."

Strayer hesitated. He could see the meeting was important to Heather. And the marshal had let Brown's daughter actually go inside his cell.

"Please, Mr. Strayer."

"Well, all right. But I can't let you in the cell. You'll have to speak through the door."

"That won't be a problem."

Strayer led Heather to Worthy's cell. The prisoner was asleep, and it took a while to rouse him. He sat up slowly. The weak sunlight barely penetrated his cell, and he rubbed the sleep from his eyes so he could see.

"You've got a visitor, Brown," Strayer said when Worthy arrived at the door. "It's a lady. See you treat her like one."

"Mr. Brown, I'm Heather Gillette, Benjamin Gillette's daughter."

Worthy pressed his face against the bars in the small window in the door.

"I'm glad to meet you. Roxanne's told me so many good things about you. I hope she isn't any trouble."

"No, no, Mr. Brown. She's no trouble at all."

"It's been easier for me knowing she's being looked after, and I thank you for your kindness."

Heather turned to the deputy. "Mr. Strayer, may I talk to Mr. Brown alone? I want him to be able to speak freely, and your presence may inhibit him."

"I don't know. . . ."

"I assure you I'll be fine. There is a rather thick door between us."

Strayer was reluctant to leave. "He can reach you through the bars, Miss Gillette. Stay back from the window."

"I will."

"And holler if he gives you any trouble."

Strayer walked down the narrow corridor casting occasional glances over his shoulder. When he was out of earshot, Heather stared into Worthy's eyes.

"Roxanne needs you, Mr. Brown. She needs you very much."

"Why are you telling me that when there ain't nothing I can do about it?" Worthy asked, his anguish evident.

"We both know that isn't true. We both know you shouldn't be in here."

Worthy's features hardened. "What do you mean?"

Heather lowered her voice so there was no chance Amos Strayer could hear her.

"Did Matthew Penny kill Caleb Barbour?"

Heather heard the prisoner's sharp intake of breath.

"Did he kill him?" Heather repeated. She tried to read Worthy's expression, but he'd stepped back a pace, cloaking his face in shadow.

"Why you asking me that?"

"I've talked to Roxanne. You weren't at Barbour's house when she and Barbour ran into the yard. Matthew was."

"That girl was shook up bad. She don't know what she's saying."

"I know Matthew killed Caleb Barbour. Otherwise, the timing makes no sense. You were arrested almost an hour after Matthew brought Roxanne to my house. Why would you stay with Barbour's corpse? Why didn't you follow your daughter to find out how badly she was injured? You didn't accompany Roxanne to my house because you weren't present when Barbour died. You didn't come to Gillette House because you didn't know where she was."

Worthy turned his back on Heather and sat down on his bed.

"Roxanne told me you weren't in the yard when she ran out of Barbour's house. She saw Matthew in the yard. I think Matthew saw what Barbour had done to Roxanne and killed him to protect her."

"I killed Caleb Barbour," Worthy replied in a flat voice.

"Roxanne needs you, Mr. Brown. Tell the marshal what really happened. Don't die for a crime you didn't commit."

"Mr. Penny would hang if I did what you want."

"If he killed Barbour to save Roxanne, he can claim self-defense. All the facts would come out in a trial. Roxanne can tell the jury what Barbour did to her."

"Ain't no one gonna believe her, Miss Gillette. They'd be thinking she was lying to save me."

"Not if Matthew backed up her story."

"And died instead of me? I thank you again for taking care of
my Roxanne, and I understand why you come here, but you have
to let this lay quiet. I killed Barbour. That's the end of it."

HEATHER HITCHED HER BUGGY IN front of the building that
housed Matthew's office and climbed the stairs to the second
floor. She found the lawyer working at his desk. Matthew looked
up. His handsome features were ravaged by exhaustion, and his
eyes were red-rimmed.

"Are you working on Worthy's case?" Heather asked.

"No, this is work for another client."

Heather hesitated then she remembered Worthy's desolate cell
and Roxanne's anguish.

"There is an easy way to set Worthy free," she said.

"Oh?"

"I've talked to Roxanne and Mr. Brown."

"About what?" Matthew asked warily.

"I know what happened at Caleb Barbour's house."

Matthew gave himself time to think by using a cloth to remove
the excess ink from the nib of his pen.

"What did they say?" he asked as he set the quill down.

Heather stared at him without flinching. "Caleb Barbour violated Roxanne. That's why she was naked. She ran from the house
as you rode up. Barbour chased her, and you killed him to protect Roxanne. Worthy Brown was nowhere near Barbour's house

when Barbour was killed. He's protecting you because you saved his daughter."

Matthew felt sick. He didn't know what to say.

"You can save him, Matthew. You must tell the district attorney. You've committed no crime. Barbour was a rapist. The law protects you. You killed to protect an innocent child."

When Matthew answered, he sounded like a man who had abandoned hope.

"I didn't remember what happened because of the blow to my head. When I remembered, I went to the jail and told Worthy that I was going to confess. He said that he would not let me take the blame for killing Barbour. He insisted that he would confess if I tried.

"I went to W. B. Thornton's office anyway. I did what you want me to do: I confessed. He wouldn't believe me. He said I was imagining the murder, and, in truth, I have no clear memory of it. I just know that I killed him. But Worthy won't back me out of a misguided sense of loyalty because I saved Roxanne."

"Roxanne will tell them what you've said is true."

"She never saw what happened. Roxanne wasn't in the yard when I killed Barbour. She was in shock, and she ran into the forest to escape from him. And Thornton wouldn't believe her anyway. He'd say she's lying to save her father from the gallows."

"This is insane. You are not a murderer. You saved Roxanne from a rapist."

"It wasn't that way," he said in a voice that was barely audible.

Heather looked confused. "What else could have happened?"

Matthew looked up. Heather had never seen anyone look so tired.

"I didn't kill Barbour to save Roxanne. I killed him in a rage after Roxanne was safe. I killed him because he insulted you."

"Insulted me?" Heather repeated, unsure she'd heard Matthew correctly.

"Roxanne ran into the woods, and I stopped Barbour from going after her. He was furious and he called you a . . . a name. I lost control. There was nothing virtuous in what I did. I was no better than a drunk in a saloon brawl."

"If you hadn't stopped Barbour, he would have pursued Roxanne. You know that. Surely it can't matter that you had two motives to strike him?"

"My motive—my intent—does matter in a court of law. In my mind I was not acting to save Roxanne. I was blind with rage."

Heather paused to think about Matthew's revelation. Then she looked at him.

"I care for you, Matthew. I care for you deeply, no matter what you've done. You're a good man regardless of what you think. I'll stand by you, and we *will* figure this out."

"There's nothing to figure out," Matthew said.

"Perhaps you'll win at trial and Worthy will go free."

Matthew shook his head. "Worthy won't let me call Roxanne as a witness, and he insists that I represent him so I can't testify to what really happened. As it stands, we have little chance of prevailing."

PART FOUR

ROXANNE'S CHOICE

CHAPTER 43

Benjamin Gillette had been furious with Heather for going behind his back and asking Orville Mason to investigate Sharon Hill, but his anger dissipated quickly in light of Orville's revelations about his mistress. Gillette had no illusions about the relationship he'd forged with Hill. It was a business arrangement. Sharon had hinted that she wanted more, but Gillette had been part of one long and exceptionally happy marriage. Marrying again at his age was not in his plans, and there was Heather's inheritance and his empire to consider.

As soon as the meeting with Heather and Orville concluded, Ben had summoned Francis Gibney and told him to look into Hill's background so he could find out if she was as corrupt as Orville's evidence suggested. He was especially concerned to learn the truth behind Warren Quimby's death. This morning, Gibney had presented his findings. Gillette could have sent Francis to the Evergreen to tell Hill that the affair was over, but he decided that he would break the news in person.

The cream-colored silk nightgown Sharon Hill was wearing clung to her body, accentuating the breasts and hips that had stoked Benjamin Gillette's desire since he'd first seen her in Phoenix, but Gillette felt no desire for his mistress this afternoon.

"Ben," Hill said, surprised by his unannounced visit.

Gillette walked into the sitting room without a word. Hill followed, puzzled by his cold demeanor.

"I have something to ask you," Gillette said.

"And what might that be?" Hill asked calmly.

"Do you know a man named Warren Quimby?"

"No," said Hill, her face betraying none of her emotions. Her rapid heartbeat, had Gillette been able to hear it, would have revealed her lie.

"You never encountered him while living in San Francisco?"

"Who is this Quimby person?"

"Someone I've been led to believe you knew quite well."

"I've never heard of the man."

"How well did you know Caleb Barbour?"

"Where is this going? Why are you interrogating me as if I were a criminal?"

"I have received some disturbing information about you, Quimby, and Barbour."

"I can see you're upset. Sit down and we'll discuss this. I don't know what you've heard, so I can't respond. I'll bring you a glass of wine."

Gillette was grateful for the brief respite. He was not averse to hard bargaining, but he'd lain naked with Sharon Hill not too long ago. Even with the facts he had learned, it was not easy to accuse a lover of duplicity.

Hill returned to find Gillette waiting for her on the couch. She handed him a glass of red wine and sat opposite him on a straight-back chair.

"No more questions, Ben. If you have something to say to me, say it."

Gillette took a healthy drink of his wine to fortify himself. "I've been told that Caleb Barbour has been alone with you in this suite on more than one occasion."

"Who told you this?" Hill asked indignantly.

"That doesn't matter."

Hill, an excellent actress who could fake orgasms and tears with equal facility, contorted her features until they mimicked the face of a wronged and anguished paramour.

"I love you," she said. "Why would I cheat on someone I love?"

"Why would you lie about Clyde Lukens stealing money from you? And don't deny it. His company has confirmed that he was legitimately in possession of the money you claim he stole from you."

"You were in Phoenix, Ben. You saw Lukens. How could you take his word over mine?"

"You still haven't denied spending the night with Caleb."

"There's nothing to deny," Hill said. "I've never slept with Caleb Barbour."

Hill dipped her head to feign embarrassment. "On the evening you celebrated the arrival of the Oregon Pony, Caleb came to my room. He was intoxicated and forward, and I sent him on his way. I swear nothing happened. I didn't tell you because I didn't want Caleb to get in trouble for something he did while he was drunk."

Gillette knew there was something wrong with Hill's protest, something the clerk had told him about an occasion when Barbour had stayed the night, but he felt nervous and edgy and his heart was beginning to race, making it difficult for him to collect his thoughts.

Hill watched him intently. "Is something wrong?" she asked.

"I'm . . . I just . . . feel dizzy."

Gillette tried to stand, but he staggered and fell back onto the couch. He could feel his heartbeat accelerating, and his face started to swell and turn purple. Hill smiled and sipped some of her wine.

"Sharon," Ben gasped. "I may be having a heart attack. Get a doctor."

"A doctor won't help, Ben," Hill said calmly. "Nicotine is a very rapid poison. Before a doctor can get to my suite, you'll begin convulsing. Then you'll become unconscious, go into a coma, and die."

"The wine," Ben gasped, stiffening suddenly as the first convulsion started.

"Yes, Ben, the wine," Hill confirmed as Gillette thrashed on the sofa. She watched him without emotion as he gagged and his arms twitched spasmodically. Then he relaxed for a moment.

During his brief respite, Gillette opened his mouth to call for help. Hill sprang forward and jammed a sofa cushion over his face. Another convulsion struck before Gillette could struggle. He flailed, and Hill jumped out of reach. Then she watched dispassionately as his lips drew back in a ghastly grimace. His limbs flew in all directions in an uncontrolled frenzy. A moment later, he lay limp and unconscious and on the verge of death.

Hill checked herself in the mirror. She wanted to look a little disheveled, so she ran her hands through her hair. When she was satisfied, she concentrated on feeling sad. As soon as memories of the beatings at the hands of Warren Quimby brought tears to her eyes, she raced down to the lobby.

A startled bellboy stared at the distraught woman.

"Help, help," she screamed. "It's my husband. He's dead."

CHAPTER 44

Benjamin Gillette was buried beside his wife in their plot in a hilltop cemetery with a view of Mount Hood. A large crowd came to pay their respects, despite the heavy rain that fell all day. Matthew Penny stood on one side of Heather, holding an umbrella to shield her from the downpour. Orville Mason stood on the other side, an arm around her shoulder, as they listened to Reverend Mason's short but intensely personal eulogy. Matthew knew what it felt like to suffer the loss of someone you loved dearly, so it caused him great pain to see Heather's shoulders shake with each heart-wrenching sob.

When the graveside service was over, Matthew helped Heather into her buggy. Orville Mason had the reins, and he led the mourners back to Gillette House. Matthew followed the procession on horseback. By dusk, all but Matthew, Reverend Mason, Amelia Mason, and Orville were gone.

"That was a beautiful service," Heather told Orville's father as the Masons prepared to leave.

"One of the saddest I've ever conducted," Reverend Mason answered. "Remember, you'll never be alone as long as we're here."

Matthew watched the family descend the porch steps to their carriage. Then he turned to Heather. She had tried to be strong all afternoon, but the effort had taken its toll and she looked very pale.

"How are you doing?" Matthew asked.

"He's gone," Heather said, breaking into the tears she'd held back during the reception for the mourners.

Matthew held her until the tears stopped. Then he helped her to a seat in the parlor. Heather leaned back and closed her eyes.

"It hit me hard at breakfast," she said. "We started each day together, talking about our plans or the weather or—"

She stopped, too choked up to speak for a moment.

"He wasn't there, Matthew. His chair was empty, and I knew I'd never see him in it again."

"He was a good man, Heather, a good father. You were lucky to have a father like Ben."

"Just as I was to have him for a husband," Sharon Hill said from the doorway.

Hatred flashed in Heather's eyes, and she leaped to her feet.

"What are you doing in my house?"

"I'm sorry, Miss Heather," the maid said from behind Hill. "I told her you weren't seeing anyone, but she—"

"It's all right," Matthew said. "You may go."

"I've come to pay my respects," Hill said as the maid retreated. "Since we'll be seeing a lot of each other I thought this might be the time to talk to you."

"What makes you think we'll ever see each other?" Heather snapped.

Hill smiled. "Let's be frank. I know you don't like me. Ben told me. It was one of the reasons we kept our marriage secret. He wanted to try to win you over before we made it public."

"Your marriage?" Heather said. "What are you talking about?"

"We were married in San Francisco."

"You're a liar," Heather said.

"I know this must come as a shock, but we were married. I have a signed marriage contract between Ben and me to prove it. And it would serve you well to accept me as your mother because this house, all of Ben's other property, and all his assets are now mine."

Matthew had finally had enough of Hill's rude intrusion into Heather's grief.

"Miss Hill—"

"Mrs. Gillette," Sharon corrected.

"*Miss Hill*, you're upsetting Miss Gillette, and I must ask you to leave."

"You have no right to ask me to leave my home."

"If you're smart," Matthew said, "you will never mention your preposterous assertion again. Remember, there are penalties for criminal fraud."

Hill's composure never faltered. She flashed a dazzling smile at Matthew.

"So Miss Gillette has a champion. Well, fortunately, I have a marriage contract."

She turned her attention to Heather. "Think hard before fighting me. I'm a poor loser. Contest my claims, and I'll throw you out without a cent. Do the right thing, and I'll be generous to you."

Heather rose and stared at Hill. Then she leaped forward and slapped Hill so hard that only Hill's hatpin kept her hat attached to her head. Hill staggered backward, and Heather struck her again, sending her to the floor.

Matthew sprang forward and pinned Heather's arms to her sides. "Get out quickly, Miss Hill, quickly."

Hill struggled to her feet. Every pretense of civility was gone as she stared with pure malevolence at Heather.

"You're going to regret that, you little bitch," Hill said before she left, slamming the door behind her.

Heather collapsed in Matthew's arms and wept.

"Shhh," he said, "she's nothing. Don't worry. She can't hurt you. I won't let her."

CHAPTER 45

S haron Hill entered the law office of Stephen Press radiating confidence, but her self-assurance faltered when the dapper lawyer refused to stand. When Press addressed her as "Miss Hill" after his secretary had introduced her as "Mrs. Benjamin Gillette," her confidence deserted her completely.

"Are you seeking to consult me about the so-called marriage contract?" Press asked, making no attempt to be polite.

"Yes, I—"

"Then you're wasting your time. I cannot . . . No, I *will* not help you."

"Won't you even give me the courtesy of listening to what I have to say?"

"I knew Benjamin Gillette quite well, my good woman," Press said sternly. "I knew his wife. My daughters sang in the church choir with Heather Gillette. If you are seeking an attorney who will help you defraud Benjamin Gillette's daughter, you must go elsewhere."

"How dare you imply that I'm involved in a swindle," Hill said indignantly.

"Madam, your marriage contract is the talk of my profession."

"Are you saying that my affairs are the subject of common gossip?" Hill asked, aghast. "What about the confidentiality between attorney and client?"

"Yes, yes, a regrettable lapse of professional ethics, but your lawsuit is outrageous." Press spread his hands out at his sides and shrugged. "I'm afraid this is a risk one takes when one attempts to perpetrate a fraud on the daughter of Portland's most distinguished citizen."

It took all of Hill's self-control to keep from striking the contemptuous little man. She tried to come up with a suitable parting comment, but she was so angry she couldn't think straight, so she left without another word.

It was the same everywhere she went. The first attorneys she visited were courteous. They had reviewed the marriage contract and even consulted with Orville Mason to discuss Hill's claim. The problem lay with Bernard Hoxie. He had employed an incompetent fool to forge Benjamin's signature. As soon as Orville explained Sharon's background and demonstrated that the signature on the contract was an obvious forgery, the attorneys declined to represent her. Now no lawyer would even give her the time of day.

The Evergreen Hotel was a short distance from Press's law office, and Hill was still in a rage when she entered the lobby.

"Miss Hill," Harvey Metcalf, the assistant manager, called out.

Hill walked toward the stairs, pretending she had not heard him. She hated the supercilious little drudge who had fawned on her while Benjamin was alive but now treated her with open contempt because Heather refused to pay the hotel's bill.

"Miss Hill," Metcalf shouted loudly, calling the attention of everyone in the lobby to her. Hill spun toward him, her face scarlet with anger and embarrassment.

"Yes, Mr. Metcalf?"

"Just a reminder that you must be out of your room by noon tomorrow."

An elderly couple seated near Sharon exchanged puzzled looks, but the bellboy, who knew everything that went on in the hotel, hid a grin. Hill mustered what dignity she had left and walked up the stairs with her shoulders thrown back and her head high. Her brave front collapsed the moment she was in her suite. Clothes were strewn around the room. The sheets had not been changed in days. Dust was collecting on the furniture. Hill had complained to the management, but they no longer listened to her. She was certain that Orville Mason had instructed them to make her life as miserable as possible.

Hill walked to the window and stared down at the bustling crowd on the street below. She hated them, hated everyone who had a home and someone who cared about them. She was smarter than they were, and she was beautiful, yet she had no one and owned only the clothes on her back and the money in her purse.

Hill fought back tears. Crying was what weaklings did, and she was not weak. She wiped her eyes and breathed deeply until she was calm. She couldn't let Heather Gillette win. She had to find a way to fight back.

CHAPTER 46

After completing his circuit, Jed Tyler returned to Portland under threatening skies. His home at Fifth and Yamhill was six blocks from the river, but there were few structures to act as barriers against the damp, chill air gusting inland from the Willamette, and the biting wind stung his cheeks and almost tore his hat from his head as he unlatched his front gate.

As soon as Tyler was safely inside, he submerged in the steaming hot bath his housekeeper had drawn for him. While Tyler bathed, Mrs. McCall heated up a pot of stew. After dinner, she went home, and the judge settled in front of the fire that had been set in the hearth in the parlor. Just before he had left to ride the circuit, a steamer had arrived bearing a gift from his brother, Gibbon's *The History of the Decline and Fall of the Roman Empire.* Tyler settled his heels on his footstool and was about to open the first volume when a knock at the front door intruded on his solitude. He carried an oil lamp into the foyer and looked through the leaded glass. Sharon Hill was standing on his doorstep.

The judge was dressed in black trousers and suspenders, his shirt was open at the neck, and his sleeves were rolled up, displaying forearms corded with a laborer's muscles and matted with black hair. Tyler hesitated before opening the door, discomfited at the thought of Sharon Hill seeing him in this state of undress. Then he remembered the inhospitable weather and opened the door quickly.

The biting cold and vicious wind had played havoc with his visitor. Even with a hat, her hair was in disarray and her cheeks had been rubbed raw, but her distress only made Hill more beautiful in Tyler's eyes.

"Thank goodness you're home," Hill exclaimed.

"Come into the parlor. I have a fire on."

"Thank you. The cold was making me faint."

"You shouldn't have been out walking by yourself," Tyler said as he ushered her in. "This is a sailor's town. There are disreputable sorts about."

"I doubt I was in danger. The hooligans probably have enough sense to stay inside on a night like this."

Tyler smiled. "Maybe so."

The judge threw some kindling on the fire, and it flared up. The flames licked the belly of a fat log, and warmth began to spread through the room. Hill held out her hands toward the heat.

"I feel better already."

"Rest here. I'll bring you some tea."

"If it's no bother," Hill said, smiling sweetly.

Tyler hurried off, and Hill looked around. The room was sparsely furnished. A chair identical to the one on which she sat faced her across a small walnut table. A couch whose back was covered by an antimacassar rested against a wall under an oil painting that portrayed a sailing ship in turbulent seas. There was a bookcase against another wall, and folded reading glasses rested on a thick volume on the table. The room had an unused feel to it, and Hill guessed that few people were entertained here.

The fire warmed her. She leaned her head against the back of the chair and opened her coat. The heat made her feel deliciously sleepy. She shut her eyes and was drifting off when the clatter of a china cup against a matching saucer signaled the return of her host. When she opened her eyes, Tyler was standing over her, motionless.

"I almost fell asleep," Sharon confessed, noticing that the judge had put on a jacket and string tie while waiting for the tea to brew. Tyler set the tea on the table and watched anxiously as his guest took a sip.

"Is it all right?"

"Perfect."

Tyler sat opposite his guest and studied Hill as she sipped her tea.

"What brings you here at this time of night and in this weather?"

Hill had seemed at peace while she recovered from the cold, but Tyler's question caused a sudden change, and he sensed desperation in the tension in her shoulders and the tight line of her lips.

"I've come to ask for your help."

"What's wrong?" Tyler asked.

"I'm being cheated by Orville Mason and Heather Gillette, and I can find no one to take my side. They're throwing me out of my hotel. The lawyers are all against me. I have no one to turn to."

"You must start at the beginning," said Tyler, who could make no sense out of her disjointed statement.

"Ben and I traveled to San Francisco. We were married there."

Sharon Hill could not have caused Jed Tyler greater pain had she shot him through the heart. If Hill was married to Benjamin Gillette, she was lost to him.

"I've shown the contract to several attorneys, but no one will help me. Mason has bought them off. It's hopeless."

"You have some sort of contract with Ben?"

"A marriage contract, duly notarized. An attorney in San Francisco prepared it. Ben signed it, but Heather Gillette swears it's a forgery, and no one will risk her anger now that she controls Ben's holdings."

"I shouldn't be listening to this. Litigation concerning this matter may come before me."

"Not you, too," Hill moaned.

Tyler felt terrible, but he also felt helpless. "You must understand—I want to help you, but I'm a judge. It's my duty to remain neutral in matters that might come before me."

Hill stood up. "I should have known you'd be like the rest. You were my only hope. I thought you would have the courage to stand up to Mason and Gillette."

Tyler rose with her. "Wait, please. Sit down. You must calm yourself. I don't understand why you've come to me if you're married to Ben. Has he denied the contract?"

"Ben's dead. Didn't you know?"

Tyler was stunned. "I've been riding circuit. I had no way of knowing."

"He died in my arms. And now his daughter is trying to cheat me and go against her father's wishes."

Tyler was torn. It would be totally inappropriate for a justice of the supreme court to intervene in a case that might come before him, but Sharon Hill affected him as no woman had before. He could not stand to see her in such distress.

"I'll help. I'll talk to Mason tomorrow. We'll get to the bottom of this."

"Oh, Jed, I knew you wouldn't let me down."

She paused and looked upset.

"Is there something else troubling you?" Tyler asked.

Hill hesitated. Then she looked him in the eye. "When you see Mason he . . . he may say things about me."

Tyler's brow furrowed. "What kind of things?"

"Bad things."

"Don't worry, Sharon. I won't believe Mason's lies."

Hill hesitated again before taking the risk she had debated taking since settling on the judge as her last resort.

"Some of what he says may not be lies. Jed, I'm going to be completely honest with you, even if it costs me your friendship. I know what I tell you will sound awful, but I can't ask for your help and lie to you. You're one of the few decent men I've met here, one of the few men besides Ben who has treated me with respect. So here it is."

Hill looked away from Tyler and into the fire. "My life at home was terrible. My father . . ." Hill looked down. "He . . . There is no delicate way to put it. He mistreated me, Jed. Then he tried to marry me to a man for money. This man was so vile that it makes me ill to think of him. I had to escape, so I ran away to San Francisco. That's where I met Warren Quimby.

"Quimby was a smooth talker. He took me in when I had nothing; he fed me. He said he loved me, and I believed him. He was sweet at first, but he soon controlled me completely. He . . . he forced me to . . . to do things with men against my will.

"I tried to run away, but he caught me and beat me within an inch of death. He kept me a prisoner in his room and starved me. It looked hopeless. Then he had a heart attack and died. I took what I could and fled to Oregon. I wanted to leave my old life behind. I wanted to be reborn. When Ben proposed, it was a dream come true."

Hill looked directly at Tyler. "When I married Ben, I respected him and valued his friendship, but I never loved him. Marriage was my way out of the trap life had set for me. He was kind and he never mistreated me. And, yes, he was rich."

Fire flashed in Hill's eyes, defying Tyler to cast stones at her. "Do you see what that could mean to someone like me, who had lived a life filled with poverty and horror? And now Mason and Heather Gillette are spreading lies about me to keep me from inheriting Ben's estate. They want people to believe I stole from Clyde Lukens even though the jury found him guilty. They're even suggesting that a heart attack did not take Ben from me, that I had something to do with his death. Heather has always hated me. She's spiteful, and she's twisted Mason until he can't see the truth."

Tyler was stunned. What Hill had just told him was almost too much to absorb. How could he not have suspected the horrors Sharon had endured? How could there be no hint of the degradation to which she had been subjected? How brave must she have been to have gone through so much and still maintain her sanity?

"The whole city is against me, Jed. Now that you know the truth, where do you stand?"

Tyler hesitated, knowing that what he said next would either send Sharon Hill away forever or bind her to him. How much did she mean to him? he asked himself. The answer to that question was easy. She meant everything.

"I stand beside you," the judge told Hill.

"I knew you wouldn't let me down."

"I'll pay for your suite at the Evergreen. They won't throw you out."

"I can't stay there. It's been like living in hell. They refuse to clean my room or let me eat in the dining room. The staff smirks behind my back."

"It's the only decent hotel in town."

"Then I'll find a boardinghouse."

Tyler made a decision. "I have a guest room in which you can stay."

"I couldn't. It would cause a scandal."

"Sharon, I've been a respected member of this community for years. If I lose that respect by helping a woman in great distress, what was that respect worth in the first place?"

"Oh, Jed, I prayed you wouldn't care what people thought. I prayed that you would stand by me."

"I will," Tyler swore. "They won't hurt you anymore."

JED TYLER FIXED DINNER FOR Sharon Hill. Then he took her to the Evergreen Hotel, where they collected both her belongings and curious stares. Harvey Metcalf was at the front desk, and Hill delighted in the assistant manager's servile attitude as he complied with the judge's demand for assistance with her luggage.

Tyler's guest room was at the other end of the hall from the judge's bedroom. When Hill was settled in, the judge bade her good night and went to his own bedchamber, but it was difficult for him to sleep knowing that Sharon was so near and knowing that the choice he had just made could destroy the life he had built for himself.

Soon after they parted for the night, the judge heard a gentle knock on his door. He opened it and found Hill standing inches from him in a sheer nightgown.

"I couldn't sleep," she said.

Moments later, Hill was in the judge's arms.

After, as they lay together, Hill told Tyler that she had fallen in love with him when he'd held the lynch mob at bay in Phoenix. Then she told him how much Benjamin Gillette was worth and how rich they would be when her contract of marriage was upheld. They would own Gillette House. They would travel to Paris. They would drink the finest wines, wear the finest clothes, and make love on sheets made of silk. They would live in a paradise on earth. And they would have the power that wealth and Gillette's business empire would bring them. Men would do what they willed, and they could do anything they imagined.

As she murmured in Tyler's ear, Sharon Hill used the skills she had learned in her profession to arouse her lover again, and each time they made love she smiled with satisfaction, knowing that she had bound one of the state's most powerful men to her through sex, the promise of wealth, and her power to make him love her.

CHAPTER 47

Justice Tyler rose shortly after dawn, despite having slept for only a few hours. Mrs. McCall arrived just as he was leaving to confront Orville Mason. It took all of her willpower to conceal her shock when she learned that the city's most notorious female was bedded down in the judge's home.

Orville Mason was surprised when his secretary announced that Jed Tyler was in his waiting room. He and Tyler were on opposite sides in the debate over slavery and in different political parties. They saw each other in court but had nothing in common other than the cases in which they were involved.

"I've come to discuss Benjamin Gillette's marriage to Sharon Hill," the judge said without preamble when the door to Orville's office closed behind him.

"Benjamin Gillette and Sharon Hill were never married," Orville stated firmly.

"I've seen the marriage contract."

"I'm confused," Orville said. "What possible reason can you have for involving yourself in this matter? You're a judge, not an attorney."

"I'm also Mrs. Gillette's friend. Perhaps her only friend, since you've turned everyone in Portland against her."

"Miss Hill is responsible for the town turning against her. Not only has she been trying to defraud Heather Gillette, but she's been exposed as a perjurer. Miss Hill lied in Phoenix when she claimed that Clyde Lukens stole from her."

"Nonsense. Lukens was found guilty by a jury in a case over which I presided. The evidence was clear."

"You were deceived. Lukens's company vouches for his honesty, and it has confirmed that the money Hill claims was hers was rightfully his."

"You weren't present in Phoenix. You didn't hear the witnesses. In any event, what happened in Phoenix is irrelevant. There is a marriage contract signed by Benjamin Gillette. Sharon Hill and Gillette were betrothed, and I demand that you perform your duties as executor of his will."

"I was Ben's attorney, and he never told me anything about marrying Miss Hill. He didn't ask me to change his will or take any other action consistent with marriage.

"More important, the contract is a fraud. When Joseph Baxter approached me on Miss Hill's behalf, I gave him a document with Ben's signature and asked him to compare it with the signature on the so-called contract. I've done the same with another attorney who wasted his time on this matter. I will give you the same opportunity to compare Ben's actual signature with the signature on the so-called marriage contract. That signature is a blatant forgery, and that is why no attorney will represent Miss Hill."

"Mrs. Gillette has given me her word that the signature is real. I accept her word."

Orville sighed. "I have no wish to quarrel with you. I beg you to compare the signature on the contract with Ben's real signature."

"You refuse to recognize Mrs. Gillette's claim?" Tyler asked.

"That is what I've been telling you."

"Then we have nothing more to discuss."

"Justice Tyler, Sharon Hill is a very dangerous woman. You have a sterling reputation. If you continue to assist her, it could ruin you."

"We will see who will be ruined," Tyler said, slamming the door as he left the office.

Orville slumped in his chair and massaged his temples. He was no friend of Jed Tyler, but he had no wish to see him brought low. He feared that would be the consequence of the judge's actions if he continued to champion Hill's immoral cause.

CHAPTER 48

W. B. Thornton pushed away from the dinner table with a contented grin. His belly grew larger every day, but he could not resist Abigail's honey-glazed ham, candied yams, and mouth-watering corn bread.

"I think I'll have a drop of brandy in the study," he told his wife as he used his napkin to dislodge a piece of corn bread that had attached itself to his beard. When he completed his task, the district attorney headed for the liquor cabinet, but a knock at the door made him pause in his journey. Thornton glanced at the grandfather's clock in the front hall and wondered who could be calling at eight o'clock.

"Good evening, Jed," Thornton said as soon as he opened the door.

"I hope I'm not disturbing your dinner," the judge said.

"We just finished. I was going to have some brandy. Will you join me?"

Thornton brought Tyler into the study and poured two snifters of brandy. Tyler took an absentminded sip, then set down his glass on the end table.

"So what brings you here at this hour?" Thornton asked.

"A delicate matter. But I must have your promise that everything I say to you will stay between us."

"Of course."

"What are your political plans?" Tyler asked.

"Well, now. I'm quite content for the moment, you know. I haven't really thought much about the future."

Tyler did not react to this obvious lie. Thornton's ambition was a frequent topic of conversation in political circles.

"Have you ever thought about a position on the supreme court?" Tyler asked.

"Of course," Thornton answered with a nervous laugh.

"I'm going to step down from the bench for personal reasons. The governor owes me several favors. I'm willing to call them in to see that you are appointed to my seat. Would you accept the position if it was offered?"

"I'm flattered," Thornton gushed. "I never thought . . . Well, there are others better suited, but—"

"You are the best choice," Tyler assured the district attorney.

"I can't tell you how much I appreciate your confidence in me. But what prompted your decision?"

Tyler's plan depended on what happened in the next few minutes, and he steeled himself by taking another sip of brandy.

"If I recommend you to the governor, he'll appoint you to finish my term. During that term, a case may come before you involving Benjamin Gillette's estate."

Thornton paled as the import of Tyler's words dawned on him. "Jed, I—"

"Hear me out," Tyler said, using a tone that commanded immediate obedience in court. "Benjamin Gillette's estate is worth fifteen million dollars. Whoever controls it also owns the majority of shares in the Oregon Railway and Navigation Company, in which, I believe, you are heavily invested. That person will be in an excellent position to help his friends."

What Tyler didn't say, but what he implied, was that the person who controlled the estate could also do a great deal of harm to anyone who crossed him.

"Sharon Hill married Benjamin Gillette in San Francisco, but they kept their marriage secret. Miss Hill—Mrs. Gillette—has tried to assert her rights as Ben's widow, but Orville Mason has launched a scurrilous campaign to discredit her claim."

The so-called marriage contract was the talk of Portland society and its legal community. Everyone knew about it, and Thornton could not understand why it would concern Justice Tyler. He learned the answer to his unspoken question when Tyler continued.

"I intend to step down from the bench and represent Mrs. Gillette to establish her legitimate interest in the estate and save her good name."

Thornton was stunned by the crudity of Tyler's approach, but he concealed his shock from the jurist.

"I've heard about the marriage contract, but I have no opinion about it," Thornton assured Tyler.

"That's good," Tyler said. "A judge must have no opinion about a case until he hears all the facts."

"Of course."

"So, shall I speak to the governor about your suitability to fill my seat on the court?"

Thornton hesitated. He was not someone who could think

quickly, and there were so many possible outcomes if he accepted the judge's offer that he was lost in the maze they created. What he could see clearly was a vision of W. B. Thornton draped in the robes of a justice of the supreme court.

Thornton was ambitious, and an appointment to the court would be a tremendous boost to those ambitions. Then there were the future financial rewards to which Jed had alluded. But Tyler had left no doubt about the quid pro quo in this Faustian bargain. Could he do it? Could he fix the result of a case? If he was suspected of fixing a case of this magnitude, he would be destroyed, but who could prove anything since only he and Tyler would know what transpired in his study?

"You can count on me, Jed."

"Then it's done."

Tyler stood. Thornton walked him to the front door in a daze. As soon as the judge was outside, beads of sweat appeared on Thornton's brow and he felt dizzy. He leaned against the door and closed his eyes. As he took long, slow breaths to calm his racing heart, he was assailed by doubt and wondered what he had gotten himself into.

AS SOON AS JED TYLER was out of sight of Thornton's house his shoulders sagged. He felt sick about what he'd just done. Thornton did not have the intellect to sit on the court, and fixing a case went against everything Tyler stood for, but he had no choice. His life had been barren without Sharon Hill in it, and he could not give her up. Her happiness meant everything to him, and she could not be happy while this stain on her dignity remained. And, of course, there was the money and power controlling the Gillette fortune would bring them.

Tyler had done well in the West, but Benjamin Gillette's success was magnificent. Once Tyler was in control of Gillette's enterprises and fortune, he would be the most powerful man in Oregon and one of the most powerful men on the West Coast of the United States. Allying himself with Sharon Hill was risky, but the rewards would be astounding if the risk paid off.

CHAPTER 49

The maid showed Orville Mason into the parlor and went to summon Heather.

"Have you come about the marriage case?" Heather asked as soon as she sat down across from her lawyer.

"No. I want to talk to you about something else that requires your attention. But I am taking some action in Hill's case that may decide the matter. Bernard Hoxie is the California attorney who prepared the marriage contract. I'm going to San Francisco to confront Hoxie and explain what will happen to him if he testifies for Hill. If he sees the light and admits the forgery, we'll be rid of Miss Hill."

"If Hoxie prepared a forged marriage contract for Hill, he's a criminal. Will you be in danger?"

"Hoxie does have a bad reputation, but I'm no adventurer. I don't plan on getting into anything I can't get out of. Don't worry. I'll be perfectly safe."

"If you didn't come to talk to me about the marriage contract, why are you here?"

"I haven't pressed you about certain matters because you've been grieving, but I don't feel I can put off this discussion any longer. Ben was the moving force behind a financial empire worth many millions of dollars. There's the bank, the shipping company, his stores—"

"I'm well aware of his business holdings."

"Then you appreciate the fact that, as Ben's heir, you must make decisions involving them. There's nothing to worry about for the immediate future. Good men are running the enterprises and I've been overseeing them, but there are some pressing matters that require your attention. Since Ben passed away I've entertained offers to buy out your interest in a number of his companies. Some of these offers have come from San Francisco, and I can discuss them with the interested parties while I'm there. That means I need guidance from you concerning them."

"What do you think I should do, Orville?"

"If you sell everything Ben owns, you'll be wealthy and independent for life. Apart from a sale, I can arrange for you to retain stock in the more profitable ventures. This will provide you with a steady, and considerable, income."

"What will happen if I don't sell?"

"It's hard to say. Ben was the driving force behind his business ventures. To a great extent, it was his personality and business acumen that made them successful. As I said, he recruited good men to help run them. We could promote some to provide continuity, but I don't know what will happen without Ben at the helm."

"Would my taking the helm provide continuity?" Heather asked.

"You?" Orville asked, taken aback by the suggestion. The idea of any woman taking control of a multimillion-dollar business empire had never occurred to him.

"I'm Ben's daughter. He discussed his businesses with me all the time, and he trusted my judgment. You and the good men my father put in place can educate me further. And believe me, if I find I'm not up to the task, I'll tell you. I have no wish to destroy what my father spent a lifetime building."

Orville recalled what he admired most about Heather. It was her intelligence and independent spirit. Looking back, he realized that there was nothing he'd discussed with her about her father's estate that she had not grasped, and there was no question that she possessed her father's tenacity and charm.

"If you help me in this, I know I can succeed," Heather said. "Will you do that for me?"

Orville smiled. "Of course I will."

CHAPTER 50

As soon as Orville left, Heather went upstairs and changed into breeches and a flannel shirt. She threw on a heavy jacket and went to the stables, where she had the stable hand saddle her favorite horse.

Heather had been to San Francisco on several occasions, but she had only been exposed to the bright side of the City by the Bay. If Bernard Hoxie was a man so morally bankrupt that he would forge a marriage contract for a slattern like Sharon Hill, Heather assumed that Orville would find him in the darker parts of the city that were explored by a gentleman only at his peril.

Orville Mason was fearless and brilliant in a courtroom or political arena, but Heather doubted that he had ever been in physical danger. Matthew Penny had confronted violence and survived on the Oregon Trail, at Caleb Barbour's house, and on the road from Gillette House on the evening of the Keans' performance when he'd been attacked. Orville was ill equipped to deal with a villain like Hoxie, but Heather trusted Matthew to use force to defend Orville if it became necessary.

Heather had another reason for enlisting Matthew as Orville's bodyguard. Killing Caleb Barbour had changed Matthew, and Worthy Brown's insistence that he take the blame for the killing was destroying him. If Worthy followed through with his plan, Matthew would go through life with the blood of two men on his hands, and Heather was afraid of what Matthew might do if Worthy was hanged.

Heather cared for Matthew. She even considered the possibility that she loved him. When they had kissed in the gazebo after the theater, her heart had soared. Rather than diminishing her feelings for him, Matthew's confession of his love for Rachel had earned her respect. And they had definitely been drawn to each other while Matthew was convalescing. Heather had no idea what would have happened between them if Matthew had not killed Caleb Barbour and if her father had not died. Those events made it impossible for their personal relationship to move forward. But there was one thing Heather knew for certain. No matter what the future held for the two of them, she had to find a way to save Matthew. She hoped that getting him away from Portland might lift his spirits.

Heather tethered her mount to a hitching post and walked up the stairs to Matthew's office. She watched him through the window. He was concentrating on a document.

Matthew looked up when the door opened. "Heather, what brings you to town?"

"Did you know that Orville is going to San Francisco?" Heather asked.

"No, I didn't."

"He's going to confront Bernard Hoxie about the signature on the marriage contract, and I'm afraid that he may be putting himself in danger. Hoxie is a degenerate and a criminal, and I don't know what he'll do if Orville upsets him."

"Why are you telling me this?" Matthew asked.

"I want to ask you for a favor. I would feel much better if Orville didn't confront Hoxie alone. Would you go with him to San Francisco?"

Matthew didn't answer right away. Heather could see conflicting emotions twisting him.

"Please. I am afraid of what a man like Hoxie will do if he feels threatened."

"You're right. Orville is ill equipped to deal with a man like Hoxie. I'll go with him."

Heather reached out a touched Matthew's hand. "Thank you, Matthew. I knew I could count on you."

"You're a good friend to Orville and to me. Don't think for a moment that I don't appreciate that."

For a moment, Heather thought that he would say more, prayed that he would. Then he pulled his hand away.

"I've got to finish my work. It's for a case," he said.

"I understand," Heather answered, though she wasn't talking about his need to complete his reading of any legal papers. "Thank you for helping Orville."

CHAPTER 51

※

Shortly after midnight, the lights of her salons and staterooms aglow, the steamship *Northern Star* drew in through the Golden Gate, passed the fortifications that guarded the narrow entrance to the bay, and steamed around the little island of Alcatraz, firing her guns to announce her arrival. From the deck, Orville Mason and Matthew Penny took in the tumultuous scene. Clipper ships filled the harbor with a forest of sails; steamers as large and showy as those on the Hudson and Mississippi lay at anchor in a blaze of light. Behind those ships, from the water's edge to the base of her three hills, and from the Old Presidio to the Mission, flickering all over with the lamps of her streets and houses, lay San Francisco.

In 1847, San Francisco was no more than a small trading post and mission station with a population of four hundred. By 1850, as a result of the Gold Rush, the population had soared to twenty-five thousand. The metropolis the two friends stared at from the deck of the *Northern Star* now had a population of 56,802 and boasted, "New York dresses better than Paris and San Francisco better than New York."

Matthew bulled his way through the throng around the gangplank to a hackney coach with Orville close behind. Orville told the driver to take them to the five-story, fireproof International Hotel on Jackson before settling into the silk-lined luxury of the coach. The driver snapped the whip, and the silver-loaded harness jangled as the horses pushed through the express wagons, handcarts, cabs, coaches, and people who filled the dockside streets even at this late hour.

Orville and Matthew were exhausted, but the manic energy of the city acted like strong coffee. Sikhs, Chinese, and Samoans jostled one another as they walked along the lamp-lit cobblestone streets past elegant, three-story buildings. Ragged children ran beside the coach begging for pennies. Streetwalkers mixed easily with ladies of unquestioned virtue and the gentlemen who escorted them. By day, the clattering hooves and wheels of commercial horse-and-wagon traffic filled the streets. At night, this racket was replaced by the laughter and music that poured out of the city's saloons and theaters.

Sidewalk musicians were entertaining the crowds outside the entrance to the International. Matthew saw young boys on the fringe of the crowd openly hawking pornographic books and pictures. The coachman carried Orville's and Matthew's bags to the hotel entrance, knocking aside a filthy urchin who tried to interest Orville in a picture portraying two buxom women engaged in an act that guaranteed them a suite in hell. The price for the short ride from the docks was extravagant, but Orville would have been disappointed if anything in this larger-than-life city had not been dear.

Their room was on the fifth floor. Orville tipped the porter, while Matthew threw back the shutters and took in the view.

"My God," Matthew exclaimed as he looked down from this unaccustomed height, "this must be the way a hawk sees the world."

Orville had experienced a similar pleasure in the belfry of his father's church, but the tranquil feeling engendered by the snow-capped mountains and virgin forests of the Willamette Valley was nothing like the electricity generated by the chaos and decadence of San Francisco.

After unpacking, the attorneys went down to the dining room for a late dinner. By the time they returned to their rooms, they could think of nothing but the pleasure of passing out in their luxurious beds. Orville was asleep in minutes, but the elation Matthew had experienced deserted him as soon as he closed his eyes.

Self-pity and a lack of hope made Matthew despair in Portland, but he had never been to sea, and the voyage coupled with the noise and lights of the City by the Bay had the effect on him that Heather had hoped it would. Once on board the *Northern Star*, tantalized by ocean breezes and the vista of an endless sea, Matthew's spirits had risen and the distractions of San Francisco had continued to keep his depression at bay. But hope deserted Matthew as soon as he closed his eyes.

After Rachel's passing, the worst time of day was the moment he settled in bed and closed his eyes. Darkness and the still of night provided no distractions from sad or morbid thoughts, and it was then that memories of Rachel overwhelmed Matthew. Now these visions were joined by a loop that replayed the blow Matthew had struck in Barbour's yard, and Matthew was reminded that human beings could never travel back in time to change their fate.

A LITTLE AFTER TEN, MATTHEW opened the shutters, expecting to be greeted by San Francisco's famous fog. Instead, the view was so clear that he could see the buildings on the wooded shore of Contra Costa across the bay. After dining, Orville went to the docks to meet with two executives from Gillette's shipping company while Matthew explored the city. Then, shortly after three, Orville and Matthew walked to Montgomery Street, the favorite location of merchant counting houses, banks, insurance companies, and auction houses. Montgomery also boasted handsome shops and fashionable hotels that made it the Regent Street of the West and every bit as elegant as New York's Broadway.

Their destination was Henry W. Halleck's unique Montgomery Block, a four-story building with nearly 150 offices built in the newly fashionable Italianate style. People laughed at Halleck when he revealed his idea, not believing it possible that he would find tenants for so many offices, but the block was now a symbol of the city's pride. It featured bronzed iron front doors framed by stone columns modeled on those of the Diocletian Baths in Rome. Each office had the novelty of gaslight and fireplace grates. An artesian well in the center courtyard provided water on each floor, and every window had iron shutters to protect against thieves and fire. The walls were solid brick.

All these features were enthusiastically pointed out by Harold Denton, Orville's Harvard classmate, as he led Orville and Matthew from the reception area to his office. Denton was short and rotund, with a paunch, sparkling green eyes, and a cheery disposition. His hair was bright red and his goatee and mustache stood out against his pale, baby-smooth skin. Being the only redheads in their law school class had drawn the men together, and fierce intellects and fiercer attitudes about social justice had cemented the friendship.

When they were seated, Matthew listened stoically as the friends brought each other up to date about their lives since leaving Cambridge. Finally, Orville got down to business.

"Tell me all you know about Bernard Hoxie," he said.

Denton's smile disappeared. "You watch yourself with Hoxie, Orville. He's a dangerous lowlife. When he's not representing whores and thieves, he prowls the bars looking for destitute seamen he can con into bringing spurious lawsuits against shipowners. And he'll do anything for money, or find someone who can do it for him."

Orville flashed an indulgent smile. "I think you're being overly concerned, Harold. Mr. Hoxie is an attorney-at-law, a member of our profession. I'm in San Francisco to discuss a legal matter with him, not to judge his clientele."

"Bernard Hoxie is not just an attorney," Denton warned. "Have you heard of Shanghai Kelly or Mother Bronson?"

"I don't believe I have."

"Those scum run boardinghouses near the docks. They use women and liquor to lure seamen into them. Then they drug their victims and sell them to shipmasters in need of a crew. Hoxie is a silent partner of Kelly, Bronson, and others of their ilk. The whores at his saloon steer these poor wretches to the boardinghouses, and Hoxie takes his cut of the sale of each piece of human cargo without ever dirtying his hands. And that isn't the only criminal enterprise in which he is involved."

"I assure you that I do not intend to take up with any ladies of the night," Orville said to humor his friend. "Now, where can we find Mr. Hoxie?"

"You're being naive, Orville," Denton said. "You're not at Harvard now. When you enter the Barbary Coast, you'll be leaving civilization behind. Lawyers like you rely overmuch on reason. Men like Hoxie are not reasonable. They are predators, and their thought processes are more akin to sharks than philosophers."

"I appreciate your concern, but there are millions at stake here, and I have a limited time in your city."

Denton sighed. "Hoxie's office is in the Dancing Bear saloon on Davis."

Orville pulled out his pocket watch and opened the face cover.

"It's after five, Matthew. We'd better be going," he said.

Denton looked aghast. "Surely you're not venturing into the Barbary Coast at night. Why don't you have dinner with me and go in the morning?"

"We can dine tomorrow, but I must see Hoxie as soon as possible."

"May I make a suggestion," Matthew said. Orville and Denton turned toward him. "I can tell by your tone, Orville, that you aren't taking Mr. Denton's warnings seriously, but I do. Men like Hoxie are not to be taken lightly. Let me go to Hoxie's place of business and reconnoiter while you dine. If all goes well, we can return to his office in the light of day."

"An excellent course of action, Orville," Denton said.

"Good lawyers are hard to come by," Matthew said. "Heather needs you."

When Orville hesitated, Matthew removed a pistol from the pocket of his sack coat. "You are clearly my superior in a court of law. Please accept the fact that I'm more at home than you in a place like the Barbary Coast."

Orville sighed. "You're right, but promise me you'll take no risks."

Matthew smiled. "I'm as fond of my skin as you are of yours. But to assure my survival, I do need to bring one thing with me."

"And that is?" Orville asked.

MATTHEW KNEW HE HAD CROSSED the border between morality and sin when the cobblestoned elegance of Montgomery Street gave way to muddy thoroughfares and plank sidewalks crowded with degenerates, low- and highborn, seeking out the most vile and degrading vices. As Matthew was navigating his way through the crowds that streamed past the brothels, dance halls, cheap hotels, gambling dens, pawnshops, and saloons that lined Davis Street, a queued Chinaman, his eyes glazed by opium, lurched into his path. Matthew stepped back against the peeling paint on a clapboard wall and paused to get his bearings. A sudden lull in the street noise brought the strains of an obscene song to his ears. Though the words were raw, the voice that sang them had a certain style. He turned toward the music and noticed a handbill tacked to the wall. It advertised the headline act of the saloon against which he was standing. The handbill pictured a sensuous woman mounted by a massive grizzly bear. At first, Matthew thought the woman was being mauled by the creature, but the text clarified what was really happening and explained that those wishing to witness the act live need only enter the premises of the Dancing Bear.

Matthew steeled himself and pushed through the saloon doors just as applause and a chorus of appreciative whistles were directed at the scantily clad woman who had sung the bawdy ballad Matthew had heard from the street. Men and women were three deep at the bar. Matthew saw an opening and wedged himself between a brooding, bearded man who was working on a frothy mug of beer and the back of a fleshy woman who was chatting up an inebriated sailor. He shouted a question, and the bartender pointed toward a balcony that overlooked the barroom.

Three different women accosted Matthew as he traversed a sawdust-covered floor made sticky by spilled liquor and the occasional spray of blood. He politely refused their advances and was halfway up the stairs when the saloon's main attraction took the stage. The buxom maiden in the handbill turned out to be a scrawny, pockmarked woman who simulated the sex act with bored detachment, and the proud grizzly was a pathetic, muzzled brown bear with patches of hair missing from its shabby coat and a drugged look in its dazed and sleepy eyes. The maiden's dance with the fierce grizzly was as big a fraud as Sharon Hill's marriage contract.

Matthew climbed over a drunken sailor who lay crumpled against the banister at the top of the stairs. There were several rooms on the second floor, but the one he wanted was at the end of the hall. Matthew knocked, and a deep, rumbling voice invited him in. The dim light of a solitary desk lamp provided the only illumination in the room. Stuffed behind the desk at the end of the room was a fat man whose triple chin and folds of fat obscured the natural shape of his face. Behind the fat man stood a muscular behemoth who looked as dangerous as Francis Gibney. Matthew let his hand caress the outline of the pistol stowed in the pocket of his coat.

"Mr. Hoxie?"

The fat man nodded.

"I'm Matthew Penny, an attorney from Portland, Oregon," he said as he presented his card. "I'm here on behalf of a client to discuss a business matter."

"Please sit down," Hoxie said after glancing at the card. "I've heard that Portland is quite the up-and-coming town, but I've never had the pleasure."

"That may change sooner than you think," Matthew said.

"Oh?"

"I'm here as a representative of the estate of the late Benjamin Gillette. A woman named Sharon Hill claims to have entered into a marriage contract with Mr. Gillette, which you allegedly prepared. I'm interested in any information that can shed light on the validity, or lack thereof, of the contract."

"Then we have a problem. I did prepare the contract for Miss Hill, but discussing it would involve a breach of an attorney-client confidence."

"The attorney-client privilege does not cover fraud."

Hoxie's bodyguard straightened up like an attack dog on alert, but Hoxie merely smiled and folded his hands across his stomach. "Are you suggesting that there's something wrong with the contract?"

"Something is unquestionably wrong with the contract," Matthew said in an amiable tone. "The signature of Benjamin Gillette is an obvious forgery. Every lawyer who has compared it with Mr. Gillette's real signature has refused to represent Miss Hill."

"I was under the impression that Caleb Barbour was representing Miss Hill."

The mention of Barbour's name made Matthew dizzy, but he hid his emotions.

"Mr. Barbour is dead," Matthew said.

"Oh?"

"And I don't think it would have helped Miss Hill if he was her attorney, especially since we can prove that Barbour was Hill's lover. And that is not the only thing we know about Sharon Hill, who has tried to portray herself as an unfortunate orphan.

"Before traveling to San Francisco, we employed the services of an investigator who looked into Miss Hill's background and the background of people with whom she associated, including you. This investigator reported that Miss Hill and a Mr. Warren Quimby were living together when Mr. Quimby died under mysterious circumstances. Poison was suspected by some. Miss Hill was present when Mr. Gillette died under circumstances remarkably similar to those surrounding Mr. Quimby's death. The only thing Benjamin Gillette and Warren Quimby had in common was Sharon Hill."

"Where is this headed, Mr. Penny?"

"Do you gamble?"

Hoxie laughed. "Asking a resident of the Barbary Coast if he gambles is like asking a priest if he prays."

"I'm guessing that Miss Hill paid you to prepare her marriage contract and to arrange for Benjamin Gillette's signature to be forged, but I'm also guessing that your expected remuneration does not stop there. By all accounts, you are a shrewd man, and I'm certain you know how rich Miss Hill will be if the contract holds up in court and she inherits Benjamin Gillette's fortune. So you're probably counting on a large sum of money if Hill prevails."

Matthew paused and stared at Hoxie long enough to remove the smile from the lawyer's lips.

"A bet on Hill winning in an Oregon court will be a very bad bet. Sharon Hill is despised in Portland, and Heather Gillette is the daughter of one of Oregon's most respected citizens. Everyone knows the marriage contract is a fraud. The public is outraged by Hill's suit. In order for Hill to prevail at trial, you will have to testify under oath in Oregon that you saw Benjamin Gillette affix his signature to the contract. I can promise you that you will be arrested for perjury and worse if you do so. No one will help you in Portland. You will be out of your element."

"Are you trying to frighten me, Mr. Penny?" Hoxie asked calmly.

"I told you that we employed an investigator to learn as much as we could about this matter and the people involved in it. So I know that you are not a man who frightens easily. I am simply pointing out that it is better to go with a sure thing than gamble on a very, very long shot."

"And what would this sure thing be?"

"Telling the truth. Reject whatever Hill has promised you to secure your perjury in favor of upholding the ethics of our profession and doing the right thing."

Hoxie smiled.

"Upholding the ethics of our profession is always foremost in my mind, Counselor, but you did say that this was a business discussion, and in business a man always seeks a profit. So besides the, uh, spiritual benefits of doing what you ask, would there be any material advantage to me if I follow the path you propose?"

Hoxie watched carefully as Matthew withdrew from his jacket a pouch filled with gold coins that Harold Denton had given him. He placed it on Hoxie's desk. Hoxie looked at the pouch but made no move to touch it.

"What is this?" Hoxie asked.

"A fee for this consultation. Should an appearance in an Oregon court cause you to incur expenses or business losses, you may expect to be compensated."

"I see."

"When considering the course of action you wish to take, I would ask you to remember that it is always better to have powerful friends than powerful enemies. Especially when you can secure these friendships simply by telling the truth."

"You've made some excellent points, Mr. Penny," Hoxie said as he pulled the pouch toward him.

"All I ask is that you consider them seriously," Matthew answered as he rose to leave.

CHAPTER 52

A clock chimed, and Sharon Hill's stomach tightened. Jed had gone to the dock two hours ago to meet the steamer bringing Bernard Hoxie from San Francisco, and he should have returned by now. If Hoxie was not on board, if he did not testify . . . She stopped these negative thoughts to keep herself from going mad. Hoxie had to come; he *had* to.

A cloud of dust signaled Tyler's return, and Hill raced downstairs and onto the porch.

"Did he come?" she asked, her fists clenched at her sides as she fought back her panic.

"He's at the Evergreen; I just left him. Everything will be fine."

Hill closed her eyes and tilted her head back. "Thank God," she sighed.

Tyler placed his hands on her shoulders. "You must take hold of yourself. We will prevail."

"Are you certain?" Hill asked as she clutched his forearms.

"I'm certain," Tyler reassured Hill, who did not know about his bargain with Thornton.

"We must win," Hill said. She sounded desperate. "It's the only way to silence everyone. Once our title to Gillette House is clear—once we control Ben's enterprises—no one will dare to treat us this way."

Tyler nodded, but he was not certain that even that great change of fortune would save them from the ostracism Portland society had imposed.

"I hate them. We'll take everything from them, Jed, everything."

"Sharon," Tyler said helplessly as she stormed into the house. He followed her, wanting to hold her but knowing that she would push him away if he tried. He understood her suffering. When they walked the streets of Portland, society passed them by as if they did not exist. Tyler had not received a single social invitation since Hill had moved in. Even Mrs. McCall had given notice because of the scandal. Sharon had no one but him, and he had no one but her.

Hill was sitting on the bottom step of the hall stairs, her head in her hands and her hair in disarray. Tyler sat beside her.

"What will I do if we lose?" she cried.

He wanted to tell her that they would have each other even in defeat, but he was afraid of what she would answer if that was the best he could offer.

"It will be all right," he said instead. "Hoxie is here We have the contract. It will be all right."

CHAPTER 53

The loft of the Coleman Barrel Company was packed with spectators, and Matthew was lucky to find a seat in the rear of the courtroom. Once he had settled onto the bench, he saw Roxanne Brown leaning against the wall on the other side of the loft, and he looked away quickly.

W. B. Thornton, who had just been appointed to fill out Jed Tyler's term on the Oregon supreme court, was hearing the case.

"Call your next witness," he told Tyler.

"I call Mrs. Gillette."

"Objection," Orville said. "Mrs. Gillette passed away several years ago. I ask the court to instruct Mr. Tyler to refer to his client as Miss Hill."

"Yes, Mr. Tyler," Judge Thornton said. "The purpose of this lawsuit is to decide if Miss Hill has the legal right to be called Mrs. Gillette."

"Very well, Your Honor," Tyler conceded, certain that Thornton was ruling for Heather Gillette now so he would seem even handed when he ruled in Sharon's favor at the end of the case.

Hill walked from her seat at counsel table toward the witness stand. An angry murmur passed through the loft. Hill kept her eyes forward, aware that no one in the courtroom wished her well.

"Miss Hill," Tyler asked after some preliminary questions, "did you take a trip to San Francisco with Benjamin Gillette?"

"I did."

"What was the purpose of this trip?"

"Ben told everyone it was a business trip—and he did conduct some business while we were in the city—but the trip was our honeymoon."

Judge Thornton gaveled for quiet as an angry buzz filled the courtroom.

"Please tell the judge the steps you and your betrothed took to solemnize your marriage."

"The California Civil Code permits a marriage by contract. With this in mind, we contacted Bernard Hoxie, a California attorney, and asked him to prepare a marriage contract."

"I hand you plaintiff's Exhibit twelve. Please identify it for the court."

"This is the marriage contract between Ben and me."

"Did you see him sign it?'

"I did."

"Where did you and Mr. Gillette sign the contract?"

"In the office of attorney Bernard Hoxie."

"Was Mr. Hoxie present?"

"Yes. He watched us sign the document."

"After you two signed the contract, did you consummate the marriage?"

Hill lowered her eyes. "We did, that night at our hotel."

"Was Mr. Gillette happy with his decision to wed?'

When Hill answered she was smiling. "Very! He looked forward to the time we could make our nuptials public so I could move into Gillette House and we could spend every possible moment together."

"Why didn't you let everyone know about the marriage?" Tyler asked.

Hill looked at Heather. "His daughter disliked me for some reason and Ben hoped to reconcile her to our match first."

"No further questions," Tyler said.

"Your witness, Mr. Mason," Thornton said.

"Thank you, Your Honor. Miss Hill, other than you and Mr. Hoxie, who knew of this so-called marriage contract?"

"Only my late husband."

"No further questions, Your Honor."

"I have nothing on redirect," Jed Tyler said, surprised by the brevity of Orville's cross.

"Any further witnesses, Mr. Tyler?" the judge asked.

"We call Bernard Hoxie, Your Honor."

Matthew had given Orville a full account of his meeting with Hoxie, but an attack of nerves still gripped Orville when the lawyer hoisted up his massive body and waddled to the witness stand. Hoxie was a vile human being who was fully capable of any deception, so Orville had no idea in which way the witness would lean. He was fully prepared to destroy Hoxie during cross-examination, but he hoped that would not be necessary.

"How are you employed, Mr. Hoxie?" Tyler asked.

"I am an attorney and a member of the California Bar."

"In your capacity as an attorney, did you make the acquaintance of my client, Sharon Hill?"

"I did."

"Tell the judge about your business dealings with Miss Hill."

Hoxie swiveled his head so he was addressing Thornton.

"Miss Hill came to my office and asked if I would draw up a contract of marriage between her and Benjamin Gillette."

Tyler crossed to the witness and handed him Exhibit 12. "Do you recognize this document?"

"Yes, sir. It is the contract I prepared for Miss Hill."

"Is this Miss Hill's signature on the bottom line?"

"It is."

"How do you know that?"

"She signed the contract in my presence."

"And is this the signature of Benjamin Gillette?" Tyler asked, turning so he could witness the reaction of Orville Mason and Heather Gillette.

Hoxie studied the signature. "I presume so."

Tyler's features clouded. This was not the testimony they had rehearsed.

"Well, sir, you saw Mr. Gillette sign this contract, did you not?" Tyler asked.

"No. That's why I said that I presume Mr. Gillette signed. You see, I gave the contract to Miss Hill. She wanted to take it to her hotel so she and Mr. Gillette could read it in case they wished to make corrections or additions."

"But Mr. Gillette and Miss Hill discussed the preparation of the contract with you in your office, didn't they?" Tyler said, flashing a menacing look at Hoxie.

In return, Hoxie offered Tyler a bland smile. "No, sir. I never met Mr. Gillette. He wasn't with Miss Hill when she consulted with me about the contract. When Miss Hill returned to my office, she was alone and Mr. Gillette's signature was on the document. She assured me that it was genuine, that she had seen Mr. Gillette sign the contract."

"Liar!" Sharon Hill shouted as she sprang to her feet.

"Restrain your client, Mr. Tyler," Thornton ordered, alarmed by Hill's look of insane rage.

"This is no good, Sharon," Tyler whispered.

Hill pointed a finger at Heather. "How much did this whore pay you?" she screamed.

Thornton pounded his gavel, and Marshal Lappeus and his deputies moved to the front of the loft.

"Control yourself, madam, or I'll be forced to hold you in contempt," the judge warned.

Tyler reached for Hill, but she shrugged off his hand. As she rounded the counsel table on her way to Hoxie, she reached into her purse and pulled out a derringer. The marshal saw the gun and tackled Hill. The derringer flew out of her hand when her shoulder struck the courtroom floor.

"Get off her," Tyler shouted as he punched Lappeus in the face. Hill was trying to gouge out the marshal's eyes, and he was helpless to defend himself against Tyler's onslaught. Tyler was setting himself to throw a second punch when three deputies toppled him. Hill reached for the derringer, but Orville raced around his table and scooped up the weapon.

"Stop this at once," Thornton shouted at Tyler. "Have you lost your senses?"

Lappeus turned Hill over to one of his deputies and dropped his weight on Tyler, who had thrown off one deputy and was trying to strike a second.

"For God's sake, Judge, don't make us hurt you," he begged.

Tyler stared at Lappeus and froze as it dawned on him how he must look. He collapsed.

"Let me be," he said. "I won't resist."

"This is disgraceful," Thornton said, his voice shaking. "You were a judge. How can you act like this?"

Tyler stood up. His face was crimson from embarrassment. Hill struggled in the grasp of two deputies.

"What should I do with them?" Lappeus asked the judge.

Thornton was torn. He had made a devil's bargain with Jed Tyler to fix the contract case, but everyone in the courtroom had seen Sharon Hill pull out her derringer and Tyler attack the marshal.

"Confine them in the jail while I decide what must be done," Thornton ordered, his voice shaking and his eyes unable to meet those of Tyler.

"I'll kill you," Hill shrieked at Heather as she was dragged out of the loft. "Gillette House is mine. I'll see you dead before I'll let you have it."

CHAPTER 54

While Justice Thornton decided what to do with them, Sharon Hill and Jed Tyler shared the cell that had been Kevin O'Toole's living quarters. Normally, Marshal Lappeus would not have permitted the unmarried couple to stay together, but it was the only cell other than the one where Worthy Brown languished that was dry enough for habitation.

"She bought Hoxie," Sharon Hill ranted as she paced the cell's dirt floor.

Jed Tyler lay on the bunk, trying to block out the litany Hill had been repeating since they'd been thrown in jail for contempt. Tyler prayed that Sharon would be reasonable once they were free, but he held out little hope that his prayer would be answered.

"She's stealing everything from me. My beautiful house, my money, my position in society."

"The judge may rule for us yet," Tyler said wearily.

"She's probably bought him, too," Hill went on, paying as little attention to him now as she had every other time he had tried to calm her. Hill's face was red, and her fists were clenched. Tyler came up behind her and tried to take her in his arms, but she jerked away.

"Don't touch me."

"Sharon, I love you. I—"

Hill turned on him. "You let Mason and Gillette make a fool of you. If you were a man, you'd kill them."

Tyler's eyes widened from shock. "You're upset. You don't know what you're saying."

"Killing those thieves would be justice, not murder."

"Keep your voice down. The guard will hear you."

"They deserve to die, like Ben," she muttered.

Tyler wasn't certain he'd heard Hill correctly. For the first time, Jed Tyler let himself see the madness to which Hill's beauty had blinded him.

Hill saw the way Tyler was looking at her. Fear replaced the fire in her eyes. She flung her arms around Tyler's neck and clung to him.

"Forgive me, Jed. I know none of this is your fault. You've been so good to me. You're my champion. Will you fight for me, Jed? Will you defeat them?"

Tyler gently pried her arms from his neck and stood back so he could see her.

"Did you . . . ? Ben? Are you saying you . . . did something to him?"

Hill realized the mistake she'd made. "No, darling. I'm upset. I don't know why I said that. Ben died from a heart attack. I feel like I killed him because I couldn't save him. You believe me, don't you? You can't think . . ."

"Of course I believe you," he answered mechanically.

Hill started to cry. "Oh, Jed, what am I doing? I'm just upset. I can't stand the idea that we're in this awful place while Heather Gillette is strutting around Gillette House."

"I know," Tyler said as she nestled against his chest.

"I love you, Jed," Hill said. "Do you love me? You must. Without you, I have nothing."

Hill's plea made him sad because her twisted idea of love was all he had. Hill's lawsuit had dragged down his lofty reputation, and many people now considered him as mad as his client. Tyler remembered the expression on Thornton's face as the judge watched him writhe on the courtroom floor in the grip of the deputies. How low had he fallen since that day in Phoenix when he saw Sharon Hill set off like a gemstone in the drab mob? How drastically must he have changed for a little man like Thornton to look down on him with such disgust?

Tyler looked at the patch of sky that showed through the cell window. He knew that he should break free of Sharon Hill, but he would be the vilest kind of coward if he deserted her in her most desperate hour. If he abandoned Sharon, he might be able to salvage something from the wreckage of his career and restore his tarnished reputation, but he could not cast her away. The sad truth was that he loved her even if she was . . . Tyler could not bring himself to finish the thought, could not bring himself to admit that the lawsuit was a fraud and Sharon Hill might be insane. If he admitted that, then he would be forced to admit that he had destroyed his reputation and career for the delusions and criminal ambition of a madwoman.

CHAPTER 55

Roxanne was dusting in the entryway when Marshal Lappeus knocked on the front door. He tipped his hat when she opened it.

"Afternoon, Roxanne. Is Miss Gillette around?"

"Yes, sir. I'll tell her you're here."

Heather and Orville Mason were in the parlor. Roxanne told them Marshal Lappeus was calling. After she led the marshal to the parlor, Roxanne left the room but positioned herself so she could hear what was said.

"What brings you here, Marshal?" Roxanne heard Heather ask.

"Judge Thornton is going to let Jed Tyler and Sharon Hill out of jail tomorrow afternoon so the trial can continue. I think Jed will be okay, but Hill worries me. Amos Strayer says she's been raving from the time we locked her in about how you stole everything from her. He heard her threaten to shoot you."

"Do you think she's serious?" Orville asked.

"I think she's unpredictable. I also think you should have Francis and some of his men watch the house and stay close when you're in town."

Roxanne listened to the conversation a while longer. Then she went into the library and thought about what Marshal Lappeus had said. Miss Heather had saved her. Now she was in danger. Roxanne had heard Hill threaten her mistress in the parlor of this very house and in the loft of the Coleman Barrel Company; she'd seen Hill point a derringer at Bernard Hoxie with deadly intent. Her father had taught her that it was wrong to hate, but she did hate Sharon Hill. Other than her father, no person on earth meant more to Roxanne than Heather Gillette. Heather was her savior and protector. Roxanne owed her life to Heather, and she would do anything for her.

Roxanne's eyes were drawn to the lower drawer of Benjamin Gillette's writing desk. The wood was stained a deep brown. She had polished the handles of the drawers until they shown like gold. The shutters in the library were closed, but a beam of light squeezed through a crack and its tip splashed against the corner of the brass handle of the lower drawer, creating the glow of a miniature sun. While Roxanne stared at the pinpoint of light she wondered how she would feel if Heather Gillette died at Sharon Hill's hand.

Roxanne walked to the escritoire and opened the drawer. Benjamin's Colt and a box of bullets still lay in it. Roxanne picked up the pistol. It felt as heavy as she remembered. Roxanne had never fired a revolver, but she was positive that she could fire this gun if it was aimed at Sharon Hill.

CHAPTER 56

Matthew Penny flipped up the cover of his hunter case and looked at his pocket watch in the pale light of a three-quarter moon. Bernard Hoxie was late. Matthew's nose was running, and his cheeks were cherry-red. A gust of cold air struck him, and he moved behind a stack of wooden crates. Matthew was waiting for Hoxie in an alley between two warehouses across from the docks. A mass suddenly filled the entrance to the alley. There was no mistaking that shape. Matthew left his hiding place.

"Mr. Hoxie?"

"Give me a moment to catch my breath," the lawyer wheezed. "I am unaccustomed to walking distances, and I'm almost done in."

A few moments later, Hoxie walked into the alley with his bodyguard close behind. Matthew was anxious to finish his business with the lawyer. He handed him a pouch of gold coins. Hoxie smiled and bounced the pouch in his hand.

"I trust this will cover your expenses and any time lost from your business," Matthew said.

"I'm sure it will be more than adequate."

"When do you return to San Francisco?"

"I leave on the morning steamer. Mr. Tyler has released me from my subpoena."

"I'm not surprised. You destroyed Sharon Hill's case. The testimony of Miss Gillette's witnesses concerning the validity of the signature should drive the nail into her coffin."

"Don't be so certain."

Matthew's brow knit. "What do you mean?"

"You know, I wouldn't mind doing more business with Miss Gillette." Hoxie held up his hand. "Not the type of business our more established firms handle. I know I'm a small fish in a large pond. But I wouldn't mind if you threw the occasional crumb my way, now that you've seen how reliable I am."

"Please come to the point," Matthew insisted.

"Yes, the point. It's the judge: he's in Tyler's pocket."

"Thornton!"

Hoxie nodded. "When Tyler met with me to prepare my testimony, he seemed serenely certain of victory. I pressed him on the wisdom of his self-confidence in light of the overwhelming public opinion in favor of Miss Gillette. He let slip that the judge's verdict had been secured."

The seat on the supreme court, Matthew thought. There had been rumors that Tyler had influenced the governor's appointment.

"If you knew about this, why did you double-cross Hill?" Matthew asked.

"When you visited my office in San Francisco, you asked me if I was a betting man, and I told you that I was not averse to placing the occasional wager." Hoxie shrugged. "In this instance, I'm betting that Benjamin Gillette had more judges and politicians in his pocket than Tyler. If I'm right, Hill won't win in the long run because your supreme court will take away any victory she secures.

"Besides, I know Sharon. She can't be trusted. She'd never have paid me what I'd been promised once she had Gillette's fortune and power. If she wins, I wouldn't be surprised if she hired someone to do away with me. After all, I'm the only witness who can contradict her about Benjamin Gillette's signature on the marriage contract. Leaving her destitute is a matter of self-preservation."

"Thank you for this information," Matthew said.

"It's my pleasure, and should things work out for Miss Gillette, I will count on your conscience to decide the reward to which I am entitled for telling you about the judge."

Matthew waited in the dark for a reasonable amount of time before leaving the alley so he and Hoxie would not be seen together. While he waited, he decided what to do with Hoxie's information. Then he went in search of Orville Mason.

CHAPTER 57

O rville!" Justice Thornton said, surprised to find the attorney at his doorstep so late in the day.

"Good evening, Judge. May I come in?"

Thornton's brow furrowed. "I don't know if that would be appropriate. Ex parte contacts are frowned upon."

"Is that what you told Jed Tyler when he approached you about securing your seat on the court?"

"I don't know what you're talking about," Thornton blustered, but his sudden loss of color told Orville all he needed to know.

"The governor is staying at the Evergreen. We just had an interesting discussion about Jed Tyler's suggestion for who should take his place on the supreme court. It's cold out here. I'd prefer to tell you what the governor said inside, where we won't be overheard. I promise I'll not stay long."

Thornton hesitated then stood back and pointed the way toward his study. Orville and the ex-DA were in different political parties and social circles, and this was one of the few times the young lawyer had been inside Thornton's house.

"You have a pleasant home," Orville said when he was settled in a chair opposite the judge.

"Thank you."

"And a good reputation. It would be a shame if scandal ruined it."

"I don't know where this is going."

Orville studied Thornton. The silence clearly made the judge uneasy.

"Are you and Jed close?" Orville asked.

"I wouldn't say that anyone is a close friend of Jed Tyler. We are of the same political persuasion and business partners. We dine together on occasion."

"Are you surprised that Jed told the governor to appoint you to his seat? The governor was. He told me that Tyler's resignation was unexpected, but not as unexpected as his insistence that you be his successor. What do you think prompted such vigorous support?"

"Well, I suppose he . . . he appreciated my legal abilities. I was the district attorney of our most populous county."

"I have been told that Jed offered to secure your appointment in exchange for a promise to rule for Sharon Hill."

Thornton colored. "That's outrageous. Who's spreading these lies?"

"Someone who had it from Tyler. If this accusation became public and the governor repeated what he told me about the passion with which Jed Tyler supported your nomination, many would believe it."

A sheen of sweat formed on Thornton's forehead, and he shifted uneasily in his seat.

"Why are you doing this, Orville? Have I ever wronged you?"

"No, Judge—not yet. But you will if you rule contrary to the evidence in this case. If you have made a Faustian bargain for your position and fulfill it, I will make certain that you do not stay on the court. I will run against you at the next election, and I will defeat you. But stay true to your calling and rule according to the evidence, and I will be your staunchest supporter." Orville stood. "It's late and I've said what I came to say. Thank you for hearing me out."

Thornton stood in the entryway after Orville left. He had feared the worst when he accepted Tyler's offer, and his sin was coming home to haunt him.

"Was that Orville Mason?" Abigail asked. Thornton had been so absorbed in his thoughts that he had not heard her enter the hallway.

"Yes."

"What did he want?"

Thornton hesitated. Then he asked his wife to join him in his study. He retrieved a decanter of brandy from a walnut cabinet and poured a glass before sitting down.

"I need your advice about what I should do in the marriage-contract case."

Abigail was surprised. Her husband rarely asked her opinion about business or legal matters.

"Do you remember the night Jed Tyler offered to put my name before the governor as his successor?"

"Yes."

"There was a condition of his support that I never told you about. Something I had to promise to do before he would tell the governor to appoint me."

"What condition, Wilbur?"

Thornton took a moment to answer. When he did, he could not look at his wife.

"Hill has no case. Her star witness says he never saw Ben Gillette sign the marriage contract. Heather Gillette's witnesses are the most respected lawyers in Portland. They'll swear that the signature on the contract isn't Ben's. Mason is going to call witness after witness to swear that Ben never mentioned marriage."

"Of course he didn't marry that woman," Abigail huffed. "Who would believe such a thing?"

Thornton drained his glass and refilled it.

"Perhaps if that San Francisco lawyer had said he'd seen Ben sign the contract . . . But how can I hold for Hill now? She's a madwoman. She menaced a witness with a derringer, and she threatened to kill Heather Gillette."

"Why are you troubled? Throw her out of court and let's have done with her. She's a walking scandal."

"It's not that easy, Abby. I . . . I promised Tyler."

"Promised him what?"

"That I would rule for Hill in exchange for the seat on the supreme court."

Abigail looked stunned. "You couldn't have."

Thornton held his head in his hands. "I wanted the seat so badly, and everything happened so quickly. Tyler didn't give me time to think. Now I don't know what to do."

Abigail sat up straight. "There is only one thing you can do. You must do what is right. You must rule in accordance with the evidence. Jed Tyler asked you to commit a crime. You can not honor a promise to commit a crime."

"You don't understand. They're both crazy. If I cross them, they might . . . There could be an attempt on my life. And if Jed doesn't kill me, he'll certainly seek revenge by revealing our bargain. I'd have to resign. My career will be finished."

"It won't be that easy to destroy you, Wilbur. You're a respected member of this community."

Thornton ran his fingers through his hair. "I'm not, Abby. People don't take me seriously. I haven't gotten where I am by being liked. The post of district attorney was a crumb tossed to me for faithful service to the party."

"You were a good district attorney. You did a very good job. You wouldn't have been reelected if the voters didn't think you'd done a good job."

There were tears in Thornton's eyes. "You're so good to me. If I lost you—"

"But you won't. And you won't lose your judgeship. Jed Tyler had no right to force you to make that promise. Stand up to him. Show everyone that you are incorruptible by doing the right thing."

"I don't know, Abby. I don't know."

CHAPTER 58

Marshal Lappeus had taken Jed Tyler and Sharon Hill directly to court without giving them a chance to clean up or change their clothes, and they had been forced to listen to Heather Gillette's witnesses with the stench of the jail still clinging to them. When all of the evidence had been presented, Tyler could delude himself no longer. He was familiar with Benjamin Gillette's signature because of the time he had spent as Gillette's tenant when he moved to Portland, but he had not seen it in years. A brief look at the marriage contract had not convinced him that the signature had been forged, and he had rationalized his refusal to compare the signature by convincing himself that Sharon Hill would not lie to him if she loved him. But he was unable to fool himself any longer after he had been shown the evidence that Orville Mason planned to introduce.

Tyler had still been confident of victory before Bernard Hoxie testified. After Hoxie's betrayal, Sharon Hill's only hope of prevailing lay with Thornton honoring his corrupt promise.

As Tyler waited for W. B. Thornton to reveal his decision, he glanced at Hill. She had shown no emotion since court started, but would she stay that way if they lost? Tyler dreaded the possibility of another outburst like the one that had sent them to jail.

Tyler shifted his attention to Justice Thornton, who would not meet his eye, a bad sign. Before rendering his verdict, the judge cleared his throat and took a sip of water. Tyler detected a slight tremor when Thornton spoke.

"This case has been difficult," the judge said. "Strong emotions have been evidenced by both sides. The plaintiff has presented to the court a signed contract of marriage and has sworn that Benjamin Gillette was a willing party to it because he was in love with her. In support of her position, Miss Hill has introduced evidence that proved that Mr. Gillette paid for her suite at the Evergreen Hotel and visited her there often, frequently staying the night.

"There is further evidence that Miss Hill accompanied Mr. Gillette to San Francisco during the week that the marriage contract was allegedly entered into by the plaintiff and Mr. Gillette. So I find that there was a . . . an amorous relationship between Mr. Gillette and Miss Hill. That, however, does not resolve the question of the final disposition of their relationship. Were the couple passionate friends or were they legally married? And here the proof becomes vague."

Tyler could see where Thornton was headed. He knew he should be furious at the betrayal, but he could not muster feelings of indignation. Love and greed had blinded him to the truth, and he was empty of rage now that he saw clearly what should have been obvious all along.

"Aside from the plaintiff, an interested party, no witness has been produced to swear to the validity of Benjamin Gillette's alleged signature," Thornton continued. "The defendant, on the other hand, has produced many witnesses who have sworn under oath that they have witnessed Mr. Gillette's signature on many occasions and have concluded that someone other than he signed the marriage contract. Most damning is the fact that Bernard Hoxie, who prepared the document, never met Mr. Gillette, and the plaintiff has produced no witness who can support her position that Benjamin Gillette ever entered into a contract of marriage with her.

"On the other hand, the defendant has produced numerous close friends and acquaintances of Mr. Gillette who have sworn that he never mentioned any intention to wed or took any steps regarding his will or other matters that would indicate such intention. Therefore, I find . . ."

MATTHEW WAITED UNTIL THE COURTROOM was almost full before finding a spot against one of the walls where he could watch the proceedings unobserved. He had not spoken to Orville since telling him what Hoxie had confided about Thornton, so he did not know what had happened during Orville's meeting with Justice Thornton. Matthew's body tensed when the judge took the bench, and it did not uncoil until he gave his verdict.

Matthew saw Heather leap into Orville's arms. Then they were lost from sight as the spectators rose as one, cheering for the verdict and surrounding Benjamin Gillette's daughter. Matthew left while chaos reigned, and he was halfway to his office when it dawned on him that he was smiling. Matthew stopped in the street. A couple walking behind Matthew almost collided with him and gave the young attorney odd looks as they passed.

Matthew savored the joy that filled him. He was happy! He

had not been happy since the night he had killed Caleb Barbour. Matthew felt tears well up. Heather was saved, and he had played a part in her victory. For the first time in a long time he had done something he could take pride in.

"I have done some good," he whispered to Rachel, and he imagined that she stood in front of him, smiling. His chest tightened, and he gulped for air. Then he sobered. Worthy Brown was still caged in a dank, claustrophobic jail cell. What he had done for Heather was a good thing, but his act would carry only the weight of a pebble on the scales that would judge Matthew's worth if Worthy Brown died for Matthew's sins.

CHAPTER 59

In court, Sharon Hill had accepted the decision without emotion, but her placid demeanor disappeared as soon as she and Tyler were alone.

"You swore we would win," she screamed when the door to Tyler's house closed behind them.

"Please, Sharon—"

"You coward. You just sat there while Thornton spewed out his lies."

Tyler felt defeated before Hill's rage, and he did not have the energy to contest it.

"The signature," was the best he could manage.

"What of it?"

"Did you write it? I've seen Ben's signature many times. There is—"

"What? There is *what*? Are you questioning me now? Will no one stand with me?"

"I . . . I still love you. It's just . . ."

Tyler could not go on. He felt weak, his immense strength sapped by his ordeal.

"You don't love me," Hill shouted. "If you loved me, you would have won. If you loved me, we would be owners of Gillette House and wealthy beyond our dreams. What will I do now? I have nothing. What will become of me?"

Tyler was suddenly tired of Hill's self-absorption. "I do not doubt that you will get on. You have your wiles and no morals to impede you."

Hill spun on him. "What did you say?"

"You heard me."

Hill saw Tyler's new resolve, and it was suddenly clear to her that she should never have trusted him. He was like every other man she had put her faith in. Hill forced her features to portray remorse. Her chin fell to her chest, and she looked at the carpet.

"Oh, God, can you forgive me, Jed? I'm so upset that I don't know what I'm saying. You are the only one who stood beside me through this, the only one I could count on."

Hill grabbed her hair and pulled it tight. She squeezed her eyes shut. "How can I treat you like this?"

Hill dropped to her knees and wrapped her arms around Tyler's legs.

"I'm an ungrateful fool. I should be whipped for hurting you. Please forgive me."

Tyler didn't know what to say. He felt sick, but he and Hill were joined to each other by their folly, and he did not have the strength to untangle himself from the snare that enmeshed him.

"Come, Jed. Let's not argue. You are my only friend, and I would be lost without you."

Hill stood. She grabbed Tyler's face and kissed him passionately. At first, Tyler resisted. Then he gave in because, if only for a little while, sex would let him forget the fool he had made of himself and everything he had lost.

When they were in the bedroom, Hill gave him everything she had and left him exhausted. Then, while he lay sated and spent, she left the bedroom and returned with two glasses of wine.

CHAPTER 60

R oxanne was dusting in the conical tower at the top of Gillette House. From its windows, she had an unobstructed view of the Willamette and Columbia Rivers and the Cascade and Coast Mountain Ranges. While Roxanne was cleaning the window that overlooked the garden, Sharon Hill walked out of the woods and toward the rear of Gillette House. Roxanne froze. There could only be one reason for Hill's stealthy approach. Sharon Hill was here to harm Miss Gillette.

Roxanne remembered Benjamin Gillette's revolver and imagined how it would feel to point it at Sharon Hill's heart and pull the trigger. Roxanne could pull the trigger in her imagination, but could she look Sharon Hill in the eye and kill her?

Hill was halfway to the house when Roxanne made her decision. Moments later, she was flying down the stairs to the main floor.

HEATHER SHOULD HAVE BEEN HAPPY now that she did not have to deal with Hill's insane lawsuit, but the anxiety created by Hill's ridiculous claim and the pressure of learning the ins and outs of Benjamin Gillette's enterprises had given her no time to grieve for her father. Now that the lawsuit was finished, the feelings she had kept inside flooded her and left her sad and drained.

The day was cold but clear, and sunshine lit up the parlor. She had come in here to remember Ben. Thinking about her father also brought back memories of her mother, and she was thinking about how truly alone she was when Sharon Hill entered the room. Hill's hair was uncombed, and her clothing was rumpled. There was a smudge on her cheek and an insane fire in her eyes.

Heather was shocked by Hill's sudden appearance. Then her shock turned to anger and she leaped to her feet.

"What are you doing in my house?" Heather demanded.

"This is my house. You stole it from me."

"Miss Hill—"

"Mrs. Gillette!" Hill said. Then she raised Jed Tyler's revolver, which she had concealed at her side. "Say it or I will shoot you now."

Heather could see that Hill was not in her right mind, and she tamped down her anger.

"Mrs. Gillette, this house will never be yours if you use violence against me. You will be put in jail. This is not the way. You can appeal Justice Thornton's verdict. The supreme court may rule for you."

Hill laughed. "You must think me a fool. You have Thornton and the other judges in your pocket. I will never get justice in the courts, but I can exact justice now." She pointed the pistol at Heather's heart. "If I can't have Gillette House, I'll make sure you can't, either."

Heather raised her hands in a hopeless attempt at defense and took a step back. Hill glared at Heather and aimed. A shot shattered the silence, and Sharon Hill's head exploded seconds before her body pitched forward. Heather gaped in astonishment. Then she turned and saw Roxanne in the doorway. Standing in front of her was Francis Gibney, a smoking revolver in his hand.

"Roxanne saw Hill approaching through the garden," Gibney explained as he walked over to the dead woman. "You owe her your life."

No one blamed Francis for shooting Sharon Hill, especially after they discovered Jed Tyler dead in his bedroom. Dr. Sharp had tested the wine remaining in the glass on the floor next to Tyler's body and concluded that he had been poisoned. The doctor thought that there was a good possibility that Sharon Hill had murdered Benjamin Gillette in the same way.

Roxanne didn't think that anyone would have blamed her if she had been the one who shot Sharon Hill, but she'd made her choice as she raced down the tower stairs. Francis Gibney was out front and Benjamin Gillette's pistol was in the writing desk in the library. She knew that she would have time to summon Gibney or grab the weapon, but she wouldn't have time to do both.

Why had she run to Francis instead of getting the gun? She had never fired a pistol, so there was a practical reason for her decision, but the real reason she had chosen to summon the bodyguard was something her father had said when she had told him about the gun in the library.

Worthy had told her that he would rather hang than know she had shot someone because he knew that guilt would haunt her for the rest of her life. Roxanne did hate Sharon Hill, and she wondered whether she would have felt any guilt if she shot Hill to save Miss Heather. She did not know what would have happened if she'd gone for the gun instead of Francis, but she did trust her father, and she was glad she would never know what would have happened had she gone to the library instead of the front porch.

PART FIVE

THE RAIN

CHAPTER 61

The weight of having to gain an acquittal for Worthy Brown crushed Matthew, and his guilt consumed him, driving him to prepare ceaselessly. He slept in fits and starts and ate only when his hunger was so great that it interfered with his concentration. Matthew's weight had dropped until he looked gaunt and unwell, and he was always exhausted and morose.

The day before the trial, Matthew walked to the jail to confer with his client. It started to rain when he was halfway there. Matthew hunched his shoulders and ran as the downpour increased in intensity. As soon as he was inside, Amos Strayer led him down the muddy corridor to Worthy's cell and locked Matthew in with his client.

"I want to beg you one last time to let me call Roxanne so we can mount a believable case of self-defense," Matthew said as soon as the deputy was out of earshot.

"We talked about this before," Worthy answered stubbornly. "I ain't going to let you call Roxanne as a witness."

"Be reasonable, Worthy. The jurors will expect her to testify. If she doesn't, they'll assume it's because her testimony would hurt you."

"I can't help what people assume."

"It may be painful for Roxanne to tell what happened to her, but you should let her choose what she wants to do. Your life is at stake. She won't refuse."

"If she testifies, Roxanne would have to do more than tell about what Mr. Barbour done to her. If she says I killed Caleb Barbour, Roxanne would have to lie after she put her hand on the Bible and swore to God to tell the truth. I can't ask that of no one but myself."

"Let me be blunt, Worthy. Witnesses who were at your court case will tell the jurors that you threatened to kill Barbour if he mistreated Roxanne. Dr. Sharp will testify that he examined Roxanne and she showed signs of being beaten. The prosecution will put on the men who went to Barbour's house to put out the fire. They'll say they saw you alone with the body in Barbour's yard. You will be convicted if we do nothing. Won't you even let me talk to Roxanne and see what she says?"

"I know what she'll do. She'll go to court and lie, and I won't have it. And don't think you can trick me by calling her against my will. If I see that child walking to the witness stand, I'll confess and put an end to it."

Matthew continued to try to persuade Worthy to change his mind. When it was clear that he was making no headway, he stood up and yelled at Amos Strayer to let him out.

"I know you're worried for me, Mr. Penny. Don't be. I'm at peace, and I'm ready to accept what the Lord has in store for me with an untroubled mind."

"You are only thinking of yourself," Matthew answered bitterly. "Other people will suffer if you hang. Roxanne will be alone in the world, and I will go to my grave with your death on my conscience."

"You saved my Roxanne and made her future possible. You are a good man, Mr. Penny, and you will come to see the wisdom in what I done. God loves you. He won't let you suffer."

When Matthew heard the deputy put his key in the lock, he turned away, utterly defeated.

THE RAIN WAS POUNDING DOWN when Matthew walked back to his office, but he was oblivious to the onslaught. Matthew shut the office door behind him and shucked off his rain-soaked jacket. It was freezing in the office, and he set a fire in the potbellied stove. Then he hung the jacket over a chair and moved it near the stove to help it dry. He started to head for the stairs to his apartment so he could change out of his wet pants, but he stopped abruptly and turned to look at his jacket.

"My God!" he whispered. Then he dropped onto a chair and ran through everything that had happened on the evening Barbour died. When he was done, he found that he was short of breath. He stood and paced, going over everything again. Maybe all was not lost. Maybe he could win Worthy's case without the defendant or Roxanne Brown taking the stand.

Matthew grabbed his jacket and hurried across town to Dr. Sharp's office. Then he found Marshal Lappeus and asked him some questions. It was after dark when Matthew explained his strategy to Worthy Brown. The decision was not one Matthew could make without Brown's consent. Worthy listened carefully and agreed to go along with Matthew's plan. Matthew was elated when he left the jail, but doubt began to edge aside certainty as he neared his office. He was gambling with Worthy's life. If the dice came up wrong, Worthy Brown would hang.

CHAPTER 62

William Page had been appointed Multnomah County district attorney when W. B. Thornton was elevated to the supreme court. Page was a sturdy, thick-chested man with a full head of curly black hair and a well-tended beard who had graduated from Miami University Law School in Ohio and practiced in Chicago before moving to the Oregon Territory in 1857. He had earned a reputation as a business lawyer, but he was also a skilled trial attorney. Matthew could not help noticing how confident Page looked when he took his seat at the table for the prosecution.

Justice Thornton had recused himself from sitting in the *Brown* case, and Justice Ruben P. Boise was presiding over the trial. Boise, a native of Massachusetts and a graduate of Williams College, had moved to the Oregon Territory in 1852 after practicing law in Chickopee Falls, Massachusetts. In 1859, after Oregon entered the Union, he was elected to the Oregon Supreme Court.

"Good morning, gentlemen," Justice Boise said as soon as court was called to order. "Shall we proceed with the selection of the jury?"

Matthew's stomach churned and his legs shook as he rose to answer the judge. Once he spoke, there was no going back.

"Your Honor, after conferring with my client, we have decided to waive a jury and try this case to the court."

There was a collective gasp in the spectator section, and Justice Boise could not mask his surprise.

"We are trying a murder case, Mr. Penny. Your client will hang if he is convicted. Is he absolutely certain this is the way he wishes to proceed?"

Matthew nodded to Worthy, and his client stood. They had discussed this decision at the jail, and Matthew had urged it on Worthy. He worried that prejudice against Negroes among the jurors might trump any reasonable doubts raised by the evidence. Justice Boise was opposed to slavery and had a reputation as a compassionate man. Matthew hoped the reputation was well earned because Worthy's fate would be in the hands of this slender, intelligent, gray-bearded jurist.

"Your Honor," Worthy told the court, "Mr. Penny and I have discussed this, and I want you to decide my case."

As his first witnesses, the district attorney called several prominent Portlanders who had visited Caleb Barbour's home. They testified that he treated Roxanne humanely, and each man swore that he'd never seen Barbour mistreat the child. During cross-examination, Matthew got these witnesses to admit that Roxanne was a servant and that Barbour never expressed any love or affection for her, but only Roxanne could testify about the way she was treated when there were no witnesses around.

Next, Page called several witnesses who testified that Worthy had threatened to kill Barbour in this very courtroom only hours before Barbour died. Then Page called Ed Grace to the stand.

Grace's friends slapped him on his massive back as he threaded his way through the spectators to the witness stand. He acknowledged the attention with grins and nods and looked more like a prizefighter headed toward the ring than a witness in a murder case.

"Mr. Grace," William Page asked, "what were you doing on the evening Caleb Barbour was murdered?"

"Objection," Matthew said. "Whether Mr. Barbour was murdered is a question for the court to decide."

"Sustained," Judge Boise said. "Please rephrase your question, Mr. Page."

"Please tell the judge what you were doing the evening Mr. Barbour died."

"I was playing poker at the Oro Fino Saloon. Amos Strayer ran in and said he needed some boys to ride out to Caleb Barbour's place because it was on fire, so I saddled up."

"What did you see when you arrived?"

"The nigger standing near Mr. Barbour's corpse and the house on fire."

Matthew stood. "Your Honor, will you please instruct the witness to refer to Mr. Brown by his name or as the defendant."

"Yes, Mr. Grace. Do not refer to Mr. Brown other than by his name or by the legal term. You may continue, Mr. Page."

"What did the defendant do when he saw you?" the DA asked.

"He ran off, but Rex Arneaux lassoed him."

"Did the defendant appear to be afraid?"

"He sure did."

"Did he submit to arrest peacefully?"

"No, sir, he did not. He kept fighting, so we had to calm him down."

"What happened next, Mr. Grace?" Page asked.

"Marshal Lappeus rode up and took charge of the prisoner."

"No further questions."

Matthew studied the witness. Grace stared back defiantly.

"You testified that you were playing cards at the Oro Fino when Amos Strayer asked you to join the posse."

"Yes."

"When did you go to the saloon?"

"I don't recall."

"Well, didn't it rain heavily that night?"

"Yeah, it was pouring."

"Was it raining when you got to the saloon?"

"It was."

"Was it still raining when you left the saloon to ride to Mr. Barbour's house?"

Grace thought for a moment before answering. "I don't believe it was. I'm pretty sure I didn't get wet during the ride."

"Okay, so you rode to Mr. Barbour's house, and I believe you told the judge that Mr. Brown appeared to be afraid when you rode up?"

"Wouldn't you be if you killed someone and got caught?"

"Your Honor, I move to strike that remark," Matthew said.

"It's stricken," the judge said. Then he turned to the witness.

"Mr. Grace," Boise said sternly, "just answer Mr. Penny's questions."

"He looked scared," Grace said.

"Had you done anything to frighten him?" Matthew asked.

"Me? No."

"Tell me, Mr. Grace, how many men were with you when you got to Mr. Barbour's house?"

"Uh, ten, twelve. I'm not sure."

"Were you on foot when you spotted Mr. Brown?"

"No, sir, we were riding."

"Riding hard?"

"Yes."

"Riding hard in Mr. Brown's direction?"

"Yes."

"Were some of the men yelling?"

"I guess."

"What were they yelling?"

"Some were yelling about the nig . . . the defendant, and some were yelling about the body."

"And I assume some of you had your weapons drawn?"

"Some."

"So let me ask you this, Mr. Grace. If you were all alone at night and on foot and ten or twelve men came riding hard at you, yelling, with their guns drawn, do you think you might be frightened?"

Grace started to say something. Then he changed his mind and clamped his jaws shut.

"I'll take that as a yes." Matthew said. "Let's move on. How much time went by between the first moment you saw Mr. Brown and the time Marshal Lappeus arrived?"

"Not much. Maybe a minute or two. Everything happened real fast."

"And Mr. Barbour was already dead when you rode into the yard?"

Grace nodded.

"You didn't see how Mr. Barbour died, did you?"

"Brown killed him."

"Did you see him kill Mr. Barbour?"

"Well, no. But who else could have?"

"Anyone who left before you arrived, Mr. Grace, anyone. Isn't that so?"

Grace paused for a moment and licked his lips.

"Well?" Matthew pressed.

"I didn't see him killed, so I can't answer," Grace said.

"That's right, Mr. Grace. You didn't see Mr. Barbour killed, so you can't tell the judge who killed him or how he died, can you?"

Grace looked down. "I guess not."

"No further questions, Your Honor."

AFTER MORE OF THE MEN who had ridden to Barbour's house testified, District Attorney Page called Marshal Lappeus to testify about Worthy's arrest.

"Marshal," Matthew said when it was his turn to cross-examine the lawman, "it rained heavily the day Mr. Barbour died, did it not?"

"Yes."

"Was it raining when you rode from town to Mr. Barbour's place?"

"The rain had stopped by the time Mr. Gillette's servant told me about the fire."

"When you arrived at Mr. Barbour's house, did you see his body?"

"I did."

"Describe the condition of the body to Justice Boise."

The marshal turned to the judge. "It looked pretty bad, Judge. Mr. Barbour was sprawled across the porch steps on his back so his face was up. The house had a covered porch, and the fire brought down the overhang. A piece of wood had fallen across Mr. Barbour's face and set it on fire, so the front of his head was burned bad."

"Did you have a chance to touch Mr. Barbour?"

"I did."

"Were his clothes wet?"

"Yes."

"So it must have been raining when he died?"

"I guess so."

"Did you see the back of Mr. Barbour's head?"

"Yeah, it was stove in. He fell backward onto the edge of one of the stairs, and the point drove into his head."

"Were the porch steps wet?"

"Yes, sir. They'd dried a little, but they were still a tad slippery."

"Now you arrested Mr. Brown, did you not?"

"Yes."

"Did you tie his hands behind him?"

"I did."

"So you were close to him?"

"I was."

"Did you actually take hold of him?"

"Yes."

"Think carefully, Marshal Lappeus. Were Worthy Brown's clothes wet or dry?"

The marshal's brow furrowed as he struggled to recall. Then his brow smoothed, and he stared at Worthy.

"I laid hands on Mr. Brown's arms to steer him toward the horse he was going to ride back. Then I grabbed hold of his legs to help him get in the saddle because his hands were tied. The bottoms of his pants were wet and muddy but he was dry from the knees up."

"Thank you, Marshal. I have no further questions."

"Nothing on redirect," Page said. "The state calls Dr. Raymond Sharp."

Raymond Sharp, the doctor Portland society consulted when it was ailing, was a robust man in his late forties with a full head of wavy brown hair, a thick mustache, and lively blue eyes.

"Dr. Sharp," District Attorney Page asked as soon as the doctor was sworn, "did you ride to Caleb Barbour's house at the request of Marshal Lappeus on the evening Mr. Barbour died?"

"I did."

"What did you find when you arrived?"

"There were two injured parties, Mr. Penny and the defendant, as well as the deceased, Caleb Barbour."

"We've heard testimony that the injuries to Mr. Brown and Mr. Penny were inflicted by the men who rode from town to help put out the fire. Please describe the injuries inflicted on Mr. Penny."

"He had been hit in the head and was unconscious."

"Was this a serious injury?"

"Very. He remained unconscious for several days."

"And Mr. Brown?"

"He had suffered several blows, but he was conscious."

"Please describe the results of your examination of Mr. Barbour."

"As I have said, he was dead when I arrived. His body was burned in spots where it had been touched by burning pieces of wood from the porch overhang, and his face was also badly burned."

"Did you determine the cause of death?"

"Yes, it was obvious. Mr. Barbour had fallen backward, and the back of his head was impaled on a sharp corner of the top porch step."

"In your medical opinion, could the deceased have been driven backward by a blow?"

"Of course."

"In your opinion, did Mr. Brown have the strength to deliver a blow powerful enough to have caused the result?"

"Yes."

"Nothing further."

Matthew stood. "Dr. Sharp, where were you when you were summoned to Mr. Barbour's house?"

"I was at Gillette House."

"Why were you there?"

"Heather Gillette had asked me to minister to Roxanne Brown."

"Please describe Miss Brown's medical condition on that evening."

"She was in shock. Her eyes were glazed over, she was obviously terrified, and she would not answer any of my questions. She became quite violent when I tried to conduct a physical examination."

"Did Miss Brown have any obvious physical injuries?"

"Several. Her nose had been broken, and there was a large knot on the back of her head. I saw many scratches and bruises on various parts of her body."

"I beg your pardon for having to make the following inquiry, Dr. Sharp, but were you able to examine Miss Brown's genital area?"

"She resisted mightily at first, but Miss Gillette was finally able to calm her enough for me to conduct an examination."

"Did you find signs of forcible sexual intercourse?"

Sharp looked solemn when he answered. "Yes, I did."

"In your opinion, had Miss Brown been raped?"

"Yes."

"You have testified that you examined Mr. Barbour's corpse when you arrived at his house."

"Yes."

"How was he clothed?"

Dr. Sharp paused for a moment and stared into space. When he responded, he spoke slowly.

"He was wearing a shirt, but it was not tucked in. Sections of the shirt had been burned."

"Did he have a jacket?"

"No, just the shirt."

"Pants?"

"Yes, he was wearing pants."

"What was the condition of his fly?"

"I remember that his fly was unbuttoned or partially unbuttoned."

"Shoes?"

"No, I'm certain that he wore socks but no shoes."

"Now you testified that Mr. Barbour died because his head struck the edge of one of the porch steps?"

"Yes."

"Were the steps slippery?"

"They were still wet when I arrived."

"But the rain had stopped?"

"Yes, it had come down hard earlier, but it had stopped by the time I left Gillette House."

"Was Mr. Barbour's house still on fire when you reached it?"

"Yes. The fire had almost burned out, but it was still aflame."

"I want to ask you a hypothetical question, Doctor. Assume when Mr. Barbour fled out the front door of his house that he was wearing socks and the steps of his front porch were slippery from the rain, is it possible that he could have slipped on the steps and fallen backward with enough force to have caused his death in the manner in which you found him?"

Dr. Sharp did not answer immediately. When he did answer it was with great seriousness.

"What you say is possible."

"Did Marshal Lappeus have Mr. Barbour's body brought to your office so you could conduct an autopsy?"

"Yes."

"Did you find any indication that Mr. Barbour had been struck by a hard blow?"

"No, but if the blow was to the face, any signs of assault may have been obscured by the fire. The face was badly burned."

"So your answer is that you saw nothing that led you to believe that Mr. Barbour had been struck by Mr. Brown before he hit his head?"

"I . . . Yes. I saw nothing to indicate that someone had hit him and caused him to fall."

"In fact, you cannot tell Justice Boise beyond a reasonable doubt that Mr. Brown had anything to do with Mr. Barbour's death."

"No, I can't."

"And a reasonable explanation for what you found at the scene would be that Mr. Barbour, fleeing at high speed from a fire in his home in stocking feet, caused his own death by slipping on his wet steps."

"Yes, that is a possible explanation."

"Thank you. A few more questions, Doctor. When you examined Mr. Brown, were his clothes wet or dry?"

"I am pretty certain that his clothes from the knees up were dry."

"But Mr. Barbour's clothing was wet?"

"Yes."

"Thank you, Dr. Sharp. I have no further questions."

The courtroom was buzzing as the doctor left the witness stand and walked to a seat in the rear of the makeshift courtroom. When the trial started, the district attorney had assumed that Matthew was going to depend on self-defense or defense of another to gain an acquittal for his client. Dr. Sharp's testimony had shaken him.

"Do you have any more witnesses, Mr. Page?" Justice Boise asked.

"No, Your Honor. The state rests."

"Mr. Penny?" the judge asked.

"I have a motion," Matthew answered as he tried to keep his voice from shaking. "I move the court to grant a judgment of acquittal on the grounds that the evidence taken in the best light for the state cannot support a verdict of guilty in this case."

The judge looked very interested in what Matthew had to say, and he leaned forward.

"State your grounds."

"Here is what the evidence shows, taken in the light most favorable to the state. Mr. Barbour's house was set on fire while he was partially dressed. I submit that he was partially dressed because he had just raped Roxanne Brown, but whether he was fleeing his home to pursue Miss Brown who was naked and battered when she fled from Barbour's home or whether he was simply fleeing the fire, he was fleeing into the rain in his stocking feet.

"There is no evidence in the record that Mr. Barbour was struck by Mr. Brown before he fell. No witness saw Mr. Brown strike Mr. Barbour. Dr. Sharp, after examining the body, cannot say beyond a reasonable doubt that Mr. Brown struck Mr. Barbour. He did say that a reasonable explanation of the cause of death was that Mr. Barbour's feet slipped on the slick porch steps and he hit his head when he fell.

"And now we come to the most telling evidence adduced at

this trial, the rain. It came down in buckets that night, and it is indisputable that Mr. Barbour was lying dead on those steps in the rain. He and his clothes were wet. The rain extinguished the flames on the board that burned his face. One thing the court knows for certain is that Mr. Barbour died in the rain.

"Another thing the court knows for certain is that Mr. Brown traveled to Barbour's house after the rain stopped. The rain soaked everything, Your Honor, but it did not soak Mr. Brown. Mr. Brown could not have had any part in the events that caused Mr. Barbour's death because his clothes were dry. No one saw Mr. Brown kill Caleb Barbour because Worthy Brown was nowhere near Barbour's house when Mr. Barbour died."

WILLIAM PAGE'S ARGUMENT WAS HALFHEARTED, and it was apparent to Matthew that the district attorney had lost faith in his case. Justice Boise granted Matthew's motion to acquit and adjourned court. Heather sent Francis Gibney to the front of the makeshift courtroom to protect Worthy, but no one tried to harm Matthew's client now that everyone believed that Caleb Barbour had died in a freak accident after raping an innocent young girl.

"You're free," Matthew said.

Worthy sat, stone-faced.

"It's over, Worthy. You can go to Roxanne. You can be together."

Worthy turned to Matthew and stood slowly. He stared at him for a moment. Then emotion overwhelmed Worthy, and he hugged his lawyer.

"You see," he said. "You see. You're free, too, Mr. Penny."

Before Matthew could respond, Orville clapped him on the back and Heather offered her congratulations.

Marshal Lappeus loomed over the group. "That was good lawyering, Mr. Penny. And I've got to say, I'm not sorry you won. I got to know Mr. Brown, and he seems a decent sort, which is more than I can say for Barbour."

"Does Mr. Brown have to go back to the jail?" Matthew asked.

"Not unless he wants to. He's got clothes there, but someone can get them later."

"You must come with me to see Roxanne," Heather told Worthy. "She knows your case was going to be decided today, and she'll be sick with worry. Seeing you free will be the best present she has ever received."

Worthy looked at Matthew.

"Go along, Worthy. There's nothing more you need to do here."

"And you must come, too, Matthew. We'll celebrate." Heather beamed at Penny. "You were magnificent."

Then Heather and Francis Gibney led Worthy out of the loft and down to Heather's carriage.

"Well done, Matthew," Orville said. "That was the most brilliant job of lawyering I've ever seen."

"Thank you, Orville."

"Shall we ride up to Gillette House together?"

"I'll meet you there. I want to bring my papers to my office and do a few things before I head up."

"Very well," Orville said. "I'll tell Heather you're on the way. She was right, you know. You were magnificent."

Matthew walked to his office without seeing his surroundings.

Worthy was free, but Worthy had never done anything wrong except try to take the blame for something Matthew had done.

Heather and Orville were right. He had been magnificent: a magnificent liar. It had all been a trick. The truth had not come out in court. A fiction had led to Worthy's release. Caleb Barbour had not slipped on a wet step. Matthew had murdered him, and Matthew believed that he would suffer for that act for the rest of his life.

CHAPTER 63

The day after Worthy Brown's trial, Matthew bathed, put on a fresh set of clean clothes, and set off on horseback up the winding road to Gillette House. He found Heather seated on the sofa in the room where they had schemed to save Roxanne on the evening Matthew had killed Caleb Barbour. Heather stood up and smiled when she saw Matthew. The windows were open, and the sun came out from behind a cloud. Heather studied Matthew in its light.

"How are you?" she asked.

"I'm better now that Worthy is free, but I'm not well, and every minute I stay in this town I grow sicker at heart." He paused and looked down. "I'm going to leave Oregon."

"Oh, Matthew."

"Nothing has worked for me here. First, Rachel . . ." Matthew's voice caught, and he paused to regain his composure. "And my law practice has not been successful." Matthew looked down. "And I will never be able to put what happened at Caleb Barbour's house behind me."

"If you leave Oregon, where will you go?"

Matthew shrugged. "Maybe back to Ohio."

"Would life be so much better there?"

"I have no idea what life will thrust upon me. It's all been a big surprise so far."

Heather's features changed from pity to stern resolve. "I wish you had the ability to see yourself as I see you. You think you are a coward because you let Worthy Brown take your place in jail, but Worthy left you no choice. He put you in a box. But, Matthew, the truth is that you saved Worthy Brown's life."

"I should receive no credit for gaining an acquittal for Worthy when he did nothing but try to take the blame for something I'd done."

"I know you are racked with guilt because Barbour died at your hands, but Barbour was a cruel and vile man, and God knows what he would have done to Roxanne if he'd gotten his hands on her again.

"No matter how *you* see yourself, I see a good and decent man who saved the life of a helpless girl. You also saved me from ruin. Orville told me about your meeting with Bernard Hoxie in San Francisco. He said that you are the person who convinced Hoxie to testify truthfully, and it was his testimony that destroyed Hill.

"I get so angry when I see you devalue yourself like this. Roxanne and her father might be dead now if it were not for you, and I have no idea what my fate would have been without your intervention. The three of us owe you our lives, Matthew. How many people can claim to have had that great an impact on the future of other human beings?"

Matthew looked down, but Heather forced him to look at her.

"I love you," Heather told him.

"You shouldn't. I'm a flawed human being."

"No, you are just a human being, and we are all flawed. But you're a good man at heart, and you've suffered more than your fair share. Stay here, stay with me. Let me help you to be happy."

"I don't know—"

"Matthew, I've just told you that I love you. Do you love me? Be honest. If your heart tells you that you don't, then tell me, but if you do love me, don't break my heart by leaving."

Matthew hesitated. He had loved Rachel more than life itself, but he could not hide from the fact that he loved Heather, too.

Heather took Matthew's hands in hers. "Don't let what happened during a split second at Caleb Barbour's house destroy your life and mine," she said. "If you love me, tell me."

Matthew flashed on his final memory of Rachel, and his chest seized up. He had lost love once, but he was being given a chance to find it again. He began to sob. Heather held him. Tears stained her cheeks, too, as they rocked back and forth in each other's arms.

CHAPTER 64

Roxanne stayed at Gillette House while Worthy fixed the damage to the cabin and cleared it of the debris that had accumulated during the months he was confined. When the cabin was fit for habitation, Roxanne moved in with her father, but they returned to Gillette House each day to work for Heather.

One afternoon, two weeks after Worthy's trial, the weather was mild enough to sit in the gazebo. Heather found Roxanne in the kitchen making the crust for a pie and asked the young girl to join her.

"Have you given any thought to your future?" Heather asked when they were seated side by side.

"I guess I'll stay here and work for you," Roxanne answered.

"Is that all you want out of life, to be my servant?"

"You've been good to me, Miss Heather. And this house is a nice place to work."

"It's a safe place, but is this what you want?"

Roxanne shrugged.

"What does your father want for you, Roxanne?"

"Freedom," Roxanne answered, the words catching in her throat. "And I got that now."

"Do you think your father wants freedom for you so you can work for me, or does he want something more for you?"

"I don't know what he wants for me past freedom. We talked about it some, but all my daddy said about freedom was that we could choose once we had it."

"Roxanne, there's a war going on. When it's over, the future of your people will be different. Slavery can't last. Once all of your people are free, they'll need to be shown what to do with their freedom. They'll need to be educated like white people if they want to succeed in a white man's world.

"You have a fine mind, Roxanne, too fine to waste as a servant in Gillette House. There's a school in Boston run by Hiram Knox, a minister of Reverend Mason's acquaintance. Reverend Knox is white, but the school is for freed Negroes. Some of the teachers are even Negro. I wrote to Reverend Knox about you, and I just received a reply. Reverend Knox is willing to accept you as a pupil."

Roxanne's eyes went wide with fear. "I don't want to leave you, Miss Heather."

"I know you're frightened. And you won't be alone. I'll make sure that your father goes with you. But you and your father have to go. Oregon bans Negroes from the state. You have no chance of success here. In Boston, there are free men and women of your race. You are so bright. Once you receive your education, there are so many things you'll be able to do."

Roxanne was trembling now, on the verge of tears. Heather cupped her chin and forced Roxanne to look at her.

"When I was sent to Boston for my education, I cried, too. I was terrified to leave my family and friends and everything I'd ever known. But I was so glad by the time my education was complete. You'll become a self-sufficient woman in Boston. You'll start a new life away from the suffering you've experienced here and among Negroes who can make choices for themselves." Heather smiled. "Who knows, you may even meet your husband there."

Roxanne flushed with embarrassment, and Heather laughed. Then she reached out and hugged Roxanne.

"You been so good to me," Roxanne said.

"You deserve goodness. You're brave, and your life has been hard. It's time you turned your back on your old life and built a new one. You love learning, and there's only so much I can teach you. A new world will open up for you at Reverend Knox's school. If you choose, you may become a teacher someday and open up new worlds for others. Think about this opportunity. Discuss it with your father. Then let's talk again."

Heather walked away, and Roxanne stayed in the gazebo to think. Worthy was free, and a future of possibilities was suddenly open to her, but the prospect of leaving the only safe place she knew and going across the continent to Boston was terrifying. Then it occurred to her that she would not have known what a continent was or the location of Boston had it not been for the education Heather had given her. Learning was exhilarating. Roxanne remembered how she felt when she grasped a mathematical concept and the wonder she experienced when Heather told her about Africa, where Worthy had been born. Heather had opened up a new world for her, but that world was confined to the library in Gillette House and limited by Heather's knowledge. There was so much more to learn, and Heather was giving her the chance, if she could muster the courage to go after it.

CHAPTER 65

Worthy Brown stood at the rail of the steamer to San Francisco, the first leg of the journey east. White sails appeared on the horizon from time to time, and a pod of whales had entertained the passengers the day before. Otherwise, there was little to break the monotony of the calm and endless sea.

Worthy heard footsteps, and a moment later Roxanne was leaning on the rail beside him.

"The ocean sure is big," she said as she looked toward the horizon.

Roxanne's sense of wonder made Worthy smile. "It sure is."

"You told me that it took forever when you came from Africa across the ocean. I didn't know what you meant by 'forever' until now. I don't know how you survived the journey."

"It was hard, but seeing you here with me now I believe that every hard thing that happened in my life was worth the sacrifice. I would do it all over again if I knew you would end up free and happy."

Roxanne smiled. "I am free, Papa, and I am most definitely happy."

Worthy laughed and pulled Roxanne against him.

"You make me proud; you make me proud."

They talked a little longer. Then Worthy went inside, but Roxanne stayed at the rail. The last few days had been a whirlwind, and it was good to have time to reflect on them.

Would everything turn out well for her? She looked out at the vast expanse of ocean and thought about her endless possibilities.

"I believe things will go well for me, Daddy," she whispered into the strong breeze. "I believe they will."

AUTHOR'S NOTE

In the early 1980s I read an article about *Holmes v. Ford*, a case from the Oregon Territory. In Missouri, Colonel Nathaniel Ford had owned Robin and Polly Holmes and their children as slaves, but when he moved to the Oregon Territory, Ford told Robin and Polly that if they helped him establish a farm in the Willamette Valley, he would free the family. The Holmeses kept their part of the bargain, but Ford kept only part of his. He freed the parents and one small child but retained several of the children as indentured servants. During this time period, Oregon was hostile to blacks. When Oregon became a state in 1859, the state constitution barred free Negroes from living in Oregon unless they had been residing there when the constitution was passed. The Holmeses, who were illiterate, had to find a white lawyer who would help them get their children back. In 1853, George Williams, the chief justice of the Oregon Supreme Court, ordered Ford to return the children, but one had already died in Ford's custody.

I thought this situation was heart wrenching. I could not imagine what Robin and Polly had gone through, and decided to write a novel inspired by the case. I set the book in 1860, during Oregon's second year as a state, and made one of my main characters a young lawyer who was grieving for his wife, whom he had lost on the Oregon Trail.

During the 1980s I spent many hours in the library of the Oregon Historical Society learning about frontier life in 1860 and, more specifically, what the practice of law was like then. I also stumbled across a memoir of Stephen J. Field, one of America's most colorful citizens. The first United States Supreme Court justice from the West, Field was also the only Supreme Court justice to be arrested for murder while sitting on the bench. I decided that a character based loosely on Field, as well as a highly fictionalized version of the case that led to his arrest, would be part of my book.

For several years on and off I worked on a draft of *Worthy Brown's Daughter*. Then, in 1993, *Gone, But Not Forgotten* became my first best seller. In 1996, I retired from law to write full-time. I wrote contemporary legal thrillers while my historical novel languished in a drawer. Sometime in the 1990s I dusted it off and reread it. After a consultation with Jean Naggar, my exceptional agent, we decided that the book still needed more work before it would be worthy of publication.

In 2010, Jennifer Weltz, another of my agents, took a look at the book and made some brilliant suggestions that prompted me to rewrite it from page one. HarperCollins agreed to publish *Worthy Brown's Daughter*, and my editors, Caroline Upcher and Claire Wachtel, worked hard to make the novel the best book I've written, and Milan Bozic designed the perfect jacket to showcase it.

I have taken liberties with some of the historical events in the book. The Oregon Pony arrived in Oregon in 1862, not 1860, and Charles and Ellen Kean performed *The Merchant of Venice* in

1864. I want to thank Chet Orloff, former executive director of the Oregon Historical Society, for reading the book and bringing other historical inaccuracies to my attention.

Special thanks also go to Ron Cinniger, who plotted Matthew Penny's cross-country trip, which did not make it into the final manuscript, and provided me with invaluable reference materials. Thanks also to Dick Pintarich for his invaluable information about the Barlow Road, and Nancy Kelton, Pam Webb, Jay Margulies, Jerry Margolin, and Virginia Sewell for their constructive comments. Thanks to my wonderful children, Ami and Daniel, and Ami's husband, Andy, for their support. And, as always, thanks to Doreen, my muse, who continues to inspire me.

Set out here is a bibliography of books I read while working on *Worthy Brown's Daughter*. Since my research was ongoing from the early 1980s, it is possible that I have forgotten to include other books and articles I relied on. If so, I apologize in advance.

Anderson, Dorothea. *Your District Attorney's Office*, 1855–
1977, Portland: Multnomah County District Attorney's
Office, n.d.

Barlow, Mary S., "History of the Barlow Road," *Quarterly of
the Oregon Historical Society 3* (1902), 71–81.

Cooling, Benjamin Franklin. *Symbol, Sword and Shield:
Defending Washington During the Civil War*. Hamden,
CT: Archon Books, 1975.

Davis, William C. *Battle at Bull Run: A History of the First
Major Campaign of the Civil War*. Garden City, New York:
Doubleday and Co., Inc., 1977.

Field, Stephen J. *Personal Reminiscences of Early Days in California*. New York: Da Capo Press, 1968.

Gilbert, Bil. "Thar Was Old Grit in Him." *Sports Illustrated*, January 17, 1983.

Harrell, Mary Ann. *Equal Justice Under Law: The Supreme Court in American Life*. Arlington, VA: The Foundation of the Federal Bar Association, 1975.

Lansing, Ronald B. *Nimrod-Courts, Claims, and Killing on the Oregon Frontier*. Pullman: Washington State University Press, 2005.

Leeson, Fred. *Rose City Justice: A Legal History of Portland, Oregon*. Portland: Oregon Historical Society Press, in cooperation with the Oregon State Bar, 1998.

Lewis, Oscar. *This Was San Francisco*. Philadelphia: David McKay Co., Inc., 1962.

Lockley, Fred. "Facts Pertaining to Ex-Slaves in Oregon and Documentary Record of the Case of Robin Holmes vs. Nathaniel Ford." *Quarterly of the Oregon Historical Society 23* (June 1922).

Lockwood, Charles. *Suddenly San Francisco: The Early Years*. San Francisco: A California Living Book, 1978.

McLagan, Elizabeth. *A Peculiar Paradise: A History of Blacks in Oregon, 1788–1940*, Athens, GA: The Georgian Press, 1980.

Meredith, Roy. *Mr. Lincoln's Camera Man: Matthew B. Brady*. Second revised edition. New York: Dover Publications, 1974.

Morrison, Samuel Eliot. *The Oxford History of the American People. Vol. 2*. New York: New American Library, 1972.

Muscatine, Doris. *Old San Francisco: The Biography of a City.* New York: G. P. Putnam's Sons, 1975.

Pintarich, Dick. "Sam Barlow's Infamous Road." *Oregon Magazine* (February 1983).

Richards, Leverett. "Mrs. McNatt on the Oregon Trail." *The Oregonian* (July 1, 1979).

Sandburg, Carl. *Abraham Lincoln: The War Years. Volume 1.* New York: Harcourt, Brace and Co., 1939.

Vestal, Stanley. *Joe Meek: The Merry Mountain Man.* Lincoln: Bison Books, the University of Nebraska Press, 1952.

Victor, Frances Fuller. *The River of the West.* Oakland, CA: Brooks-Sterling, 1974. First published in 1870 by R. W. Bliss and Co.

ABOUT THE AUTHOR

PHILLIP MARGOLIN has written seventeen *New York Times* bestsellers, including his latest, *Sleight of Hand*, and the Washington Trilogy. Each displays a unique, compelling insider's view of criminal behavior, which comes from his long background as a criminal defense attorney who has handled thirty murder cases. Winner of the Distinguished Northwest Writer Award, he lives in Portland, Oregon.